'I am a regular Norfolk Dumpling.'

'Doubtless if Gilly had lived we might have roved the world together. As it was, we visited it in our imaginations.'

'Gilly?' Alex repeated, surprised into bad manners by her absolute determination not to be ruffled.

'Ah, I forgot,' said Harry. 'Your cousin Gilbert, my late husband. The despised and rejected of men, I understand, seeing that his father had the bad taste to marry for love and not for lands and money.'

She had left herself open to him. His reply was quick and savage. 'Unlike yourself, madam, I believe.'

Paula Marshall, married, with three children, has had a varied and interesting life. She began her career as an assistant in a large reference library and ended it as a senior academic in charge of history teaching in a polytechnic. She has travelled widely in Europe, Russia, the USA, Scandinavia and New Zealand, has been a swimming coach, embroiders, paints pictures, and has appeared on *University Challenge* and *Mastermind*. She now lives in Leicester.

She has always wanted to write, and likes her novels to be full of adventure and humour, her heroes to be intelligent and virile athletes, and her heroines witty and spirited. This is her first book for Masquerade.

COUSIN HARRY

Paula Marshall

First published in Great Britain 1991 by Mills & Boon Limited

© Paula Marshall 1991

Australian copyright 1991 Philippine copyright 1992 This edition 1992

ISBN 0 263 77583 6

Masquerade is a trademark published by Mills & Boon Limited Eton House, 18–24 Paradise Road, Richmond, Surrey, TW9 1SR.

Set in 10 on 10½ pt Linotron Plantin 04-9202-84883 Typeset in Great Britain by Centracet, Cambridge Made and printed in Great Britain

CHAPTER ONE

'I ASK you, Emily, to understand how I felt, when I returned from the wars to find that my grandfather had willed away my entire patrimony to a cousin whom I did not know existed. That Racquette, which I have always loved, and was my home, was not to come to me, and was lost to my line. It was a blow which, if not mortal, struck me to the quick. Never mind that I have my mother's inheritance, which is grand enough, I know, and makes my concern at losing the Templestowe lands seem mean, but it is my home I have lost.'

Gilbert Alexander Ashburn, seventh Earl of Templestowe, Alex to his friends, a man in his early thirties, was pacing the rose garden at Rule, his house on land which marched with that which he had hoped to inherit, his maternal aunt, Emily, Duchess of Hornsea, walking by his side. It was a fine cold day in April, 1816, and the rest of his guests were scattered about the garden, taking the air before luncheon.

Alex fell silent. His aunt, a pretty little woman in early middle age, looked at him. 'You must know how sorry I am, Alex,' she said gently—everything about her small person was gentle, but she had the unthinking authority of the great lady she was. 'But you know how capricious your grandfather was. Your successful career in the Army, far from pleasing him, as one might have expected, annoyed him. By contrast with his own early failures, one imagines. And then his constant quarrels with your father. . .'

Alex made an impatient movement of his hand. 'It is hard to pay for my father's and grandfather's failures, and have my own success, modest though it was, count against me.'

Emily looked at the tall length of him, at his hard face, eagle's profile and flaming red hair. All the Ashburns had tempers to match their hair, and Alex's was rather milder than most. His grandfather's had been legendary—he had quarrelled with everyone, except Alex, until on Alex's father's sudden death he had sent word to the Spanish Peninsula, where Alex was campaigning under Sir Arthur Wellesley, demanding that he sell out and return home immediately. He said it was Alex's duty as the new heir to marry Arabella Temple at once. Alex had refused to do any such thing in the middle of the campaign, whereupon, enraged, his grandfather had immediately set in motion the arrangements which were to disinherit him.

Never mind that years before he had quarrelled with the dead younger son, who was the new heir's father, and sent him away, never to speak of him, or to him, again; it was Alex's supposed offence which was the more recent and heinous, and was to be severely punished, even if it meant rewarding a hitherto unknown grandson.

Alex had never really thought that his grandfather meant what he said. He had been the old man's favourite, and could not imagine that his duty as a soldier, to his superior officers and to his men, would be held against him.

He remembered standing in the library at Racquette, still in his worn officer's uniform, having left his regiment in France to return home at a moment's notice, when his grandfather had died. He remembered also the lawyers' faces, the faces of his relatives, his younger brother, Ned, standing beside him in mourning black, waiting for the formality of the Will-reading, himself impatient for it to be over so that he might be off, back to his duties, and then the stunned silence when the lawyer had read out, in his emotionless voice, the words which bequeathed Racquette and the Templestowe lands and fortune to Gilbert Ashburn, the cousin he hardly knew existed.

The only other Ashburns mentioned were his brother Ned and a distant cousin, both of whom had been left small annuities of the kind normally given to servants— indeed, several servants had been left larger ones. It was as though to emphasise his distaste for his blood relatives that the sixth Earl had been remarkably generous to his staff, whom he had constantly mistreated in life.

'I take it that the Will is good, sir,' Alex had said.

'Unbreakable,' smirked the lawyer, almost proud of the furore he and the late Earl had created between them. 'Cast iron, as your grandfather so wished.'

'Then I bid you good day, sir; I am a stranger in this house, and do not wish to stay.'

He had turned on his heel, taken his tired self to his horse, the old steward lamenting behind him, Ned following, climbed on it, and begun to ride away. Nearly two years later the memory was still with him. He had made for the nearest inn, and begun to drink as he had not done since he was a boy, and there Ned had found him.

'For God's sake, Alex, there must be something we can do.'

'You are a good fellow, Ned, but you may be sure our grandfather and his advisers knew what they were about. Leave it; I am not poor, and nor are you. Mother's lawyers saw to that.'

'But it was your home,' Ned had said, 'and now it goes to someone we none of us know. Why was not the estate entailed?'

The drink was beginning to take hold, and soon he would be stupefied and would sleep. 'Our distant ancestor broke the entail to spite *his* heir. We have a habit of it. God grant I do not treat a son or grandson of mine so.'

Ned had stayed with him, and began to drink, too, and for the first time Alex did not discourage him.

They had both gone to sleep, their heads on the inn table, and in the morning he had sent Evans, his sergeant, to Racquette to collect Ned's belongings, and the two of them had driven back to London, Ned to stay at Alex's town house, and Alex to return to the Army, Racquette in a stranger's hands and lost to him forever.

He returned to the present, and to Emily and to the latest turn of Fortune's wheel. They were so near to Racquette that to see it they merely had to leave the rose garden and walk along the Downs a little, and it would appear gleaming white in the watery April sun. It was a walk he would never take.

'You have heard the latest news,' he said. 'I had not thought to be so. . .touched again.'

Emily nodded. 'Only the gossip, which may not, of course, be the truth.'

'Lumsden, my lawyer in London, told me the truth of it before I left for Rule. You know that they could not even find my cousin. The old man took no steps to do so. I suppose it added to his pleasure to think of the trouble he was causing after his death. And when they did find him, it was his grave they discovered.'

'I had heard that, yes,' said the Duchess, 'and wondered what it would do to the inheritance—if there were any way by which you could regain it?'

'Oh, no, my dear. Failing all else, it reverts to the Crown. But there was no need. The rest of the story beggars belief. Lumsden told me, just this last week, though I gather it is already round the town—God knows how—that my cousin had been a dying man for the last years of his life, and a year before his death he married some penniless adventuress, or so the local Rector said, and left her all he possessed. Which, although he never knew it, by then included Racquette, and all that went with it, as he died after my grandfather.' He paused. 'And she is there, at Racquette, now. You see the irony of it, I'm sure. Ned is on fire. But what is the use of that? She is the greatest heiress of the day, and is sure to marry again, and Racquette will be gone. Not even Ashburns in it, now that my cousin is dead, and left no children.'

'It is not like you to be bitter, Alex,' said Emily, as they stopped near the hedge which divided them from what was still Ashburn land, although, as Alex had said, for how long? 'But I do understand your feelings. You are sure that your cousin's wife is as Lumsden says?'

'He spoke to Heriot, who went there to see her, and also spoke to the Rector—Frith by name—where she lived. An unseemly marriage to a dying man, he said. Harriet Ashburn is her name. A demure harpy, he called her.'

'Well, that's a striking thought,' said Emily, laughing. 'I should like to see what one looks like.'

Alex laughed, too. 'If it were happening to another, one would be entertained. I own that to be true. But that rankles as well. To enter a room and be pointed out as Templestowe, you know the man I mean. . .and all the meaningful looks, and the sideways sneers. I never did like London Society much, but I must do my duty there, and attend while Parliament sits. I also own I spend but little time at Rule now, because of its nearness to Racquette; I prefer my estate at Allerton in Nottinghamshire, but I have my duty to my tenants.'

'Indeed,' agreed Emily, thinking that, whatever his other faults, Alex would do his duty if the heavens fell, which made his grandfather's behaviour the more provoking.

'Did you learn anything of your cousin?' she ventured.

'Only that he was reputed to be extraordinarily intelligent and learned for so young a man. He was barely twenty-three when he died.'

'Surprising that he should marry an adventuress, then.'

'Probably knew nothing of women,' said Alex curtly. 'Would you like to go in, Emily? The air is quite keen.'

'Not yet.' She thought that she would turn the conversation away from these sad matters, and try to cheer her nephew up. She had been almost a mother to him, since his own mother had been a semi-invalid for many years

before Ned was born, and Aunt Emily was treasured by
the two brothers. She was acting as Alex's hostess at
Rule, and had been partly responsible for his guest list—
'You must not be a hermit, or you are in danger of
following in your grandfather's footsteps, to say nothing
of my husband's,' she had told him, almost severely.

Alex had said God forbid to that, but not all her guests
were to his taste—the widowed Lady Lansden and her
young daughter, Louisa, for instance, although he could
guess why they had been invited. Together with Pearson,
the Duchess's companion, they came over, since it was
evident that Alex's private conversation with his aunt
had ended.

More general talk ensued. The weather, the prospects
for the season, the Regent, his daughter and her marriage, the King's illness, until it seemed to Alex that to
read out the Court Circular might be more exciting. He
had hardly thought this when excitement in their own
lives was upon them.

Their conversation had been almost drowned by the
sound of hoofs and a man shouting, and, as they turned
at the sudden noise, a figure came sailing over the hedge
to land appositely at Alex's feet, missing the Duchess,
who, with a face of alarm, dropped on her knees to the
sward beside the sudden newcomer, who lay stretched
out and semi-conscious before them.

It was a young woman in a shabby green riding habit,
her hat gone, her black hair, longer than was fashionable,
streaming loose, and her face white. She was trying to sit
up, and to speak, but as Alex, too, knelt down beside
her, she fell against him, clutching at him and saying,
'Oh, you must forgive me, I really did not mean. . .'
before losing consciousness completely, and falling headlong into his strong arms.

CHAPTER TWO

HARRIET ASHBURN, whose late husband Gilbert—
Gilly—Ashburn had always called her Harry, rode out
from Racquette, the great country house which she had
so strangely inherited, her head groom Phelps behind
her. He had chosen from her stable a solid black horse,
Caesar by name, guaranteed, he said, as to his sober
character, perfectly fit for a young lady to ride.

While Phelps prepared him for her she thought briefly
of her many visitors during the fortnight which had
passed since she had arrived at Racquette. Most of the
county had visited her, eager to meet the new heiress.
Every young, middle-aged and old man who needed a
wife had sized her up—as though I were a promising
mare, she thought—and some had sent their mother or
their sister to look her over as well.

Today she meant to avoid them, and to enjoy silence
again. Phelps, coming up to her, after they had left the
Home Park, approved of her lack of chatter, her quiet
manner and willingness to be instructed. 'Not too far, or
too fast,' she had said. 'To the nearest boundary, perhaps.' Together they quartered the smooth and smiling
countryside companionably, until they came to a copse
where single file was necessary, and where Phelps fell
behind a little, adjusting his saddle-girth, so that as
Harry emerged into another wide stretch of parkland,
with a distant hedge screening another great house, she
was alone.

She was never to know quite what happened next—
whether a bird started up and frightened Caesar, but,
whatever it was, that usually reliable horse threw back
his head with a shrill neigh and bolted, with such savage
speed that she was almost thrown immediately. How she

11

kept her seat she never knew, but she refused to panic,
and concentrated on trying to stay aboard and to control
Caesar's flight, if that were possible. Behind her, Phelps,
who arrived in time to see Caesar bolt, gave helpless
chase as horse and rider fled across the park towards the
looming hedge.

There was no hope that the hedge could be avoided,
so Harry set her teeth and prepared to hang on for dear
life as Caesar collected himself for the jump—and then
as suddenly stopped. Earth, hedge and sky swung around
her in a mad kaleidoscope until she felt herself falling.
She had an impression of noise, shouting, people scatter-
ing, before she found herself on the ground, bruised,
dazed but still alive.

Someone was kneeling beside her, supporting her. For
some reason she felt that she must explain her sudden
appearance. She clutched at the man holding her, and
said, 'Oh, you must forgive me, I really did not
mean. . .' but, before she could complete the sentence,
the broken scene before her disappeared into the dark.

How long she was unconscious she did not know. She
returned to life to find herself still on the ground, a man's
strong arms about her.

'She's conscious again.' A woman's voice, anxious,
concerned.

'Yes, and not badly hurt, I think. Shaken, perhaps.'

She looked up, and there looming over her was a man's
face—Gilly, her dead husband's face, but harsh and cold
as his had never been.

'You are with us again, madam,' said Gilly's altered
face, 'but, good God, what possessed you to set Caesar at
the hedge? You are fortunate that you did not kill
yourself, or him, or any of us.' His voice, thought Harry
dazedly, was almost Gilly's too, but deeper, authoritative, the voice of a man used to giving orders, and to
seeing them obeyed.

'For shame, Alex,' said the woman's voice, when he
had finished speaking. 'The poor creature hardly knows

who or where she is. Ned, help your brother to carry her into the house before he commits any further *bêtises*. For shame,' she repeated.

'It is of no consequence.' Harry tried to speak briskly, but to her horror her voice was as weak as she felt. 'If you will only assist me to rise. . .' And she tried to stand, but everything swung about her again, and she gave a great sigh and lay back on the man's strong arm once more.

After that she half lost consciousness to regain it to find herself still in the rose-garden, on a rustic bench, a shawl over her, and a pretty little woman holding her hand, while the man with Gilly's face glowered in the background. Phelps had arrived.

'So, you are a little recovered,' said the unknown lady gently. 'Take no notice of Alex; his manners were always deplorable. He was greatly shocked, and feared at first that you were—severely hurt. He advised us not to move you yet, in case anything was broken. But it seems that you have been fortunate.'

'I did not mean to jump the hedge,' said Harry defiantly, through her shock and pain. 'I hope Caesar was not hurt. It was an accident.'

'Indeed it was, Mrs Ashburn,' said Phelps, his face ashen. 'I assure you, my lord, Caesar bolted without warning, and I not near enough to help.'

'Caesar bolted?' The dark eyebrows rose. 'He's usually the mildest of beasts.'

'Yes, my lord, who would have thought it? I blame myself for not being nearer, but the mistress is a useful horsewoman, and has been well taught.'

'Gilly had me taught,' offered Harry, thinking as she spoke, 'My lord', so this must be Gilly's cousin. The man she had unwittingly supplanted. The resemblance was explained, and so, too, was his cool and distant manner.

The unwanted heiress of Racquette had arrived in his presence in the most dramatic fashion possible. I only

needed a trap-door and a wand to be the bad fairy in
person, thought Harry dreamily, and there I was, preparing to meet him in the most cool and dignified manner
possible   to   reassure   him   as   to   my   innocent
respectability. . .

She moved restlessly at the thought, and the lady, who
was still holding her hand, said suddenly, 'When you
have all finished prosing, we must take Mrs Ashburn
into the house and make her comfortable. She will need
to rest.'

'Yes, Your Grace, I will carry the mistress.'

'Your Grace?' Something in Harry's slight movement
as Phelps said this alerted the Duchess, who smiled and
said, 'While arriving among us in such an unconventional
way, my dear, somehow does away with the formalities,
I must restore us to equal terms, as Phelps has told us
who you are. It is only proper that I inform you that I
am Emily, Duchess of Hornsea, and that cross-looking
gentleman is Alex Templestowe, your late husband's
cousin, and the eager young man who has just arrived is
his younger brother Ned. The three ladies present are
Honoria, Lady Lansden, her daughter Louisa, and my
companion Laura Pearson. Before you is Rule manor
house, where we must take you to rest and recover.'

As Phelps moved forward, Alex Templestowe said
abruptly, 'No need; I will carry Mrs Ashburn in—you
had better try to find Caesar, Phelps. Ned will help you.'

Harry found herself easily lifted by the same strong
arms which had supported her earlier.

'Take her upstairs,' said the Duchess as they entered a
manor house of Tudor aspect, all rose brick and mul-
lioned windows. 'Into the tapestry-room, Alex. Dr
Chartley must be sent for, to see whether she has suffered
any serious hurt.'

Harry realised that there were other ladies present,
and that two of them were following Alex and the
Duchess in, their faces curious rather than worried.
They, too, had witnessed her descent into the rose-

garden, but had made no offer of assistance. They must be the Lansdens whom the Duchess had mentioned, and they were apparently willing to allow the Duchess to organise matters.

The older lady stopped Alex to peer at her, and asked, 'Do I collect, my dear Duchess, that this is Mrs Ashburn?' Her drawl was inimical. 'Alex's cousin by marriage. What a coincidence, if, of course, it be one!'

As though, thought Harry crossly, I were capable of setting Caesar at a hedge and being certain that he would not break my neck.

She moved in Alex's arms at the thought, and wished to be anywhere other than where she was. He must have sensed her distress, for he said immediately, 'We cannot stand here talking—I must take Mrs Ashburn upstairs. Perhaps——' he turned to the Lansdens '—Honoria, or Louisa, one of you would care to accompany me.'

It was Louisa Lansden's turn to drawl. 'I think not, Alex. Surely the Duchess's maid, or her companion, could help.'

'No,' said the Duchess firmly. 'I am the one who disposes of my women. Pray do not put yourselves out, either of you. I will accompany Alex.'

'Oh, that would never do.' Honoria Lansden was all bland concern. 'Louisa——' She got no further, the Duchess raised her hand.

'No! I am quite determined. Alex, upstairs with you before you become fatigued enough to drop your burden. Honoria, Louisa, resume your important affairs. I will be Mrs Ashburn's *dame de compagnie* until her own arrives from Racquette.'

A woman after my own heart. The words drifted through Harry's head as the jolting ascent sent it spinning again, and made her grateful for the comfortable bed and the Duchess's kind assistance in removing her clothes once Lord Templestowe had gently laid her upon the bed and departed.

'Lie there, my dear, and do not fret. We shall send for your maid and your companion. Now you must try to sleep.'

But Harry could not sleep; running through her head was all that had happened to her in the past few years, and this last adventure, which had deposited her at the feet of the man who of all the men in the world must most resent her, was almost too much. Between the pain of her body and the pain of her troubled mind there was little to choose. She saw Alex Templestowe standing there, so like Gilly, yet so different. She knew immediately what he thought of her, and the Lansdens, too. An adventuress, who had somehow now insinuated herself into their lives. Only the Duchess's freely given kindness soothed her a little, and as she lay there everything that had passed since her stepfather's death paraded itself before her as she slowly sank into a troubled sleep. . .

She had lived all her short life in Netherdene village in Norfolk, her mother's only child. She did not remember her father, John Grey—he had died when she was little more than a baby, and her mother had married again, to Captain Richard Minster, a stern naval officer on half-pay, much older than she was, and kind only to her mother. He had had little time for Harry, although he had insisted that she took his name.

There had been few children of her age and class in the pretty village, miles from the nearest town, and from her earliest days her constant companion had been Gilly Ashburn, the son of their neighbour. He was a kind, clever boy who never teased her. They learned their letters together with the elderly Rector, Mr Wentworth, and Gilly had helped her with them, for he was older than she was, and he had taken her with him, fishing, climbing trees and birds' nesting, as though she were another boy. His red head and her black one were always together.

'A hoyden, a proper hoyden!' her mother exclaimed, as she ran across muddy fields, clutching jars of tadpoles, or tiddlers, climbed stiles, and played cricket with him with a home-made bat. 'What Gilly does, I can do,' she replied defiantly, which was not quite true after he had begun to acquire a man's strength.

When Gilly was eighteen and she was fifteen, Gilly's parents and her own mother died in one of the epidemics of high fever which occasionally struck the village, and the Rector became his guardian, although Gilly was so sensible, the Rector said, that he did not need one.

This was only the first of the disasters which seemed to overtake her life and Gilly's, which until then had been idyllically happy. First, Gilly had suddenly begun to fall ill with a slow, wasting illness which no doctor appeared to be able to diagnose or assist, and they no longer roved the fields, but worked quietly together, concentrating on their intellectual life, for Gilly's brain remained as keen as ever even though his body was gradually failing him.

And then Mr Wentworth, their kind mentor and teacher, died in his sleep, and was replaced by a new man, cold and thrusting Mr Frith, who disliked Gilly, calling him patronisingly, 'our poor invalid', and speaking to him as though his mind were as feeble as his body.

At first, Mr Frith, who felt that he needed a wife, had come 'a-courting' Harry, as Hannah Pye, her elderly maid and companion since her mother's death, had said. Harry could not like him, he was so unkind to Gilly, but her stepfather had insisted that she become more of a conventional young lady, and less of a tomboy turned bluestocking, as he hoped to see her married, and soon. Mr Frith seemed just the thing.

But Mr Frith's interest in Harry suddenly declined when he grasped the full extent of the Minsters' poverty, concealed beneath their genteel show. Her stepfather had professed to believe that she had discouraged him and driven him away, and was harsh with her, particularly after Mr Frith had married a plain widow with money, and the pair of them had extended their unkindesses from Gilly to the Minsters.

Harry was truly relieved that Mr Frith had abandoned her, and told Gilly so. It was a sunny day, and he was lying on a sofa on the lawn at the time, wrapped in shawls, for he was always cold, and they had been reading Cicero's *Letters* together.

He put down his book and said, 'But you will wish to marry one day, although not someone like Frith, I hope. He has a mean spirit and would have made you unhappy.'

'Oh, I never want to marry,' she replied with all the confidence of eighteen. 'I want to stay here forever, with my books and my garden, and you to talk to.'

Gilly looked at her. She was not a beauty like her dead mother, but the dark eyes in her ivory face were striking, and there was something irresistible in her gentle but resolute manner. Her odd life with him had given her an athletic body and the confidence which went with it.

'Oh, you will marry, I am sure,' he said, regret in his voice, thinking of his own slow death, and the future with her, for which he had once hoped. 'And you will be happy. You are made for happiness. Think of me a little when you are.'

'You are not to talk so,' she said rapidly. 'I shall become an old maid. Very learned, thanks to you. What man am I ever going to meet, here in Netherdene?'

'You might not be here forever,' he told her. 'Who knows?' And Harry laughed, and shook her head, and changed the subject. She did not like to speak of the future when Gilly so plainly did not possess one.

Then the next blow had struck, and it was a hard one, which brought her to her knees. Her stepfather had died suddenly of a syncope, brought on, the doctor said, by the heavy drinking he had indulged in since her mother's sudden death, and she was left quite alone, the old maid she had thought to become, before she was twenty.

She had not greatly loved Richard Minster, nor he her, but she would miss him. It would be hard to return to an empty house, to live there alone, for she assumed that the house would be hers, and that she would inherit the small income on which they had lived.

But, as she stood, dazed, after the funeral, drinking sherry wine and eating stale Madeira cake, she overheard what was not meant for her ears. Mrs Frith was saying in her hard, dismissive way to a friend, 'One supposes that she will go for a governess now, seeing that there is nothing left for her here—and who would marry a gel without a portion?'

'So I understand,' the friend replied. 'Quite penniless. Poor little squab; I feel for her.'

Nothing left? Penniless? What could they mean? Harry's heart began to beat wildly. It could not be true. There was the house and the furniture, and surely Papa would have left her something to live on. She would not need much; her wants were few. No, they must be wrong, but she looked around for Mr Flewitt, Netherdene's only lawyer, who had asked to see her alone once the mourners had left. She must speak to him.

When Mr Flewitt finally closed the door on the last mourner, and bade her sit down, his kind face was so grave that she clasped her hands together in unconscious supplication, and for the first time he saw in her face a resemblance to her beautiful mother, strengthened by the promise of a character which offered more than mere prettiness could.

'My dear,' he began, 'I have two pieces of news for you—one sad, and the other—well, you shall judge for yourself.' He paused. 'Do you have any notion of your stepfather's and your own financial circumstances?'

Harry shook her head. 'No, I had assumed that my stepfather's income—I knew that it was small—and this house would be left to me. As you know, all that my mother possessed was a small annuity which died with her.'

Mr Flewitt's hesitancy grew, then he said resolutely,
'My dear, I am afraid that your situation could hardly be
worse. Your stepfather possessed his half-pay, which, of
course, died with him, and he, too, received an income
from an annuity which, like your mother's, ended when
he died. This house is rented by the quarter, and all that
he had to leave you are the few sticks of furniture
contained in it, and a few personal possessions.'

Mrs Frith's unkind words echoed emptily in her ears.
I am both portionless and penniless, thought Harry
giddily, and I have no home. I must not faint.

Her pallor was such, however, that Mr Flewitt rapidly
poured her another glass of sherry and urged it upon
her.

'Which brings me,' he continued, 'to my second piece
of news. Mr Gilbert Ashburn, who is aware of your sad
plight, would like to see and to speak with you
immediately.'

'Gilly?' She looked up at him. 'He knows?'

'He made it his business to know,' said Mr Flewitt.
'He cares for you, and, like you, is alone in the world.
He is aware that your circumstances are desperate.'

'We are both orphans,' said Harry, white-lipped.

And both brave, thought Mr Flewitt. He had expected
hysterics, tears, protests. After all, to discover that you
had no home, no relatives who cared to know of you, no
money and no prospects, would be overwhelming at any
age, but at barely twenty—— He shuddered, and
repeated gently, 'Mr Ashburn would like to see you as
soon as possible. May I ring for your maid?'

My maid, thought Harry wildly. What have I to do
with maids now? But her voice as she answered was
composed; it was not the voice of someone before whom
a large pit had opened. She allowed Hannah to place a
cloak around her shoulders, and Mr Flewitt to take her
arm and lead her to the door. . .

Her memories had reached this point when she became
aware of the present again. Someone had entered the

room and walked over to the bed. She thought that it was Hannah, forgetting for a moment that she now had a companion, and the soft hand which felt her forehead was that of Sarah Whitmore, and not Hannah's harsh palm.

'You are awake?' Sarah asked.

'Yes,' said Harry, 'but stupid, I fear.' She was still half in the past, and was about to speak to Gilly, and it was suddenly important that she did so, and that this horrid present would disappear. If only she could be back with him, not faced by his stern cousin, and all these great people among whom her life now lay, and who all too obviously regarded her as an adventuress, knowing nothing of Gilly and his compassion for her. Restlessly, she thought that even Sarah's gentle kindness seemed an intrusion.

'I have brought you a tisane to help you sleep,' Sarah told her. 'The Duchess has sent it.'

Harry sat up, head swimming, and drank the warm, scented liquid obediently. She lay down again, and let it take her away on a slow tide. Gilly was waiting for her, as he had done on that morning nearly two years ago. . .

He was in his bedroom, but for once was not in bed. He was propped up in a large armchair, a chess-board before him on an occasional table. 'So, there you are,' he said cheerfully, moving his white Bishop down a long diagonal, pinning his black King. 'As you see, I cannot fail to win, whatever I do, being both black and white.' If his cheeks were pale and thin, his eyes were bright and his red hair flamed against the white pillow.

'Harry, my dear, you know how sorry I am that I could not support you today. But I had to fight Dr Wyatt even to sit in this chair.' He caught his breath. 'But John Coachman tells me that all was proper. Come and sit here a moment. Flewitt shall pour you some Madeira, and then he may leave us a little while we talk—if you so agree.'

'Please, no wine,' said Harry. 'I shall be happy to talk to you alone.'

Mr Flewitt put down the decanter he had taken up on Gilly's instructions. 'I shall be in the next room, Miss Minster. I do not think that Mr Ashburn will be long.'

'And you may leave the door open,' smiled Gilly, 'so all will be correct.' He pulled the blanket tighter around his shoulders.

'Harry. . .' he looked at her, his expression an odd mixture of shyness and daring '. . .as you know, like you, I am an orphan. My father was the younger son of a great family which cut him off for a marriage with a shopkeeper's daughter, whom they considered unworthy of him. He prospered mildly in trade, and has left me enough for a comfortable life, which, seeing that I can follow no occupation, is to my great good fortune.'

He paused. 'Our mothers were bosom friends when we were children, and we have been friends and allies for as long as I can remember. We learned our *amo amas* together, and you were always as good a scholar as I. . . I am really putting this quite badly. . . You know that I have not long to live——'

Harry brought up her hands suddenly to grasp his.

'Dear Gilly, no.'

'Oh, Harry, yes.' He disengaged his hands gently. 'It will not do to pretend otherwise. Because I have not long to live, and because I love you, and were things different we could have had a real marriage, I am going to offer you your freedom. Harry, my dear, please marry me. It cannot be a real marriage but I can give you financial security and leave you a little house and a little income. All shall be yours when I am gone. Now you must answer me, and, of course, you must say yes.'

'Oh, Gilly——' she slipped to her knees beside him, and took the black King from his hand '—you must not talk so; I cannot bear it.'

'And I cannot bear to think of you turned on the world quite penniless. Flewitt has told me all. Do not blame

him. I compelled his answer, and rightly so. You must
not be thrown away. Say yes, and Frith shall marry us.
Think how it will displease him. There is nothing that I
should like more than to disoblige our neighbours while
pleasing myself and you.'

Harry picked up the white Queen from the board and
placed it beside the black King. 'I must be honest with
you, Gilly. I love you like a sister, not at all as a girl
should love her husband. You are my dear brother. . .'

His eyes were bright and steady and fixed on hers.
'And you are my dear sister, and that is all I ask for, or
can ask, and for my dear sister I must and shall provide.
I have so little time that we must marry as soon as the
banns can be called. The black King must have his white
Queen, and the game must be played until Mate is
called.'

Harry bent her head to hide her tears, shed for both of
them, she thought, and then lifted it again as Gilly took
her hands in his.

'If you wish, and. . .if you will allow me to help you.
But I fear that my prowess at chess is sad indeed.'

'I shall teach you,' said Gilly decisively. 'And now we
must call Flewitt, who shall arrange our affairs.'

'There are few enough of mine to arrange,' sighed
Harry.

'Or of mine.' His grasp tightened. 'Oh, Harry, you
shall not regret this, I promise you.'

Nor did she. For if the bewilderment and the sense of
being abandoned had almost overwhelmed her after her
stepfather's death, the necessity to leave her home at
speed, to arrange her affairs, to prepare for her sudden
marriage—which, as Gilly had rightly prophesied,
shocked their neighbours—all gave her little time for
grief or worry.

Some small mysteries remained as she sorted through
her stepfather's possessions. Her mother's sudden death
had left him with what might have come directly to

Harry, but as she went through his boxes she discovered little belonging to any of her parents, other than her mother's marriage lines to Richard Minster, carefully stowed away, and naming her as the widow of the late John Grey, gentleman, but there were none for her marriage to Harry's father.

Futhermore Harry's own registry of birth was missing, and for the rest there were her stepfather's books and his naval dress sword, and decorations. Tucked away in a lacquer box were her mother's few jewels, including a pendant from which a great pearl, artificial surely, dangled, and with it a delicate miniature of an unknown and handsome young man in the dress of over twenty years ago. Perhaps this was her father, whom she had never known, but nothing on it said so.

It was, however, in her mourning black, with the pendant around her neck, that Harry was married to Gilly Ashburn by a cold and disapproving Mr Frith. He had seen it as his duty to approach Mr Flewitt, citing the authority of his cloth and Harry's minority, and demanding that Harry's relatives be informed before he consented to perform the ceremony. Mr Flewitt had looked at him over his gold-rimmed spectacles, and had reiterated that Harry had few relatives, and that they had washed their hands of a penniless girl whom they had no wish to support.

'Moreover,' he said, 'Mr Gilbert Ashburn may be ill in body, but his mind is more clear than that of most of us. I honour him for his wish to care for and to protect Miss Minster—and so should you.'

'But the world will think the worst of this marriage to a dying man,' began Mr Frith.

Mr Flewitt stopped him again. 'The world always thinks the worst,' he said acidly. 'But a man of the cloth, such as yourself, should take a more charitable view.'

So, on a clear January morning with a cold sun shining, Harry rode from church with Gilly to make the short journey to his home, which was now hers, and where a wedding breakfast and some few half-scandalised guests waited. Mr Frith had swallowed his reservations, and, with his wife on his arm, joined in the toasting of the newlyweds—though none dared predict a long marriage for them. As Mrs Frith sneered later, Mr Ashburn looked like the ghost he was so soon to be.

When all the guests were gone, Mr and Mrs Gilbert Ashburn turned to each other for comfort, and it was John Coachman who carried an exhausted Gilly to his bed, which he did not leave again until nearly a year later he slipped from life as quietly and bravely as he had lived it—although not before, as Harry said, he had finished her education which Mr Wentworth had begun.

'You play a wicked game of chess, my dear,' were almost his last words to his wife, and he was buried with the black King and his white Queen in his hand.

Harry slept at last, and in her dreams Gilly had Alex Templestowe's face, or was it the other way round? The Duchess came in to look at her as she slept, and thought that, if *this* was a harpy, then what did a virtuous woman look like?

CHAPTER THREE

'MY DEAR Alex,' said the Duchess, raising her eyes from her embroidery that evening, 'pray stop towering over me and sit down. The fire does not need your attention.'

'My apologies, Emily.' The hard face softened a little. 'I did not mean to be a boor. Particularly as I wished to speak to you urgently before the rest of the company arrive.'

'Indeed.' The Duchess put her needle down. 'And do I infer from this that you wish to speak of our unexpected morning visitor?'

Alex gave a short laugh and moved across to the vast armchair on the other side of the hearth. His aunt considered him for a moment. He was turned out point device, red head suitably dressed, its wild curls brushed into order, his suit was black in the manner Brummell had made fashionable, but he was just short of the dandy, and he shared nothing of the boy's prettiness which his brother Ned still possessed, and which had been his at Ned's age. But his face was full of character, a face which had experienced and suffered.

'Yes. Our visitor. I was wondering what you made of her?'

'What I made of her?' returned the Duchess. 'She's your cousin by marriage. I would have thought your opinion the more apt.'

'Good God,' he said, jumping up again and restlessly pacing the long room. 'I haven't an opinion any more. As I told you, from what was said about her by the local Rector I pictured a demure harpy, who was only too ready to marry a dying man for his small fortune, and then suddenly found herself the mistress of a great one,

26

ready to take on the world. No fit mistress for Racquette. But now. . . I don't know. . .' And his voice trailed off.

The Duchess picked up her needle again and waited. He stopped his pacing and flung himself into his chair. He looked every inch the soldier he had once been. 'Did you ever see such a white-faced scrap? Heriot said that she had no manner—but that's not true. Even through her pain and fright she showed herself to be dignified and composed; anything less like a greedy harpy I have seldom seen. But yet. . .'

'But yet, there's the marriage,' she finished.

'Indeed, and also. . .' He paused again, and shook his head.

'And also,' she finished for him, 'there is what Honoria Lansden has, oh, so delicately, suggested. What a way to disarm you—to arrive here in such a fashion.'

He shook his head again. 'That would be to presuppose too much. That she knew that I was here in residence—that might be easy, but how could she also know that I would be in the garden? And to set Caesar at the hedge. Too risky.' And he thought of the little figure in the shabby green riding habit. After months of having a fortune to spend she was still dressed as she must have been as mere Mrs Gilbert Ashburn. Most women would have rushed to re-equip themselves in suitable magnificence. Or was that a clever trick, too?

'Though a greedy harpy might be only too willing to take risks,' the Duchess said mildly, her eyes on his troubled face. 'And would be able to turn circumstances to her own advantage.'

'But for what, one might ask? After all, she has my grandfather's fortune. Surely that must suffice.' He stopped, struck. 'But, of course, my title and social recognition by the world. Is that what you are trying to say?'

'No,' said the Duchess, folding her embroidery. 'But you are unmarried, and I've no doubt that the Honoria

Lansdens of the world will draw such inference from today's happenings.'

'If you think so little of Honoria, then why is she here?'

'Because you needed me as a hostess, I wanted to visit Rule, and Honoria and her daughter were at hand to confer respectability to my stay at a gentleman's home.' She said this with a laugh, and he responded in kind.

'Nonsense; you are my aunt. I see your real reason. Louisa is eighteen and pretty—if you like pink and white—and I am still unmarried, and need a Countess, you think?'

'There is no harm in your inspecting pretty girls of good family,' she asserted equably.

'Good God, Emily, I never thought to see *you* promoting the marriage market.' His tone was a reproof, but she was equal to it again.

'Louisa is no better, and no worse, than a dozen others you might marry.'

'And there you state the reason why I have never married. I can enjoy wit and zest in a mistress, where marriage will give me a green girl without character, and no aptitude other than to breed dull children.'

'Now, Alex,' said the Duchess severely, 'you go too far. One thinks these things. One does not say them. When you were a soldier you might be forgiven, but this is pretty talk for a diplomat.'

He gave an unwilling laugh. 'If I cannot be honest with you. . .'

'I know and I sympathise—but we have no choice in these matters. We marry and are given in marriage to hold together our land and our names. At least you, as a man, may exercise some right of choice, but we women are simply the spoils of marriage, no more,' she said steadily.

'You shame me,' was his curt reply.

'So, you do not think me a hyena in petticoats, as

Horace Walpole said of Mary Wollstonecraft when she proclaimed the Rights of Women?'

He dropped to his knees beside her, and took her hand and kissed it. 'You know that you are the mama I never had, and I know that you were married to the Duke without ever having seen him before your wedding day, and that he has neglected you for most of your married life. Forgive me.'

'Then be a little kind to Mrs Ashburn. I, too, suspect that she is not what they say. She may or may not be the adventuress the world thinks her. You might care to consider that she has Sarah Whitmore for a companion— a most worthy woman, and discreet. But I note that Sarah appears to like her, which says something for her. And be kind to Louisa, too; her mother is desperate to marry her off—the Lansdens are strapped for money, and you are filthy rich, even if you didn't inherit Templestowe's wealth.'

'So long as my kindness to either of them doesn't extend to marriage, I'm happy to oblige,' he returned. 'Although as to Mrs Ashburn, I'll reserve my final judgement on better acquaintance.'

Harry awoke the next morning a little refreshed. She was bruised and aching all over, but her head had cleared. Whether this was the result of the Duchess's tisane, or her own resilience, she was not sure. Perhaps both. She announced her intention to leave her bed at once. Hannah and Mrs Whitmore both stared at her, and urged her to further rest there, but, despite her respect for them, she refused.

'To placate you I shall remain in my room this morning, and join the company this afternoon. The sooner I am ready to return home, the better. I am well aware that I am an unwanted intruder. Lord Templestowe cannot wish me here, knowing that I have deprived him of his real home, and my presence must be a constant reminder of that.'

'Your feelings do you credit,' said Mrs Whitmore,
while Hannah scowled at her.

'Stop thinking black thoughts, Hannah,' said Harry
cheerfully, smiling at Mrs Whitmore, although Hannah's
frequently expressed loyalty warmed her.

Later, dressed and seated in a large chair by a latticed
window which overlooked the rose-garden, she mused
on her changed fortunes, while Hannah fussed about
her.

After Gilly's death she had lived the quiet life she had
expected in the modest and secure comfort he had
promised her. Her days were pleasant, if lonely—she
missed him more even than she had thought to do—and
they stretched out in front of her into an apparently
settled future, until the one on which an astonished Mr
Flewitt had brought the Templestowe lawyer, cynical
and suspicious Mr Heriot, to her. . .

It had been teatime, and in the unchanging rhythm of
her life she had laid her book aside as Hannah came in
with the tea-board, saying disapprovingly, 'Reading
again, Miss Harry?'

'But not for long,' replied Harry. 'Mr Flewitt has
asked to see me—put the tea-board in the window,
Hannah. He will be here directly.'

'Oh, aye,' said Hannah, disapproving again. 'It's only
old men you ever see,' and, hearing the door-knocker,
she went to let in Mr Flewitt, who was accompanied by
a strange, sleek gentleman with a hard white face, who
stared about him at the comfortably shabby room and at
Harry in the half-mourning lilac she had worn since
Gilly's death a few months ago. 'No black for me, please,'
he had said, and the lilac instead of black was one more
indictment of the Ashburns' strange ways.

The stranger bowed low and extravagantly over her
hand, and took the chair which looked out on the street,
and on the elderly Misses Habergeon, who daily passed
at four-thirty, so that, as Hannah said, you could set
your clock by them.

'Quiet here, Mrs Ashburn,' he offered, after Mr Flewitt had made him known as Mr Heriot, a brother officer of the law.

They drank tea, and Harry looked from one to the other, wondering what chance had brought this fashionably dressed gentleman to quiet Netherdene, and why Mr Flewitt should see fit to bring him to her. But she had learned the art of waiting, and presently Mr Flewitt put down his cup, and said to her in his kind way, 'Mrs Ashburn, I think that you know little of your late husband's family.'

'Only that they cut off Gilly's father so completely that they never had any intercourse with him—did not even know, Gilly said, where he lived. Gilly's father informed his family of his birth, but gave no clue as to his whereabouts. He wanted nothing of them, Gilly said, or they of him.'

'Indeed, so I understood, which makes Mr Heriot's news all the stranger.'

'Strange, indeed,' offered that gentleman smoothly. 'Would you believe, madam, that we have been searching for Mr Gilbert Ashburn ever since his grandfather Lord Templestowe died just over a year ago?'

Harry looked from one to the other in surprise—a surprise which grew as Mr Heriot unfolded his news to her. That Gilly was to have inherited all the Templestowe estates and wealth. That the new Earl, a man in his early thirties, once a soldier, but now a diplomat, had been disinherited, in favour of the great-nephew the late Earl had never known.

'But what is this to do with me?' she said, bewildered. 'The inheritance was Gilly's, not mine.'

Mr Flewitt looked at her, and thought how proper Mrs Ashburn was in all her ways, with little thought for her own advantage.

'Since your late husband died *after* Lord Templestowe, he inherited without knowing, and, since he bequeathed all that he owned to you, without reservation, then, my dear, *you* have inherited the great house of Racquette, and this immense dower.'

The clock ticked in the silent room. Harry wondered dizzily what the correct etiquette was for a young lady who had been made such a remarkable present. She hardly knew what to say, and, with Mr Heriot's sardonic eye hard on her, asked her questions of them, wondered if the new Earl had been left penniless, learned that he had inherited his mother's vast estates, secured to him by settlement on her marriage to his father. That there was nothing she could do but accept; Lord Templestowe had arranged for his estates to revert to the Crown in the unlikely case of their rejection. 'And you would not want that, madam; the Crown has enough already.'

Mr Heriot's manner grew ever more patronising as he instructed her, and his smile was knowing and sarcastic when she expressed her pity for the new Earl, deprived of his patrimony '—and I know that my late husband would have felt the same,' she concluded.

Mr Heriot rose and bowed to her. 'Your sentiments do you credit, madam,' he told her, and it was plain that he did not believe a word she said, and he sat down again with a flourish of his coat-tails which reminded her irreverently of the demon king in the pantomime whom she had seen on her one visit to the theatre in Norwich, and wished she could share the joke with Gilly.

She knew at once, from Mr Heriot's manner, what the world would think of her: a fortune-hunter, and Gilly's kindness demeaned to the gulling of a dying man. Well, that could not be helped, either, and her manner to the London lawyer was so cool and composed that he expressed his admiration for her sang-froid to his colleagues when he returned. 'A demure piece, indeed, as the local Rector informed me, who swallowed a plain bun when she married her victim, and found that it was a currant one. I take my hat off to her.'

She did not know that he had said this of her, but, from the expressions of those she met after her great good fortune was known, she could guess it, and on the way to her new home she summoned up her resolution. She would not allow what others might think to overset her, and as Racquette came into sight at the end of her journey she looked from the window of her little chariot at it, admired its beauty, as it nestled there, a white Palladian jewel-box, set on the Sussex Downs, and thought of the man who had lost it.

Racquette was neither as large as Blenheim, nor so magnificent as Chatsworth, but its elegance was its own. Whatever the violent temper of previous Earls of Templestowe, their taste was exquisite, and its furnishings were beautiful beyond belief to a girl who had lived a quiet life in the wilds of Norfolk.

Harry's arrival was celebrated in princely style. As Mr Flewitt handed her down, with Hannah all agog behind her, the housekeeper Mrs Marshall and Gibbs the butler advanced to meet her, walking towards her through an avenue of servants and estate workers, underservants, gardeners, grooms, gamekeepers, footmen, and some small children whom she found were lamp-boys, who stared at her like the rest. She made her way between the curtsying and bowing lines, aware that her plain mourning lilac, her pleasant, but not remarkable face, and her lack of manner, as rumour had it, added an element of farce to such pompous grandeur.

Once up the stairs and inside, however, the beauty of the classically pillared hall, the elevated glass dome, and the Italian mosaic floor with its guardian dog barking at her drove all else from her mind. Mrs Marshall led her through the entrance hall to the grand staircase, and then through a long picture gallery, where dead Ashburns, with faces reminiscent of Gilly's, stared at this intruder from the walls.

'And this, madam, is the west wing, where your apartments are ready.'

Her private drawing-room was light and airy, and through tall windows looked out on an informal garden,

with classical statuary standing about, Pomona vying
with Flora in girth. She sank on to a flowered bergere, as
Mrs Marshall, head bent, enquired if tea would suit her,
and commanded a rosy-cheeked maid to bring the tea-
board for madam, and place it on the laquered table
before the crackling fire. 'It being cold in April, Gibbs
thought to make you comfortable here,' she explained.

Gratefully, Harry began to pour the offered tea, and
the housekeeper, who had stayed to draw the fire, turned
and said, 'Mrs Whitmore is waiting to see you, madam.
I believe that Mr Flewitt has informed you that she
would be most suitable to be your companion and *dame
de compagnie.*'

Say rather my duenna, thought Harry irreverently,
but she realised the necessity for a newly widowed young
lady of great wealth to observe the proprieties. 'Pray
send her to me, Mrs Marshall.'

Mrs Sarah Whitmore proved to be middle-aged, gentle
and easy to please, an Ashburn poor relation found by
Mr Heriot.

'I had not thought you to be so young, my dear. Far
younger than my poor Alex. . .oh, dear.'

'Alex?' said Harry.

'Your cousin by marriage. The seventh Earl. His
friends call him Alex; he is properly Gilbert Alexander. I
did not mean to reproach you, my dear, when I called
him poor Alex, although it was not tactful of me.
Particularly when you might meet him any day.'

'But I thought that he was in Paris or Vienna, helping
to settle the peace,' Harry said, dismayed to discover
that she was so soon to encounter an angry young man
whom she had deprived of his inheritance.

'Oh, he was, he was,' replied Mrs Whitmore, harassed,
bringing her handkerchief into play again. 'But he has
returned to settle his affairs, now that. . .now that. . .'

'Now that I have been discovered,' finished Harry,
amused at the woman's distress, and touched by her
delicacy.

'Exactly.' Mrs Whitmore was aghast to discover that she had initiated a conversation of such evident impropriety. With an air of quiet desperation she smoothed her gown. 'I understand that he may be surrendering his diplomat's career, but that could be idle gossip. For the rest, Mr Heriot thought that I might be helpful to you as you begin your life in Society. Your wardrobe, whom you might properly meet. Life in the ton can be most difficult for the unwary.'

'I have not yet decided whether I wish a life in Society,' said Harry firmly.

'Oh, but you must,' insisted Mrs Whitmore. 'You have inherited all this. You have a duty, my dear. You are young, you will marry again, and you must marry the right person who will help you in the task of ordering these great estates, not someone who will prey upon you.'

For all her apparent vagueness, thought Harry, Mrs Whitmore seemed to have a firm grasp of the practical. Her own thoughts and musings had not yet included a future husband, although undoubtedly Mrs Whitmore was correct in assuming that she would be a target for fortune-hunters.

But she did not wish to marry again, or, at least, not yet. Amid all the excitements of the last few months she had become aware that, however little she might have wanted or expected the enormous fortune thrust upon her, it was giving her the opportunity to have a life of her own choosing. What that life might be, she could not imagine, only that it would be very different from the one which she had been living, safe in dull Netherdene on what now seemed a mere pittance.

Mrs Whitmore continued with her advice. She wished to see Harry's wardrobe in order to pronounce upon its suitability. She urged Harry to consult *Burke's Peerage* to learn about Gilly's many grand relations, some near and some distant, whom Harry would certainly meet.

'The most famous of all, of course, is the Duchess of

Hornsea, Templestowe's aunt. She is known as the Little Duchess, or Duchess Emily. The Duke is now a great recluse—he was quite a rake in his youth, they say, and he's much older than Duchess Emily, you know.'

Harry did not know, but deemed it politic to smile diplomatically.

'It's a pity,' Mrs Whitmore rambled on, 'that there are no suitable younger sons for you there.'

'Oh, please,' urged Harry, 'let me become used to my new life before I husband-hunt.'

'Oh, they'll hunt *you*, my dear,' said Mrs Whitmore. 'It's a matter of you choosing. . .'

Her conversation with Mrs Whitmore echoed in Harry's ears as she dressed herself, with Hannah's grumbled assistance, after lunch. Well, at least there was one man who would not hunt her, judging by his expression, and she was certainly not going to hunt him. She was safe from Alex Templestowe for sure. So that when she met him, coming in from the garden, after she had walked downstairs, her manner was as cool to him as his was to her.

He stared dubiously at her pale face, with its slightly bruised temple, and said, 'Should you be up, Mrs Ashburn? Where is your maid or your companion? You should not be alone.'

'I am not alone,' she retorted tartly, 'I am talking to you,' and there was no answer to that, she thought. But she mistook; he had been, or still was, a diplomat.

His mouth twitched a little and he replied, 'You are prevaricating, I think. You were alone when I met you.'

Somehow she felt impelled to reply, 'Is anyone ever alone in this house? It seems full of people to me. Guests and servants. There has been quite a lengthy procession of them through my room this morning. More than I saw in a week at Netherdene.'

This show of spirit appeared to amuse him a little. 'Well, you do not want for an answer, madam. Allow me to escort you into the garden-room. The Duchess will probably be joining you there soon. Until then I shall remain with you, in case you feel overcome.'

Now what could she say to that? Only, 'You are too good, sir,' in a tone which subtly implied the opposite.

Which had no effect at all, as he took her by the arm, with, 'Allow me,' and walked her along the corridor into a pleasant room, full of plants, and sat her down on a comfortable old-fashioned settle, like the one in her drawing-room at Netherdene, and drew up a chair opposite to her.

Alex was intrigued by her, by the great dark eyes in her ivory face, and the quiet pride of her manner. She was still shabbily dressed in what probably passed for fashion in the backwater from which she had sprung. To some extent this impressed him. Although he was usually impeccably turned out, fashion meant little to him, and he had been at his happiest in the battered uniform in which he had campaigned in Spain. Evans and his valet Forbes were always lamenting that their master had to be compelled to show himself off to advantage. Perhaps Harry's women felt the same about her; on the other hand, an adventuress might seek to disarm by not appearing one.

He turned his hard grey eyes on her as she sat there, the owner of Racquette, having done nothing to earn it but leap into bed with a dying man—he must not forget *that*, must not be seduced by a composed manner and a cool charm into thinking that she was other than what she was.

Harry remained calm under his stare, which was more inimical than he realised. There was no help for it; there was little she could say or do to disabuse him of what he was undoubtedly thinking, and she waited for him to initiate the conversation. Which he did, thrusting out his two booted legs in a somewhat cavalier manner, and eyeing her with more than a little severity, as though she

were a recalcitrant and slightly disobedient young lieutenant about to be disciplined.

'So, madam, how do you find Sussex? After living in
Norfolk for so many years, you must find it strange.'

'All my life,' said Harry gently. 'Remiss of me, I
know. I should have made the world mine oyster—but
oysters are expensive.'

'Oh, indeed,' he agreed, with a short laugh, as though
the young lieutenant had shown spirit, but needed to be
chided a little for it, she thought. 'But some of us know
how to remedy that.'

The devil got into Harry. If he must think me an
adventuress. . . 'Oh, yes,' she replied. 'Where there's a
will there's a way, you know. One of the first lessons I
learned in life—a most valuable one, too.' And let his
high-nosed lordship of Templestowe make what he
would of that!

By his frown he disliked it. 'You never visited outside
Norfolk, then?'

'No,' said Harry. 'I am a regular Norfolk Dumpling.
Doubtless if Gilly had lived we might have roved the
world together. As it was, we visited it in our
imaginations.'

'Gilly?' he repeated, surprised into bad manners by
her absolute determination not to be ruffled.

'Ah, I forgot,' said Harry. 'Your cousin Gilbert, my
late husband. The despised and rejected of men, I
understand, seeing that his father had the bad taste to
marry for love and not for lands and money.'

She had left herself open to him. His reply was quick
and savage. 'Unlike yourself, madam, I believe.'

'Oh, yes,' agreed Harry. 'One has one's way to make.
Broad acres and a mansion have always seemed more
attractive to me than a cottage.' And God forgive me,
Gilly, she thought, for so ennobling our own little home
and its tiny garden, but seeing that a bad-tempered
nobleman wishes to regard me as a vulture—or is it a

vampire?—we must oblige him. I am sure you would have approved.

Alex was a little ashamed of his rudeness, the more so as he could not break her grave serenity. The slight smile on her face never wavered, and he felt himself to be a mannerless churl. But such self-control was in itself, he thought, indicative of a will and temper strong enough to carry out any plot, however devious, and, despite what he had said to the Duchess, her arrival here smacked of the arranged, although God knew how she had managed it.

Harry for her part thought that if she had any regrets about depriving this rude man of his inheritance she was rapidly losing them. 'And you,' she said sweetly, 'I understand, have made your way about the world. Are you like the man in the tale who said that the only benefit he derived from travel was that he could swear effectively in ten different languages and be unable to hold a polite conversation in any one of them?'

Alex stared at her, hardly believing his ears. He must have misheard, so grave, so politely enquiring was her face, head a little on one side, her whole manner Gilly at his bland and wicked best, baiting Mr Frith or some other monster who thought a dying invalid fair game. Of all the lessons Gilly had taught her, the ability to hold her own in a tight conversational corner was the finest and the most useful.

So, madam has a ready wit, thought Alex, an unwilling grin touching the corner of his mouth. I wonder, I really wonder, whether she is equally cool in the sexual lists, and what will happen when I joust with her there—as after this I surely will. Still waters run deep, I'll be bound, and she has already snared one man, at least, if not more. Just wait, my fine, impertinent young woman, until you have recovered a little, and I can test you to see how you fare in a rougher game.

Aloud he said, 'Oh, my Spanish is adequate enough for me to make apt comments on anything,' and he came out rapidly with a proverb in that language to the effect that the best treatment of a talkative and impudent young woman was with a broom-handle first, and a vital article of male equipment second, and his mocking eyes defied her to ask him for a translation.

Before Harry, who knew by his expression that he had said something insulting, could answer, Ned came in exclaiming, for he had not seen her presence, 'Is she down, yet, Alex? I am determined to be polite, but not too much so—oh. . .' and he made an almost comical face when he realised that it was not the Duchess to whom Alex was paying such attention, but the harpy, as he privately thought of her.

But she was not such a harpy after all, perhaps, for she pretended that she had not heard what he had said, and Alex said, 'Really, Ned, think before you speak. Sit down, do, and address your cousin properly,' suddenly feeling shame at his own treatment of Harry on hearing how someone else's rudeness, however unwitting, sounded, and Ned accordingly did so, face scarlet, to gaze furtively at her.

Harry was not at all discommoded by Ned's rudeness, but smiled at him and said, 'I am surprised that you are indoors on such a fine day.'

Eager to make up for his discourtesy, he smiled back, saying in his easy manner, 'Oh, I have been out riding, but I have to see the Rector this afternoon. He is preparing me for when I go to Oxford this autumn, but I am not a scholar, as Alex was, you know, and I need his help. No, do not frown at me, Alex; you are aware that I think going to Oxford is a waste of my time, but all the Ashburns go there. It is a thing. Did Cousin Gilbert go?'

'No,' said Harry. 'We were educated by the Rector and ourselves. Mr Wentworth said that Gilly was a natural scholar. He loved activity, though, and it saddened him to be confined to bed for so long.'

'Oh, indeed,' said Ned heartily. 'It does not bear thinking about. I could not stand it.' And he smiled at her again, wondering what his unknown cousin was like, noting in his practical way that her face lit up whenever she spoke of Gilly.

She was being vaguely cheeky to Alex, too, he rapidly gathered by her manner and Alex's expression, which amused him. No one was cheeky to Alex. He was so grand and serious and unapproachable that even Ned, who loved him, wished that he would unbend a little.

Alex was not best pleased, Ned saw, that he had confessed to his reluctance to go to University, but it was difficult to persuade Alex or change his mind over something which he saw as a principle, and it was a matter of principle to him that Ned, although a younger son, should receive a good education. However, Alex did unbend a little to say to Harry, 'If young men must go to University, then young ladies, even married ones, must have their come-out. I gather that my aunt is prepared to sponsor you when you arrive in London for the Season. It will, of course, be the Regent, not His Majesty, to whom you will be presented.'

This was really too prosingly bad of Alex; one might think him ninety and a dowager, not still comparatively young, thought Ned, with all the careless ease of eighteen contemplating thirty-one, and he was delighted to see such heavy patronage paid back by their new cousin, after a fashion both brothers soon came to recognise as her own.

For she looked at Alex, and said, her face grave, as though she were discussing the Rector's sermon, 'Oh, dear, I know that this will be all too much for me. Country mice are not trained for such magnificence. Would the Regent mind, do you think, if I asked to be excused?' And Alex almost took her seriously, and began to answer her until he, Ned, laughed, and cut in.

'But she is roasting you, Alex,' and she said, quietly, 'Oh, never; Lord Templestowe is much too grand to be roasted.'

Even Alex began to laugh at that, and the Duchess,

coming in a few moments later, found them all talking together quite easily, Ned being particularly taken by her to the extent that he said suddenly, 'Now, what shall I call you? Mrs Ashburn is too formal, Cousin Harry too informal—I shall call you Mrs Gilly,' for Gilly had come into their conversation, when she had asked Ned if he played cricket, and, on his answering yes, had told him of Gilly's love for it before illness had struck him down.

'And he taught me to bat, when I was a small girl, and bowl a little, too.'

Colour had come back into her cheeks, and her face was alight as she spoke. The brothers stared at her, amused, even Alex half succumbing to her grave charm, and the Duchess laughed and said, 'A woman of parts, I see.'

For a moment Harry was happy, and forgot her difficult situation until, without thinking, she remarked, 'And the lawn at Racquette is so smooth one could use it for a pitch, only one might ruin the flower-beds,' and Alex's face closed and shut, and the rapport of the last few minutes was gone in an instant, and she was an intruder again.

Matters were not helped by Honoria Lansden, who arrived with Louisa in tow, hunting Alex down, all four of them in the garden-room separately and uncharitably thought.

She stared at them, apparently happy together, for Alex had recovered a little after Harry's slight gaffe. 'Oh, Mrs Ashburn, you are up already, I see.' A remarkably redundant statement, thought Harry. 'Are you sure that this is wise? Rest, and only rest, will restore you.' Behind her, Louisa nodded her head, her usual accompaniment to her dominant mama's conversation.

'But a little exercise cannot hurt, and might help,' said Harry. 'I am not accustomed to lie abed in the afternoon.'

'No doubt, no doubt,' drawled Honoria. 'But then, you are not accustomed to a dramatic arrival in a rose-garden without your horse, either, one supposes.'

'Well, I could hardly arrive with him,' said Harry reasonably, 'seeing Caesar stopped dead at the hedge. It would have been difficult to have dragged him over behind me.'

Ned gave a snort of unruly laughter at this. 'Oh, splendid, Mrs Gilly. What a picture. Caught you there, Lady L.' And even Alex and the Duchess allowed themselves to smile a little.

Lady Lansden's expression was acid indeed. This impertinent young woman must be put in her place.

'One sees that you were not mentally afflicted by your unfortunate experience, Mrs Ashburn. What a relief for you.'

'Yes, indeed,' Harry agreed cordially. 'To have descended into idiocy might have amused others, but would hardly have benefited oneself. Unless, of course, one hired oneself out to a fair as a raree-show.' This came out so pleasantly that for a moment her hearers hardly realised what she had said. Lady Lansden went slowly red, and Alex glared at Ned, whose delight was patent. He disliked Lady Lansden, who lost no chance to patronise him—younger sons were of no interest to *her*— as she was now trying to patronise Harry. That young woman was lying back on the settle, an expression of sweet forbearance on her face, as though she hardly knew what she was saying, an expression which Gilly would have recognised, and laughed at in private.

After that Lady Lansden surrendered, flouncing out dragging a reluctant Louisa behind her, claiming urgent letters to write, no time to stand about chattering, your pardon, Duchess. Duchess Emily surveyed Harry, and then her two nephews.

'Well, one thing is certain,' she said approvingly. 'It will be some time before poor Honoria attempts to put you down again.'

'Oh, famous,' declared Ned. 'What could impel you to invite her, Aunt Emily? She is always a bore. And that soggy marshmallow, Louisa—oh.' He looked from the

Duchess to Alex, and before she could speak said,
'Never. You are never trying to foist Louisa on Alex!
That would not do at all. She would drive him mad in a
week with her nodding head and her blushes. Alex is a
good fellow, but he needs a girl of spirit who will stand
up to him and give him what for.'

Harry could not prevent herself. She broke into a fit
of the giggles at this frank and tactless statement of fact,
and Alex's face on receipt of it. Efforts to turn this into a
coughing fit were all too successful; Ned was sent for
water by the Duchess, and Alex, standing by, smiled
unwillingly as she gasped to such a degree that the
Duchess sat by her and patted her back.

'You are rightly served,' he said cheerfully. 'You and
Ned make a good pair of naughty children. This will
teach you to roast poor devils who have done nothing to
deserve it. You note I do not include your treatment of
Honoria in my strictures.'

It was the most natural speech he had made to her yet,
and she welcomed it. He would never forgive her for
taking Racquette from him, but there might be a truce
between them, she thought, if he could see her as a
human being, and not. . .a vampire. This further
thought worsened the giggles and the choking. Only
Ned's return with water and, 'Your pardon, Mrs Gilly, I
did not mean to drive you to this,' brought relief.

CHAPTER FOUR

DUCHESS EMILY refused to allow Harry to return to Racquette immediately, even though Harry asserted firmly that she had suffered no more than shock from her fall.

'No,' said the Duchess. 'Your head was a little injured, and where the head is concerned one must not take chances. Chartley fully agrees with me.' So, Harry was constrained to remain at Rule, as Alex's guest. She discovered that the manor house had come to Alex from his mother, who, together with Emily, was the last of a family whose lands had marched with the Ashburns' for three centuries.

'A most convenient pair of marriages,' said the Duchess drily. 'I took the northern estates to Hornsea, and Caroline brought these and the Midland ones to the Ashburns. My poor sister died young. She was an invalid after Alex's birth, and died at Ned's, and they were left to the caprice of their father, who, like his father, the late Earl, quarrelled with everyone before he, too, died young.'

'And Alex resembles them?' half stated, half queried Harry.

'No,' said the Duchess, 'Alex and Ned are more like their mother, particularly Ned. Caro had a happy wit, although constant illness dampened it a little. I admit both share the Ashburn tendency to a strong will, but in them it is not allied to caprice.'

Duchess Emily had been kind to her, so Harry did not reply. Alex's manner to her remained reserved, and she frequently found him observing her in a way which puzzled her. She was puzzled, too, by the reputation which she had undoubtedly acquired of being a fortune-hunter when she had married Gilly. More than one overheard remark since her elevation had made this known to her.

And then, seated one day with Ned, who rapidly made his liking for her plain, she found the answer. They were playing backgammon together, as the weather had turned chill and stormy, and at the end of the session he had leaned forward to pick up the pieces, saying in his frank way, 'You're a good sport, Mrs Gilly. You're not at all like that fellow Frith rumoured you to be. . .' and then he had flushed at what he had said, with Harry knowing that Mr Frith's spite had pursued her here, and partly accounted for Alex's attitude.

She had, however, completely won Ned over. The weather worsened further, and one morning she was playing Ned at chess as a heavy shower beat against the windows of the long room.

She had left off her mourning lilac, and wore a deep blue high-waisted dress, trimmed with fine lace, and the Duchess's personal maid, Poins, had cut Harry's hair fashionably short, after the manner of Caroline Lamb, at the Duchess's insistence.

Ned had generously offered to handicap himself by reducing his pieces before they began to play, but he soon discovered that Mrs Gilly was more than a match for him. Both were so enthralled in the game, dark head and red head bent over the board, that neither heard Alex enter.

He stood a moment, watching them, and laughed as Ned threw back his head, and said in pure disgust as Harry checkmated him, his King pinned by Queen and Knight, 'Oh, Mrs Gilly, you've won again. Thank God we're not playing for money.' He looked at his brother. 'You should play against her, Alex. She has me beat every time.'

Without thinking, Alex replied, 'I'm sure I should be no match for Mrs Ashburn's guile,' and then half wished he could recall his thoughtless words as Harry's face first flamed red, and then turned white. She was dismayed. At the end of the conversation in the garden-room she had thought that there was a growing understanding between them, but what he had just said appeared to show that his suspicions as to her motives and conduct were still very much alive. She was not to know that they were, but that he had also decided to go warily with her, in the hope that he could compel her to drop her guard and betray her true self, the self which had trapped his cousin, and which he was determined would not trap him. It was no part of his plan to make her wary of him—as he had just done.

'Indeed, my lord,' Harry said as formally as she could, 'you do me too much honour. My husband taught me to play, and it is his craft you should praise, not mine.'

Alex cursed himself for his clumsiness, but, before he could speak, Honoria Lansden drawled, 'A most unladylike game, chess. I'm sure I would deplore Louisa learning it.' Louisa nodded vigorously at this.

Harry dropped her a great curtsy. 'I doubt there's much chance of that, madam. Ned, my lord, Lady Lansden. You will excuse me. I think that it is time I went home.'

Alex moved forward, still angry with himself at his careless words; he had not meant to provoke this scene. 'You will grant me a game, Cousin Harry, before you go, I trust.'

It was the first time that he had not used the formal Mrs Ashburn to her, but Harry was not to be mollified. Her head high, she replied, 'No, my lord. It would be too great an honour,' and she curtsied to him, too, and made for the door, only to find him there before her.

'Cousin Harry,' he said again, 'you mistake me. I did not mean. . .'

'No, indeed,' she agreed. 'You meant nothing, nothing at all. Pray allow me to pass.'

He moved aside, and whether his anger was greater with himself for his carelessness, or with her for her

steadfast refusal to compromise in the face of what
appeared to her to be an insult, he could not say. He was
not accustomed to apologise, nor, when he did so, for his
apology to be ignored. He was unhappily aware that he
had cut a poor figure without meaning to, and to no
purpose.

As though I care whether or not Alex Templestowe
considers me an adventuress, thought Harry angrily, as
she mounted the stairs to her room. But she had to
acknowledge that she *did* care. For some reason which
she could not identify she wanted his good opinion, if for
no better cause than that she could not bear that someone
who looked so like Gilly did not approve of her.

It was odd, she thought, that Ned, who did not
resemble Gilly greatly in appearance, actually possessed
his gentle good humour, while his elder brother, whose
character was so different, not only looked like him, but
had a voice which caused Gilly's to reverberate in her
memory every time he spoke.

Oh, but Alex had character, too. A kind of fierce
integrity behind the harshness with which he treated her,
in the belief that she was the worst kind of adventuress.
She could imagine what a good soldier he had been, and
what demands he had made of himself and his men.
Hateful to be despised by such a man, and to be able to
do so little about it.

Only the thought of what Gilly would have said to her
kept the tears from falling. 'Come, you must be a good
soldier yourself.' Yes, that was it. The very next time
that 'my lord' began to take her down for her supposed
wickedness, she would let him have it, straight between
the eyes, no quarter, bugles sounding, cavalry ready to
charge. These military metaphors brought on the giggles,
and when she met the Duchess after luncheon her
manner was so cheerful that, although she asked if she
might leave, the Duchess did not feel that it was because
naughty Alex, as the Duchess privately thought him, had
completely upset her new protégée.

Talking to Harry, the Duchess had discovered that the Templestowe's harpy was, in fact, the daughter of old friends with whom she had unaccountably lost touch many years ago, in a fashion which the Duchess had always considered a little mysterious.

Drawing Harry out, Emily had found that she knew little of her parents' past, her father having died when she was a child, and her mother having done so before Harry was of an age to learn or care much about old friends and relatives. Her stepfather's refusal to acknowledge Harry's mother's first husband had also helped to keep Harry innocent of the past.

'How strange,' Harry said, 'to think that you once knew Mama and Papa; I had no idea. . .' and then she stopped and coloured a little, before finishing, '. . .no idea that they possessed such grand friends. I hardly knew that we had friends or relatives at all. I never questioned it before, but now it does seem odd, to say the least.'

'I suppose your parents and your stepfather had their reasons,' said the Duchess gently, but she privately wondered what they could have been, and how it had happened that Harry had needed to make such a marriage as the one she had made with Gilly. Even Emily, with all her tolerance, thought that a marriage with a dying man was a little strange, unless, of course, it was truly made for his money. But the more she saw of Harry, the more she liked her, and, unlike Alex, who had lost home, lands and a fortune, she felt that she was prepared to give her the benefit of the doubt over it. Besides, Alex had other reasons for mistrusting women.

So, when Harry said that she would like to return to Racquette in the morning—she did not like to call it home, thinking that Alex's relatives might find her tactless—the Duchess said gently, 'You must forgive Alex his manner, my dear; I do not wish to gossip, but he does have reasons for suspecting the motives of women.'

Harry moved her hands restlessly. She had no desire to distress the Duchess, who had shown her nothing but kindness, but she thought that Alex's manner to her was more severe than a mere dislike of women in general. It was personal, and directed towards herself. Her own sense of guilt at depriving him of what he reasonably might have expected to inherit was strong, but how could she convince him of that? Gilly had always said that excuses and explanations were signs of guilt, not innocence, and that must apply not only to explanations of her personal innocence, but also to her own regret at his grandfather's behaviour. She knew that her reply was stiff, but that could not be helped.

'I am sure that Lord Templestowe usually has a good reason for all he cares to do or say.'

The Duchess sighed a little at this. 'Indeed, child. Men are not like us, you know. They do not have to consider their words as we do. Now, I collect that you are to visit London soon. I warn you that I intend to launch you on Society, which should open many doors to you. After the Season I insist that you come to Oldheath. I cannot promise that you will see the Duke. He sees nobody, but I like your company, and should wish a little of it before you return to Racquette for the winter. Promise that you will inform me when you arrive in London.'

Harry was only too happy to agree. She was not so naïve that she did not realise all that a powerful protectress like the Duchess could do for her. Few would care to antagonise or put down a Hornsea protégée. However little London life or even visiting Oldheath Priory appealed to her, all her advisers had impressed on her the necessity for her to enter and become a part of the great world.

That evening, her last at Rule, at the Duchess's request, she read aloud from a novel by a lady of whom she had not heard. As the early chapters of *Pride and Prejudice* unfolded, she found herself falling under the

spell of both the writer and her creation, Elizabeth
Bennett. Harry even wondered mischievously if Miss
Jane Austen had ever met Alex Templestowe; he seemed
so like Mr Darcy.

'You read well, my child,' said the little Duchess
kindly. 'I only recall one other lady reading as well as
yourself, but that was long ago, and she was your dear
mama. She was very skilful at rendering *The Mysteries of
Udolpho*, very different from my dear Miss Austen's
gentle prose.'

'My mother taught me to read aloud,' said Harry.
'And Gilly found it passed the time for him when he
could no longer sit up to read himself. Pray, shall I
continue?'

Alex, who had been playing chess with Ned, and had
just mated him, looked up as she finished speaking, to
say, 'If the Duchess will allow, Cousin Harry, I should
be exceedingly grateful for a game with you. I cannot let
you leave Rule without giving me a chance to defeat you.
In all fairness, madam——' and his manner was as
pleasant as he could make it, for he was determined to
win this battle of wills with her, come what may '—you
must allow me to test your skill. I issue you a formal
challenge,' he concluded, and his eyes were brilliant on
her, as she sat there, quiet, the book in her hands.

'But not before I have finished my reading,' insisted
Harry, smiling a little, but equally determined not to
give way, if it were at all possible. 'We are all agog to see
how Miss Elizabeth Bennett deals with her clerical
suitor.'

'Oh, as to that,' said Alex, carelessly, 'she'll send him
away with a flea in his ear, mark my words. That's all
clerical suitors are fit for in novels.'

'Now, Alex, it is not like you to talk nonsense,'
remonstrated the Duchess. 'Nor are you to spoil Harry's
reading for us. Be patient for a little, and then she will
do battle with you, I am sure.'

In the face of this Harry could not refuse Alex his

game, however much she might wish to do so, and she
continued to read until the Duchess said gently, after
poor Mr Collins had been given his congé, 'Enough, my
dear. Accept our thanks. Alex, I hope that Mrs
Ashburn's skill at chess equals her ability to render prose
entertaining. You will be hard put to achieve your usual
success on the board, if so.'

There was no help for it. Harry put the book down,
and took her place at the small games table opposite to
him. A chess-board was laid out in marquetry, and the
pieces on it were exquisite. They were Indian in origin,
the Knights were elephants, the Bishops, Viziers, and
the King and Queen were a Rajah and a Ranee. Playing
with Ned it had been a pleasure to handle them. She was
not sure how she felt about a game with Alex, as there
was something about the set of his mouth which she
found disturbing.

He had already laid the board out for play, and 'Come,'
he said, 'I will offer you the white pieces,' and his eyes
as he spoke were challenging her again; the new owner
of Racquette was to be kept in her place, the usurper was
to be punished a little, perhaps, for her presumption in
inheriting over the heads of those to whom the lands
rightly belonged.

'No need,' Harry replied quietly. 'Let us draw lots for
white. I was always used to do so with Gilly.'

'Doubtless,' he said, with a sardonic smile. 'But I
insist. You must allow me a little deference to a lady.'
Judging by the manner in which he drawled out the word
lady, he was offering her no deference at all.

It was useless either to argue with him, or to deny
him. The eyes of the others were on them, and Harry
suddenly tired of prevarication.

'Then, I suppose, when a *gentleman* insists so chival-
rously, a lady must give way,' she returned, and her
stress on the word gentleman was a polite and mocking
echo of the way in which he had spoken of her as a lady.

'Bravo,' he said, after he had watched her make her

first moves, quite unexceptional as they were, with the King's pawn putting a tiny foot in the water of the Ganges, to get at Alex's black minions. 'I see that we have an excellent skirmish ahead of us.'

'A rapid judgement for you to make on so conventional an opening,' said Harry drily, considering his move carefully, 'but perhaps being a soldier allows you to judge your campaign on the nature of your opponent's first step.'

'Rather say,' he answered after a lengthy pause in which he surveyed their positions, 'that I judge my strategy by the nature of my rival, as well as by the moves he or she makes. One plays the person as well as the pieces on the board.'

Harry was silent in her turn, the only sound in the room being the ticking of the clock, and Ned's noiseless tread as he came over to watch them, only to retreat when Alex glared at him for breaking his concentration.

'My late husband would have agreed with your last remark,' said Harry thoughtfully, as she castled. 'That was a favourite saying of his.'

'We seem to share a number of things in common,' said Alex with a grin. 'I hear that he had red hair, too. Perhaps there are others of his possessions and attributes that I might have a part of also, Cousin Harry?'

Harry deemed it politic to make no answer to this, contenting herself with studying the board with the kind of concentrated dispassion which Gilly had always said was the essence of the game. She had the feeling that Alex had underrated her, had been a trifle too contemptuous in setting out to defeat a woman, and a woman whom he deemed an upstart, and had consequently been a little careless in making his early moves. She meant to make him pay for it if she could.

Alex decided that, whatever else one felt about Cousin Harry, for this was the sobriquet that the party at Rule were beginning to adopt, she at least had the merit of knowing when to be quiet. She did not chatter while he

pondered the position on the board, and, after a long
silence, he moved his Knight to a point where it seemed
to threaten Harry's whole position.

She looked across at him with a slight smile, and,
before she touched her own piece, said, 'I hope you
realise that your forward Knight is in great danger.'

'Not so,' he replied. 'It is your Bishop which is at
risk.'

'I think not,' Harry answered. 'I fear you might have
overlooked the fact that my Queen is powerful and
protects him. Take my Bishop, and you will lose your
Knight, two of your pawns, and your whole left side will
stand exposed.'

A little disconcerted, Alex stared at the board. 'Oh,
you aim straight for the heart, I see. You play an
aggressive game for a lady, but I should have expected
that, I suppose, all things considered.'

She looked straight at him. 'But, we are agreed, I
think, that I am not a lady. And you as a nobleman are
hardly a gentleman. Let us proceed on these assumptions
and the game will be easier.'

He had underestimated her, he saw, both on the board
and in life. He concentrated on his position and wished
that he had not been so careless of her skills. His cousin
had taught her well. And then, suddenly, after they had
been playing for nearly two hours, just as he judged
himself finally lost, she made a move which unstitched
her own position completely, and handed him the
victory.

For a moment, Alex thought that it was carelessness,
a loss of concentration, but as he at last looked up, almost
disbelieving, and met her steady gaze, he knew that she
had done it deliberately, and thrown the game to him.
He felt an enormous and extreme anger grip him. How
dared she be so contemptuous of him, to throw him a
win as though she were throwing a naughty dog a bone?

Harry hardly knew why she had done it. Only on
mature reflection these obvious cat-and-mouse tricks had

sickened her, as had his assumption of her guile, his belief that she had cheated her way into Gilly's life, and was now cheating her way into his. Well, there was more than one way of being a cheat, and by this version of it she was handing him a worthless and undeserved victory—and making a mock of him while she did so.

It would be interesting, to say the least, she thought, to see how his haughty lordship dealt with that, and she smiled to herself as he stared at the board, and worked out exactly what she had done. She met his enraged eyes, thinking, Oh, not so cool now, my lord, not cool at all. Two can play games, and I have been well taught.

She rose, yawned politely behind her hand, bowed and smiled, the picture of composed dignity, unruffled, in command of herself, and said, 'Oh, I give you best, my lord. The field is yours. My men lie dead upon it. You must find a better opponent to give you a worthier game.'

Lady Lansden, unseeing, blind, drawled from across the room, 'I see that you are beat, Mrs Ashburn. Ladies are hardly fitted to play gentlemen at such a game.'

'Oh, yes,' agreed Harry, her smile broadening as she took in Alex's angry and baffled face, 'my poor brain is quite exhausted at the effort of dealing with Lord Templestowe. I am sure that he will allow me to retire. A night's rest is needed to recuperate. You will allow.' And she bowed her way out of the room with all eyes upon her. Alex she left in a fury, for in some manner she had robbed him—of what, he hardly knew—and, on top of his resentment at her existing at all, he now had a sudden reckless desire to assert his mastery over her in a way which would teach her not to play such games with him. This desire was roaring in his head, to the degree that he was almost blind and deaf with the need to satisfy it.

As the door closed behind Harry's retreating back, Alex rose, swept all the pieces from the board with a blow of his hand, and then, face aflame, strode rapidly to the door to follow her, his progress watched by astonished eyes. He closed the door behind him with a sound like thunder, making for Harry, who had reached the foot of the stairs.

CHAPTER FIVE

HARRY, pleased a little at having, as she thought, demonstrated to Alex Templestowe her refusal to be categorised, half turned as she heard the noise of the closing door, followed by Alex's rapid footsteps. Seeing that he was apparently following her, she turned back again to mount the stairs. She had no wish for further conversation with him.

But Alex, still in the grip of the kind of rage he had not felt since he was a youth, saw her turn away, and the sight almost undid him.

So! She thought to ignore him. He caught her by the shoulders and swung her round. Startled, her face suddenly white, Harry quailed a little as she met his blazing eyes and felt the strength of his hard hands. She had meant to provoke him a little; she had not expected to render him so purely murderous. His whole body was a symbol of roused masculine aggression—and she was its target.

Harry controlled herself and her voice with an effort which was almost physical, feeling his hands tighten further on her arms and seeing his head drop towards hers, so that he confronted her point blank, as he might an enemy he intended to destroy.

'My lord, consider what you are doing.'

'Oh, madam, I am full of consideration.' His voice was frightening, too. It was so low, so hard, and the control he was exercising was patent within it. If *this* was how he behaved when he was controlling himself, what would she face when control was gone? He continued, repeating himself, 'Yes, full of consideration. Consideration of your conduct. What game were you playing with me in there? For sure, it was not chess.'

Harry held her own breath, widened her eyes, and attempted to show him the face of innocence. Useless, for he merely tightened his hands on her shoulders and shook her slightly.

'Answer me, my fine madam. Why did you throw me the game? I am not a fool, although I played like one, and you played me for one. Why did you do it? Answer me, I say.'

'How I play a game of chess,' said Harry, her voice still firm, betraying little of her very real fright at his altered aspect, 'is my concern, and not yours.' She tried to shift in his grip, but he held her as a cat held a mouse, ready to pounce and to maul. 'Accept that I made an error.'

She would not plead with him to let her go. He would not face down Harry Ashburn, however much he might terrorise others.

His failure to discompose her fed Alex's rage further. Anger almost choked him. 'Oh, no, I won't accept that. Whose vanity were you feeding, madam? Yours, or mine?' It was so long since he had lost his control over the famous Ashburn temper that the usual checks he kept on himself were gone, and his desire to master and to destroy was written plain on his face.

And now Harry was really frightened. She had no wish to create a real scandal by shouting for help. That could not be borne. She would ruin them both.

Surely if she kept her head she could persuade him not to persevere with this attempt to bully her into some kind of ridiculous admission of guilt—for what, she was not quite sure. She owned that she had meant to taunt him, to show him that she, too, had teeth, and could use them, and if he chose to think her a devious fortune-hunter he could, but she had not meant to raise the devil.

'Accept this,' she said, keeping her voice as slow and deliberate as her fear would let her. 'That I did not feel the need to win. Or perhaps, that I do not know why I did it.' And that last was the nearest to the truth, God help her, for by his expression he did not believe, or even really pay heed to, a word she was saying. His world had shrunk down to the pair of them, and to his need, to do what? Alex hardly knew, for something else was beginning to happen to him, something he had not quite bargained for when he had grasped her and brought her so near to him.

And that something was a desire for mastery to be physically complete, for him to have her, here, at the foot of the stairs, within earshot of the polite company in the drawing-room, a man and a woman together, damn all else, the exquisite pleasure of making love to this composed. . .mermaid. . .of seeing her wild in the grip of passion, and finally fulfilled beneath him, the harpy, the lightskirt, the temptress used, whether she would or no.

'Oh, yes,' he said through his teeth. 'What I will accept is how you won my cousin.' And his terrible desire to shatter her composure, her calm, was strengthened further. For even now, in the face of his strength and his anger, she still clung to some remnants of her grave stillness, although her face was ashen, and her eyes dark stars in it, and her coolness rested on a knife-edge.

'And this pretence that you are a débutante, an innocent, so eager to feed male vanity for your own ends, that you will offer a man anything, even a worthless victory, let us test it, madam, by all means let us test it.' And his control finally snapped, and his mouth was suddenly hard on hers, fierce and demanding, and his hands rifled her body. . .

The sensations which swept through Harry as she underwent this sudden explicit onslaught were novel to say the least, as despite herself her mouth opened under his. In the physical sense she had never experienced any real contact with men at all, never really ever been near to one, except for Gilly in his last illness, and that was different—he was a patient and she a nurse, a contact purely sexless. She was, indeed, a complete sexual innocent, although Alex did not know that—indeed thought quite otherwise, seeing her as an experienced married woman, and a vicious harpy to boot—fair game, in fact.

Oh, Harry had lived in the country and seen the animals, and knew exactly what men and women did together when they made love—Gilly had made sure of that, for she needed to be able to protect herself, he'd said. But her knowledge was intellectual and theoretical, not emotional; as she had rightly said to him, she felt for him as a sister. She had wondered why on earth anyone ever did it, the whole thing seemed so impossible and unlikely, and was alien to her, and she had said so to Gilly, who had answered sadly, 'Oh, you will know why, one day.'

She should have been affronted, shocked, as Alex continued to caress her, but her whole body seemed to flower and open at his touch in the oddest way. Even the slight violence that he was using seemed exciting and, as her mouth responded to his long kiss, by opening itself to him, his tongue flicked delicately into it, meeting hers, which took on a life of its own, responding to him, as though she had done this often before, instead of it being for the first time.

She was full of a passion which she was not aware that she had possessed, and what was worse—or was it better?—she knew that the pull of him was strong, that he had fascinated her from the first moment when she had seen him in the rose-garden. The strong resemblance to Gilly, allied to the splendid physique, and a mind as good as Gilly's, harnessed to a determination which was as resolute as her own, had all done their work on her and brought her to this fierce acquiescence in the shock of his lovemaking.

And if she were honest the fascination was stronger for the touch of fear he excited in her, the sense of playing with a tiger, only half controlled by civilised life, and his own formidable will.

She tried to assert herself, to wrench her mouth away,

to turn her face, only for his kisses to travel across her cheek, into her hair-line, and for his tongue, having teased her mouth into submission, improbably to enter her ear, creating yet another new set of experiences, so that she gave a great passionate sob. Hearing it, he dropped his right hand to cup her breast, his thumb stroking it through the thin muslin of her dress, while with his other hand he supported her head, which suddenly seemed too weak to hold itself erect.

The stroking hand produced a sensation so extraordinary and exquisite in the depth of its pleasure that Harry's whole body was consumed by it, her knees turned to water, and she feared that she was on the verge of fainting. At the same time he dropped his head and began to kiss the cleft between her breasts revealed by the low neck of the fashionable gown she was wearing, the kisses travelling downwards. *Any more and I shall be lost. Oh, God,* Harry thought, *I'm like a moonstruck housemaid, about to be seduced by the master.* And simultaneously, *So this is why men and women make love, and women are betrayed;* and the thought brought her to her senses. This time when she turned her head away she meant it. Her hands had, quite unconsciously, as though they, too, possessed a life of their own, risen to clasp him round the neck to make their embrace easier, and, with an effort of will which almost hurt, she placed them on his chest to thrust him from her.

'Oh, let me go. Please let me go. You disgust me.'

At the sound of her voice the rage left Alex as suddenly as it had come, and he was shamefully aware that he would. . .he had. . .and he left the thought unfinished, in case the finishing inflamed him further, stepping back and letting his own hands fall.

'No, I think not. Although I disgust myself a little. But that should dispose of the notion of innocence, I think.'

He realised, but with little pleasure, that he had achieved his aim. Her composure was in ruins, her breathing was reduced to gasping, and she was on the verge of tears. His last statement, jeering at her innocence, had finally almost destroyed her. She no longer had the will or the strength to assert her innocence. Useless, in any case, to do so. His mind was made up, and her passionate response had merely served to confirm his belief as to her duplicity—her maidenly reserve was a mask behind which Circe, the siren, exercised her wiles. Grimly Alex surveyed her shattered state.

'Don't toy with me again, madam,' he said, and his voice was iron. 'Accept that, however much you succeeded in snaring others, you face a harder game with me.' Oh, he could see how she had managed his cousin. Such sugar-sweet surrender when his mouth was on hers, followed by a pretence of such coy and maidenly reserve—a stratagem which would undoubtedly work with an inexperienced young man; but she would need to do better than that to capture Alex Ashburn, that seasoned campaigner on the fields of love and war.

And yet. . .and yet. . .for a moment, she had looked at him with such sorrow in her great drowned eyes that he almost could have sworn she had been sincere in her responses, that the maidenliness and the modesty was genuine. He half felt himself a cur for treating her with such harsh severity. Alex shrugged, impatient with himself and his weakness before a pair of fine eyes. How could he be so foolish?

And look, the speed with which she recovered herself! He watched sardonically as Harry straightened up under his cold stare, and swallowed the tears which were a compound of shock and shame. Shock at discovering the demands of the body—demands which she had always denied existed. Shame at the strength of her own passionate response to them.

She lifted her head high. Her confusion and sense of guilt for having co-operated so enthusiastically in her own downfall were both dismissed. She was Harriet Ashburn, Gilly's composed wife again, ready to do as he always said, and face down the world, refuse to let an arrogant nobleman destroy the castle of integrity which she carried within her.

'You must think what you please,' she said. 'For what you think cannot alter the truth. And your conduct shames not me, but you.' And she walked by him and up the stairs without a backward glance.

And now that the rage was spent, and the wave had broken on the shore again, and stranded him in a limbo where his body, so long denied, ached in an agony of unfulfilled desire—and all for a worthless woman who would treat him as she had treated his cousin, only this time it was a title which she wanted, not money and lands, the mansion and broad acres which, as she herself had said, she had gained when she married Gilbert Ashburn—his thoughts, too, were a compound of shock and shame.

Shock that she had possessed the power to rouse him so, when, after Arabella, he had sworn that no woman would ever do so again. The further shock was that he now recognised that the rage had been largely sexual in its nature and in its demand that he master and control her. Both shock and shame in that once he had begun to make love to her he had not wanted to stop, because she was so soft and yielding in his arms that she seemed to belong there. And finally pure shame, in that he, with his high-flown notions of honour, should force himself in such a fashion on any woman, even one who deserved it as much as the harpy who had married his cousin and taken his lands.

He straightened himself, stared at his reflection in the long Venetian mirror which graced the hall, and reluctantly compelled himself to return to the drawing-room. The whole distressing episode had hardly taken any time at all, he found, and the mirror showed him someone unchanged—neither a victim nor a monster.

Alex knew very well what was wrong. Whatever happened he must not touch her again. Laying hands on

her in his anger had been a gross mistake. There was no
excuse; he should have known better, known that such
intimate contact between a man and a woman grappling
together would rapidly turn into something sexual in
nature. To be so near to her, feeling her warm, living
and breathing beneath his hands, feeling her tremble at
his touch, was dangerous. In an instant the rage had
been transformed into profound sexual desire, a desire
so strong that he could hardly trust himself, had almost
been swept away.

No, in future he would be pleasant and civilised,
would avoid putting them both in a position where such
an. . .earthquake could happen again. It was not wise,
not politic. If Emily were bent on taking Harry up, and
he knew that she was—reputations meant nothing to
her—then he would perforce be compelled to meet his
cousin frequently, and by all the conventions of polite
Society their intercourse must be civil and civilised. It
would not do to put himself in a position where her
existence was a temptation to him because of physical
proximity.

That was it. He must be as grand and cool as Ned
frequently complained that he was. The only thing which
he could not understand was why she had made such a
powerful impression on him. Mere continence alone
could not account for it. He had been in company with
other women, many of them more beautiful and more
desirable than Harriet Ashburn, and he had not been
overcome by this insane determination to make love to
them.

Perhaps it was because she owned Racquette. But he
did not think that it was that, either. Much though he
wanted his home back, its pull was not sufficient for him
to behave in this odd way. Exactly what it was that drew
him, that attracted him while annoying him, he did not
know.

Enough. Like most men, Alex was not given to
examining the entrails of his own emotions over-much.

Again, like most men, he left that to women. In general, women had played little part in his life. True, he had loved Arabella Temple passionately—but look what that had led to.

Oh, damn all skirts, he thought irritably, as he tried to compose himself for sleep—with one last thought: How was *she* faring?

And Harry? Harry was in little better case than her tormentor, and for much the same reasons. How dared he treat her so? And how dared her own body let her down so cruelly? For he had known, he had surely known, the sensations which had come over her at his touch. What in the world had happened to cool, composed Harry Ashburn, that a man could discommode her so easily? And what was worst of all was to be overcome by such a cold and arrogant monster as Alex Templestowe was, for all his courage, honour and pride. Was she, who had always kept the world at bay, to be so undone at the touch of a man's lips and hands? Was it possible that she would respond to any man who cared to assault her physically? The thought was not to be borne.

Her mind went round and round and came back to the beginning. How dared he treat her and speak to her as though she were an adventuress, sneering at her innocence? How dared a man who had never known hardship or faced penury sit in judgement on her, without even knowing the truth about her?

It was bad enough that she should feel guilt at having deprived him of his home and inheritance without his assuming that she had cheated her way into Gilly's life and was now trying to cheat her way into his. Was it his title he thought she was after? If so, he could rest in peace. She wanted neither it nor him. Truth to tell, she wanted nothing from him, or any man. . .and as she thought this she sat up suddenly in bed, aflame, for her body told her that *that* statement, at least, was no longer true.

He was wrong, oh, so wrong. She had been physically unawakened, but his actions, and his alone, had deprived her of her innocence. Thinking her guilty, he had made her so!

She was so *distraite* that night, and the next morning too, that Mrs Whitmore and Hannah thought that she must be sickening for something. She feared that she was, and, what was worse, it was not *something*, it was *someone*, and of all persons it was the man whom she and Gilly had dispossessed. What was worst of all, he was a man who hated and despised her.

She must be going mad—and she tried to think of Gilly, and what he would have said to comfort or advise her, but all that she could conjure up was Alex's face as he had bent to kiss her—and he had never looked less like Gilly.

CHAPTER SIX

THE music of a waltz, played by a barrel-organ in the
street, floated in the soft summer air through the windows of Templestowe House in London, and caused
Harry, seated at her escritoire, to look up and sigh.

Mrs Whitmore, seated across the room, said anxiously,
'Harriet?'

'It's nothing. I was thinking.'

'My dear,' remonstrated Mrs Whitmore earnestly,
'you should never think. It ruins the complexion and
gives one wrinkles.'

'Make my mind a blank, you mean,' said Harry
cheerfully, thinking how much Gilly would have enjoyed
her companion's chatter.

'Indeed. It is, I find, much the best way to cope.
Embroidery is helpful, too. It prevents one brooding.
Reading, now, unless the book be very light and enter-
taining, is not to be over-recommended.'

Her tone was again so earnest that Harry, who had
been unsympathetically enjoying this remarkable conversation, looked across at her, and realised suddenly that
Mrs Whitmore's situation—poor, helpless and dependent, might have been her own, and that she, too, might
have been only too willing not to think, but simply to
endure.

She rose. Her discontent seemed suddenly stupid and
childish. On impulse she crossed the room and kissed
her startled companion on the cheek. 'Sarah, I was
wondering why my life seems so empty when I have so
much. Tonight I go to Almack's with the Duchess, and
yet, and yet. . .'

'Will Alex Templestowe be there?' said Mrs Whitmore
inconsequentially.

67

Harry was startled. 'I'm sure I don't know,' she
replied, almost crossly. 'The Duchess told me he's due
in Town any time now—but that's of no consequence to
me. I'm sure I haven't missed *him*.' Which, uncomfort-
ably, she knew was not true. Since the night of their
passionate encounter at Rule, he had seldom been far
from her thoughts.

Harry came back to the present with a start as Mrs
Whitmore said in her usual slightly *distraite* manner,
'Well, at least you do not lack for admirers. You will be
surrounded by them tonight at Almack's. . .'

'I suppose,' replied Harry slowly, 'that that is what is
troubling me. In prospect I quite liked the thought of
admirers, but in reality I find them troublesome.'

'Yes, indeed,' agreed Mrs Whitmore. 'You don't like
being kowtowed to. A little argument, but not too much.'

'And some manly independence,' Harry said. 'Well,
you did warn me about fortune-hunters and every time I
say something absurd, and some otherwise sensible man
agrees with me, I wonder what his motives are. It does
not make for comfort.'

And at least Alex neither agreed with me needlessly,
nor kowtowed, she thought. Far from it. I wonder what
I do want?

'Well, you have the Duchess and myself to protect you
tonight. Not to mention Lady Cowper and all the
dragons who run Almack's.'

Dragons, yes, thought Harry later, as she sat drinking
inferior lemonade and watching the passing show. All
the men had been compelled to discard their trousers for
silk knee-breeches—even the Duke of Wellington himself had been refused to Almack's when he had arrived
trousered. She could almost hear Gilly's voice in her
ear—Well, at least it leaves us free to admire a gentleman's legs—but she did not voice this sentiment aloud.

Seated between the Duchess and Mrs Whitmore,
approved by the Patronesses, not snubbed by the
Templestowes, Harry had truly arrived on the social

scene. All the same it was with some relief that she watched Ned making his eager way to her.

'So, there you are, Cousin Harry. I told Alex you would be here already, but I suppose he is doing his usual imitation of a Spanish don, and will only arrive to speak to us when he has done his duty to everyone who matters. What it is to be such a paragon.'

Harry's pleasure at meeting him again was unforced, and, while they sat in the supper-room together, eating ices, she told him so, and asked him how he had left Sussex, and how long he expected to be in London.

'This is my first time at Almack's,' he said, after saying that both Rule and Racquette were looking splendid with all the summer flowers coming into bloom, and then, gazing around at the company, 'I do wonder, indeed, why Alex comes at all. Thrashes like this aren't usually his line. But something or someone has brought him here. I do hope it isn't Arabella Harrendene. I don't think it can be. He is over there with Lady Jersey, and seems to be trying to avoid her. What a relief. I couldn't stand for him to go through all that again. The first time was bad enough.'

Arabella Harrendene; it was the second time this evening that Harry had heard her name. The first time had been when the Duchess had said to her, shortly after they had arrived, 'Quickly, my dear, down this corridor, away from the crush. I am determined to avoid Arabella Harrendene. She is bound to ask all sorts of impertinent questions of you, and I'm sure you would rather endure that later rather than sooner.'

Straightforward tactics seemed to be the thing. She said in her lightest voice, 'Ned, who is Lady Harrendene, and why should both the Duchess and Alex be trying to avoid her?'

Ned looked incredulously at her. 'Do you mean that no one has thought to tell you about Alex and Arabella? Oh, you really ought to know about *her*. Save you from saying the wrong thing. Everyone but yourself knows

that Arabella Harrendene and Alex—she was Arabella
Temple then—were inseparable. Oh, I wasn't very old
at the time, but I remember how jolly Alex used to be,
before he went to the wars and lost her. Said she'd wait
for him, when he asked her to marry him before he left.
It's my belief,' said Ned fiercely, 'that she knew all the
time that he wouldn't stand for her racketing around
when he was away, once she was his wife. His honour,
and all that. And when Grandfather told him to sell out
of the Army in the middle of the campaign, return home
to marry her, and get an heir, all at the double, he
refused—his honour again—said she would understand,
if you please. They say that when Grandfather read
Alex's letter from Spain he roared at his secretary, "By
God, if Alex thinks to disoblige me, I'll make damned
sure I disoblige him," and set about disinheriting him.

'The next thing Alex knew was that he had a letter
from Arabella telling him that she had married Lord
Harrendene, a man old enough to be her father, and far
richer than Alex would be, once he had lost the
Templestowe lands.' Ned's indignation was such that he
had difficulty in retaining his composure and his
grammar.

'Two blows for him at once, you see, just like the man
in the fairy-tale. Quite changed poor Alex; he'd been
such a happy-go-lucky fellow. Not at all the grim milord
he is now. Particularly as Harrendene allows Arabella to
do exactly as she pleases—and what she pleased was to
have the impudence to try to keep Alex for a lover, after
refusing him as a husband. Alex, of all men! She didn't
know my brother. I can't see you behaving like that!' he
finished artlessly.

'No, indeed,' Harry said, laughing, but thinking, Poor
Alex, no wonder he is suspicious of women. 'I have no
intention of marrying a very rich man old enough to be
my father, and enjoying myself on the town.'

'Oh, no. One sees that,' said Ned approvingly. 'You're
not at all like Arabella—except you both have dark eyes.

So there you are. Good thing she showed the cloven hoof before marriage, but you can hardly expect Alex to see that. Hates all women now. From one extreme to the other, you see—quite a ladies' man in his day. Never looks at 'em now.'

That he had been a ladies' man didn't surprise Harry after the interlude on the stairs. But what a dreadful tale. It explained so much. Alex had done his duty, and the heavens had fallen. No wonder he was bitter.

'But he kept his honour,' she said, voice resolute, 'and did not desert his men in their darkest hour.'

'No, indeed,' agreed Ned, his pride in his brother apparent, for all his gentle mockery of him for his high seriousness. 'I suppose my cousin Gilbert was like that, from what you say of him?'

Harry thought for a moment of Gilly's resolution in the face of death, and his loving rescue of her.

'Yes,' she said, 'there was a resemblance. Gilly would always do what he saw as his duty.'

More than one pair of eyes looked at them curiously as they sat there, talking so companionably together, and watched with interest as Ned gallantly escorted her back to Mrs Whitmore, who was looking even more harassed than usual. The Duchess had disappeared, removed by an imperious Mrs Drummond Burrell, one of the more powerful of the Patronesses. Mrs Whitmore's distress was soon explained.

'Arabella Harrendene has been demanding an intro-duction to you,' she began, 'and I am not certain how Lord Templestowe, or the Duchess, would feel if you were to be taken up by her.'

'It is, perhaps, more to the point what *I* would feel about being taken up by her,' said Harry gravely. 'But I do understand, and you may trust me to be discreet.'

'Ah, Ned has been explaining matters to you, I see,' sighed Mrs Whitmore, who concealed her intense common sense behind her feather-headed manner. 'Be alert, my dear. Here she comes.'

Dark eyes, Harry thought, were the only things she shared with Arabella. Her manner was imperious, her gown a deep burgundy trimmed with saffron lace, and her garnets, in an elaborate setting, encircled a haughtily held neck. She was like an offended swan, thought Harry irreverently, as she drawled her way through Mrs Whitmore's introductions, extended her fingertips, flirted an enormous fan, and arched her head so that she could survey the passing show as she patronised Harry.

'My dear.' Her drawl as she prolonged the dee-ah was almost a parody of the Devonshire House set. 'I simply had to meet you to find out what could lure Templestowe, of all people, to Almack's. Your presence here, they say, is responsible for his own. You should be flattered, although I suppose his devotion to his household, of which you are now a part, is the principal reason for his being here.'

She makes me sound like a newly taken on housemaid, thought Harry, and I am not part of his household, either. One supposes I ought to reply, Charmed, I'm sure, and bob a dutiful curtsy. Instead, she raised her own dark brows slightly and said in her gravest manner that she was sure that Lady Harrendene overestimated her importance in Lord Templestowe's eyes.

'I think not.' She looked straight at Harry for the first time. 'Alex—I've known him for years—is an absolute stickler for the proprieties. Honour and all that. So dull in a man of his age. You agree?'

'I hardly know him well enough to entertain an opinion,' returned Harry, her manner as charmlessly submissive as she could make it.

The great fan shut with an angry snap as the fish rejected the bait for the second time. Arabella's eyes passed over her, and Harry could almost hear the drawling voice passing judgement on her—'No manner, dreadfully dull turn-out, drab bluey grey; what farmyard did the Templestowes rescue her from?'

At this juncture Alex arrived with the Duchess to

rescue Harry—although she needed no rescuing. He was looking extremely fine in his formal dress. Silk knee-breeches, and all that went with them, merely served to show off his remarkable physique. His manner to them both was icily formal.

'Lady Harrendene. I see that you have already been introduced to my cousin.'

'Alex,' she drawled, 'you are always Alex to me. Yes, and now I meet you. . .' A long forefinger leaped out to pull at the pleats in his cravat. 'You really need me, Alex, to keep you *à point*.'

'Not so. I have no intention of rivalling the dandy set. I came to ask Cousin Harry to stand up with me in the Quadrille. You will excuse us.'

'Cousin Harry?' She repeated this as though Alex had said something exquisitely amusing. 'Ah, Mrs Ashburn; I see. Oh, I will always excuse you, Alex, for everything,' and she drifted away, just like the proud swan of Harry's imagining.

The Duchess, too, moved away, to leave Alex and Harry alone together for the first time since the stairs at Rule, and for both it was a moment to test their composure. They had met briefly on the morning in which Harry had left Rule for Racquette, but that meeting had been in company, and coldly formal.

'My lord,' said Harry, her manner as coolly distant as she could make it.

'Cousin Harry——' Alex's tone was equal to her own, neither friendly, nor unfriendly, dispassionate '—I am Alex to my family.'

'I thought,' said Harry, determined not to yield an inch, 'I thought that you had shown me that I am Mrs Ashburn to you, and most definitely not needed in your family circle.' Her composure was admirable, her voice uninflected, the dark eyes met his resolutely.

'I, too, have thought,' said Alex carefully, watching her as he spoke, as determined as she was, but determined also to restore relations between them to some-

thing of what they had been before their last disastrous
encounter, if only for the sake of social propriety, 'and I
am compelled to admit that my behaviour towards you
on your last night at Rule was reckless and wrong—quite
out of my usual style, I do assure you. I offer you an
apology for it. Whatever the circumstances in which we
find ourselves, through my grandfather's actions, rather
than our own, I had no right to treat you as I did. May I
ask that you have the goodness to forgive me, and allow
us to return to the footing on which we stood before?'

Despite the memory of her hurt feelings on the night,
the very real shock, and the emotional turmoil which had
followed his actions, Harry had to restrain an inappropriate amusement as she heard this grand and ample
apology. Ned was right. A Spanish grandee, no less.
How did this exquisite formality accord with the behaviour of a man who at one moment had seemed ready to
ravish her almost in public?

'You are my late husband's cousin,' she said slowly,
'and, as Arabella Harrendene has reminded me, you are
also the head of the family to which I now belong. I
cannot refuse to accept an apology so generously and
freely given. We may be a little friendly again, Cousin
Alex.'

It was said. There had been no clash of wills, both had
surrendered. He put out his hand, for a moment almost
fearful of touching hers, lest it provoke another
explosion.

'You will take the floor with me, then?'

Harry nodded agreement as she accepted his offered
hand. Suddenly supremely aware of everything about
him, she noticed how strongly beautiful it was, and she,
too, was fearful of her reactions to his touch. Fortunately
for them both, their first coming together again, although
electric in nature, created no such scene as had occurred
in Rule; both, however, secretly admitted, much against
their respective wills, that an alchemy was at work

between them, and in consequence they carefully held themselves a little apart.

Looking down at her dark head, Alex thought to lighten the occasion a little by some stupefyingly normal conversation.

'I am sorry that you were subjected to Arabella Harrendene's quizzing,' he said, as they waited for the dance to begin. 'You must not let her set you down.'

'No, indeed,' agreed Harry. 'Such a tiring person. Two sentences, and I was quite exhausted. I shall never be a star in Society. Too much is asked of one. Such perfect finish as Lady Harrendene has achieved is quite beyond me.'

He looked sharply at her. 'Now, why do I think that *you* are quizzing *me*?'

'Not at all. That would never do. You are the head of the family, always to be respected and deferred to, or so Arabella tells me. For example, it would never occur to me to think your cravat underdone. *I* thought it a veritable work of art.'

Alex smiled at her for the first time. 'Now I know that you are quizzing me. I am coming to recognise a certain expression you wear. What judgements are you passing on us as you sit there so quiet and so pleasantly agreeable?'

'No judgements. That would be impertinent. But I confess that the company entertains me greatly. I can imagine how much Gilly would have enjoyed himself.'

'So, my cousin had a savage wit?'

'Far from it,' replied Harry spiritedly. 'He was gentleness itself, but he greatly appreciated what he called the little absurdities of life.'

'One would hardly describe Arabella as one of life's little absurdities, however.'

'No, indeed. A large one, perhaps?'

Alex could not prevent himself reacting to this gravely offered remark. Her playful coolness undid him. Never mind that he half thought that it was part of the armour

she assumed to win men over; he could not prevent a
spontaneous laugh at this, loud enough to turn heads. If
Harry was aware that she had created a minor furore, she
did not betray it. Come what may, she meant him to
acknowledge not only that she existed, but that the
adverse judgements he had already made on her integrity
were incorrect. But to do so she would not compromise
herself—Gilly would not have expected it—and she
would not surrender, for one moment, her own spirit.
He must accept her as she was: Mrs Harriet Ashburn,
Cousin Harry, who had a right to be herself, and to be
accepted as herself.

In consequence her look at him was almost challenging
as the music began and they took their places with the
other three couples, and went through the lively move-
ments of the dance. As it ended he took her hand again,
lightly, and led her to the supper table.

His action was noted by many. Knowledge that gossip
about her was rife, as it had been since she had arrived
in Town, lent Harry courage rather than deterred her.
She took the plate of cold food from Alex, and sat with
him by an open window.

'I am sorry the food is so poor,' he said, 'but one does
not come to Almack's to eat.'

'No, indeed,' Harry answered, 'I have been trying to
decide why one comes at all. The place is comfortless
after the great houses I have entered since the Season
began.'

'To be seen,' he said, 'to be here, is a social accolade,
as I am sure you know. To be accepted at Almack's is to
be accepted everywhere.'

'And that is important?' Harry's tone was dry. She
was not yet quite sure what she thought of Society.

'I am sure it is important to *you*,' he said, unable to
prevent himself making some slight reference to her own
invidious position.

Harry was equal to it. 'More important for me, I
think, is that you and the Duchess accept me.'

'Oh, I accept you,' he assured her, and then, to take a little of the pleasure of that statement away, added, 'To do otherwise would hand me over to the gossips as a poor loser. That would never do.'

'So that is why you offer me a truce,' she replied, and her smile was as ironic as his. 'I was told that you were a diplomat as well as a soldier. You have proved it tonight—as you proved you had been a soldier at Rule!'

Alex coloured a little at that, and said stiffly, 'I thought Rule was to be forgot.'

'Did you so?' she said gently. 'Pray, tell me truthfully. Have you forgot it?'

He was not to be drawn. 'I had hoped that you had.'

The last food remaining on Harry's plate was a cluster of grapes. She removed her lace mittens and began to strip the fruit from its sprig, eating each purple globe with delicate appreciation.

'Verbal chess,' she remarked, after making him wait for an answer, 'might prove as dangerous as the real thing. I choose not to reply to that. An exchange of pawns, I think.'

Oh, but she was quick-witted, he thought. A mistress of allusion and evasion. He clapped his hands together lightly. 'Bravo, Cousin Harry. Tell me, did you teach Cousin Gilbert, or did he teach you? To achieve such a mastery of elliptic conversation at so early an age is an achievement in itself.'

Harry relished the last grape, as it broke against her palate. 'Oh, Cousin Alex, my late husband was not only learned, but, as I told you earlier, had a pretty wit. We taught each other.'

'I had thought him an invalid,' said Alex idly.

Harry's smile was cold. 'Ah, that is the mistake many made. Seeing his body so broken, they assumed his mind to be the same. I assure you, your cousin kept his intellect to the end.'

A pretty pair, thought Alex. If it be true they were a match, how did she snare him? And for the first time

there was a breach in his confident belief in Harry's
wiles. But he had no intention of relaxing his guard, for,
after all, was not that the impression which she sought to
give?

If Harry sensed Alex's changing reactions to her, she
gave him no sign of so doing. She handed him her empty
plate, and murmured, 'Now you may dispose of the
remains of my superb feast.'

'Willingly,' he said, and carried both their plates to
the table. Returning with lemonade for her, and wine for
himself, he told her gravely, 'At least campaigning in
Spain prepared me for such Spartan fare, but you, I
think, have had no such training.'

'No,' said Harry. 'Norfolk Dumplings, however, are
more used to being eaten, than to eat, I would remind
you.'

Alex's laugh was light and spontaneous again. Yes, he
thought, he would in future have no difficulty in keeping
his head in Cousin Harry's somewhat provoking presence. His loss of control at Rule must have been a freak,
not to be repeated. And even as he thought this he caught
her eye, and at the same time the light scent of her
person, lavender mixed with essential Harry, reached
him, and had a most extraordinary effect on him. Not
quite the same as at Rule but, again, a desire to hold her,
to kiss the slight curl at the corner of her mouth. How
totally ridiculous, he thought, seeing that she is no raving
beauty; what can it be about her which disturbs me so?

Watching him, Harry urged herself to caution. All the
more because his presence was having a peculiar effect
on her. She was so aware of him. Sitting by him, she
could almost sense him without seeing him, as though
she had developed an extra and somewhat inconvenient
talent. And she smiled pleasantly at him, trying to give
the appearance of being totally at ease.

CHAPTER SEVEN

'DOLLY, my love,' drawled Arabella Harrendene, 'what do you know of the little nobody who married Alex's cousin and inherited Templestowe's fortune?'

Adolphus Harrendene looked up from the folio he was reading. 'I know that she's hardly a nobody, my dear.'

Arabella trailed a light hand on his grey head. 'Then you know more than the rest of the world. It is quite convinced that Mrs Ashburn is a social nonentity.'

'As usual, the world is wrong,' he said with finality. 'Is this conversation leading anywhere, Arabella, or are we merely indulging in idle chatter? If so, I wish to end it.'

'You should know by now that my chatter is seldom idle.'

'Then I assume that you are interested in Alex's cousin because you are still interested in Alex. I have already warned you to take care, Arabella, in your dealings with him. Alex is a most determined and straightforward young man. Oblige me by dropping him, and choosing a more amenable lover. You know that there are plenty of handsome young men who would be only too willing to take you to bed. Order your affairs with more discretion, if you please. I want no scandal.'

Harry would have recognised the angry swan as Arabella arched her lovely neck.

'You should know me better than that, Adolphus. My interest in Harriet Ashburn runs beyond Alex, I assure you. If she is not a nobody, then who is she?'

He sighed. 'I see that you will give me no peace until you have had your way. Her mother was Henrietta Manners, of the Mannerses of Wortleigh in Hampshire. As for her father, he was John Grey, of a most respectable

branch of that family. Her mother married again, after
her father's early death, another unexceptionable gentleman—a half-pay officer in the Royal Navy. Both are
dead, and that must suffice. Again, I trust you to be
discreet. Do not meddle with either the young woman or
Alex. Good cannot come of it. You would be wise to
remember that I allow you to go your own way only so
long as you do not damage my good name.'

Her thanks echoed in his ear as she left him to his
reading. Arabella intended to regain Alex as a lover; her
failure to do so since he had returned from Spain had
piqued her—she was not used to failure, and now there
was a new problem for her. The unknown cousin who
had so suddenly appeared and who now owned Racquette
posed a double threat. Her attraction for Alex not only
lay in the fact that marriage to her would restore to him
what he had lost, but the whey-faced milkmaid apparently held charms for him as well.

How she knew this, Arabella could not have said, but
where Alex was concerned her senses were subtle. She
had watched them together, and others might have seen
nothing, but the eye of jealousy was keen. There was
more between Alex and his new cousin than one might
think. Only let Alex be fixed with Cousin Harry, and
she, Arabella, could kiss him goodbye, and she had no
intention of doing that.

Standing beneath the giant chandelier in the centre of
the ballroom at Melbourne House, magnificent in an
orange gown that no one else would dare to wear, a collar
of topazes worth a king's ransom around her throat,
Arabella's eyes quartered the room, and she, in turn,
gathered all eyes on her.

Harry, seated with Mrs Whitmore, thought sadly, I
can never compete with her in looks and manner, and
watched a tall and handsome man in his early to middle
forties make his way to Arabella.

Was he handsome? Harry could not quite determine
that. Certainly his features were regular and pleasing,

and his physique was as impressive as Alex
Templestowe's. The black and silver suit he wore, the
badge of an order on his breast, served only to enhance
his appearance. His dark hair had a frosting of silver on
it, and the bow he gave over Arabella's outstretched
hand was impeccable. Harry wondered who he was. She
had not encountered him before in her short stay in
London.

Arabella's eyes lit up as Harry's stranger greeted her.
He was no stranger to Arabella. Her pleasure at seeing
him was the greater because her husband had frequently
begged her to avoid him. It pleased her to be contrary.

'Ah, Nun'ster, well met. I did not know that you were
back in Town.'

'Yesterday, I arrived yesterday. I see you are in high
fettle, Lady Harrendene. As remarkable and lovely as
ever.' And Nun'ster held her hand a trifle long, and his
smile was a trifle too bold. 'Worth the journey from
Yorkshire merely to see you.'

Hervey Beauclerc, fifth Marquess of Nuncaster, whose
family name had been abbreviated to Nun'ster these
hundred years, turned the full force of his considerable
charm on her, and for a moment she wondered why this
should be so. He offered her his arm, and they began to
stroll away from the centre of the room towards some
seats in one of the windows. A few curious glances
followed their progress.

'I hear Society is favoured with a new star this Season,'
he said, a touch of malice in his voice, as they seated
themselves. Arabella liked to think that she was Society's
only star.

'Oh?' replied Arabella, shrugging, and opening yet
another of her wonderful collection of fans which she
used almost as weapons in her domination of London
Society. 'And who might that be? Surely you cannot be
speaking of the nobody who has usurped Templestowe's
lands and home?'

'A nobody?' repeated Nun'ster, raising his brows.

'You have met with her, then.' And he half turned to
survey the room. 'She is here tonight?'

'She is everywhere,' said Arabella, snapping her fan
shut viciously.

'An heiress worth winning, surely.'

'Now why should you care about that, Nun'ster?'
asked Arabella, laughing. 'You are rich enough already.'

'Oh,' he said, laughing in his turn, 'no one is ever rich
enough. You should know that, Arabella. You'd have
married Templestowe otherwise.'

'Not so,' she replied, almost vicious in her determination to deny him. 'All that honour and nobility bored me
too much to marry it, Nun'ster. Your star, your heiress,
is over there. Emily Hornsea has seen fit to make a
protégée of her; God knows why. A dowd, a very dowd.'

Nun'ster's glance was idle. His interest in Society's
new star was minimal. He had mentioned her merely in
order to annoy Arabella. It pleased him to cause distress.
As he turned his head, she said unkindly, 'The one in
white, no jewels, just that great pearl pendant she affects.
I cannot see why everyone is so taken with her.'

Arabella was so busy venting her spite on Harry's mild
success that she failed to notice how still Nun'ster had
gone when she had spoken of the pendant, and he had
identified it and its wearer.

He swung back to her, the strangest expression on his
face. 'You know her? Your husband is the Duchess's old
friend. You must know her. You are almost of her set.'

Arabella laughed an angry laugh. 'You, of all people,
can hardly wait to be introduced to such a bread-and-
butter miss! You cannot seriously wish to marry her for
her fortune. The great bachelor to surrender himself to a
milkmaid? The scourge of women caught at last?'

'Oh, you do dislike her, then?' he observed mildly.
'Never tell me that Alex Templestowe likes bread and
butter after the caviare you promise him,' and his eyes
turned back to Harry again, and this time his expression
was unreadable.

'Who is she?' he asked, almost shortly. 'I know she married Templestowe's cousin, but where did she spring from? No one seems to know.'

'Dolly knows,' said Arabella, and she passed on to him what her husband had told her earlier that day. 'Still a nobody,' she finished, 'plucked from a country village, marrying Alex's cousin for his money, they say.'

This time she knew that something which she had said had touched Nun'ster. He spoke to her abruptly, quite unlike his usual smooth self. If Arabella used a fan to seduce and to threaten, Nun'ster's chosen weapon was his voice. 'Introduce me, Lady Harrendene. I wish to know her.'

'Oh, you are like everyone else,' she said crossly. 'Another man to worship her in order to gain Racquette.'

He turned his head and his eyes glittered. 'Now, why should you mind that? You should be pleased if I remove her from the board. I leave your path open to gain Alex Templestowe. Far from resenting my interest, you should be offering me a reward.'

She stared at him. 'A reward, for what?'

'For taking her off your hands. Redeemed when I. . .gain her.'

'You do not say marriage?' said Arabella, her eyes glittering too now.

'Not my way,' he denied impassively. 'But she is not to know that. And what shall be my reward?' he asked again.

'My thanks, of course, my eternal thanks,' she replied.

'Not enough. How about a share of your less than eternal bed, Bella?' And he used her name for the first time, jeeringly. 'I surely deserve something for taking a whey-faced nobody off your hands.'

She struck him lightly with her fan. 'Don't call me Bella; I'm not a housemaid.'

'No, indeed,' he said. 'We are agreed on that.' And he pushed the fan aside. 'No bed, no help—and, what's more, I expect you to help me. You do want him still,

Bella, I hope? Not given up yet, surely?' His voice was
alive with mockery. If Harry had seen him then, she
would hardly have thought him handsome.

'Well, when you've got what you want, not before,'
she agreed shortly. She did not like being held to
ransom.

'Done,' he said, smiling. 'Now introduce me, and
smile yourself. You scarcely look as pleased as you
should.'

Harry sat in the supper-room, a plate of food on her
knee; she seemed to do nothing but eat indifferent fare
at these grand thrashes. Alex, who was ever-present these
days—she suspected the Duchess's hand in this, and
found it difficult to deny her—had taken her in to
supper. But almost before they had begun either to eat,
or to engage in the verbal fencing which seemed to form
the staple of their conversation, he had been claimed by
their hostess, Lady Melbourne, a person so grand that
her manners were her own.

'You will forgive me, Mrs Ashburn,' she had said,
knowing that Harry could do no other, 'but I need
Templestowe immediately to settle an argument in the
library about the Peninsular campaign. My husband and
Fred Ponsonby cannot agree about the Duke's tactics,
and I have been sent to fetch Alex to end the matter. I
promise to return him when he has given his verdict.'
And she had walked Alex off without a backward look,
and Mrs Whitmore, seeing her abandoned, had come
across to her.

'How exactly like our hostess,' she sighed. 'Every
attractive man must be carried off as a prize on some
excuse. One would think her still twenty, not in the sere
and yellow.'

It was at this point that Arabella arrived with Lord
Nun'ster in tow. Earlier, Harry had observed him in the
main salon. She had been aware of his eyes upon her,
and had been a little surprised that a seasoned man of

such mature years should regard her so curiously. Nearer to, she saw that she had been correct. He was a handsome man, but she found something inimical in his cool stare.

As Arabella went through the forms of introduction his eyes never left Harry. The pearl she was wearing obviously took his interest.

'So happy to meet you, at last,' he said, and again, although his voice was deep and pleasant, there was a note in it as if he did not quite mean what he said, or his meaning was not what his hearer thought.

Nun'ster's eye was on her pearl as he spoke, or was it her bosom which interested him?

'I knew your lovely mother,' he said. 'We were all young together—Hornsea, Harrendene, and myself, and now I meet her daughter, so fresh, so. . .charming. . .' He cannot call me beautiful, was Harry's amused inward gloss on this. 'Oh, Mrs Ashburn, such glowing youth makes me feel old.'

Well, you are not exactly young, Harry would have liked to say, so that is not surprising, and wondered why she was responding to him in this fashion. Gilly had said once that she had good instincts, and it was true that sometimes she had these feelings, and they rarely failed her. She was, for instance, wondering why Arabella should foist him on her, and remain hovering—presumably he was there to look after Arabella's supper, so why did he not do so?

For very decency, as he continued with her, she was compelled to ask him to sit with her, so there they were, apparently conversing amicably and intimately, when Alex returned, still supperless, and his face darkening as he saw Nun'ster bending towards her, talking earnestly of the happy days of his lost youth, of the delights of the Season, of the Opera, of anything. And, of course, Arabella was there to take Alex in tow, and he doubtless thought that she, Harry, had fixed herself on Nun'ster, but that could not be helped. The man was charming enough, and appeared to possess an interesting and

informed mind, and his manners were so impeccable that
she could not imagine why she had first thought there
was something strange about him as he fetched an ice for
herself and a cool drink for Mrs Whitmore.

The more he talked the more she began to think her
initial judgement of him too harsh. The scepticism with
which some of Society regarded her was perhaps creating
unnecessary suspicion on her part.

He asked her what her preferences were in the drama,
and, when she said that a visit to the Theatre to see Kean
had been a source of great satisfaction to her, said
smoothly, 'Ah, Mrs Ashburn, a devotee of the Bard,'
and began to quote from *Othello*. 'Jealousy,' he commented, watching her, 'is as cruel as the grave, you see.
But probably beyond the comprehension of such a young
lady as yourself. Now you must feel for Desdemona.'

'Oh, indeed,' replied Harry gravely, 'but a useful
manual of etiquette might have deterred her from so
unequal a marriage, and convinced her of the necessity
to obey her poor papa. Think what being a dutiful
daughter would have saved her.'

As so often, it took Nun'ster a moment to detach the
ironic nature of what she had said from the innocent way
in which she said it. When he did, for the first time his
laughter was genuine and unforced, and Harry could
suddenly see his charm.

'Oh, I heard you were a wit, Mrs Ashburn, and for
once rumour has not lied. No, you are not much like
your mama after all. She would never have been as
pointed as that. How fortunate for Society that you
rescued yourself from your Norfolk fastness. A blossom
wasted on the desert air.'

Come, thought Harry, this is a little much on a first
introduction. 'Oh, I know,' she said cheerfully, 'I cannot
hope to rival my mama in looks. I may seek to follow my
papa in his interests.'

For no reason she could discover, this did not please.

'Oh, yes, your papa,' he said curtly. 'He died early, I believe.'

And that, I note, did not displease you, was Harry's reaction to that, but she merely smiled and replied, 'Yes, I never knew him, but I suppose that you did?'

'Long ago,' he said. 'Before you were born or thought of.'

'And he was part of your set, too, and my mama?' she asked, remembering what he had said at the beginning of their conversation, and being surprised again.

Nothing she had heard at Netherdene, from her mother, or her stepfather, had suggested such grand connections. But there was the pearl pendant, and the half-understood feeling that it was not only her sudden elevation as Racquette's owner which excited Society's comment.

Nun'ster, however, did not enlarge on this, only saying, almost carelessly, 'Oh, yes. We were all part of a group round the Duke of Hornsea, your patroness's husband, who is a recluse now. The happy days of our youth. . .' This was almost sentimental in tone, but there was nothing sentimental in his voice or expression, and he immediately went on to speak of other things. 'I gather that you will be part of Margaret Askham's al fresco afternoon tomorrow. I hope to see you there. I seldom enjoy such invigorating conversation with a lady. Now I am afraid that I must leave you; I have another engagement to fulfil. You will forgive me.' And he rose to take his leave.

Now, what do I say to that? thought Harry, as he bent over her hand, turning it, of all things, palm up, to kiss it, conscious that Alex was hovering, looking as black as thunder. Well, she had only been talking to the man when all was said and done—not dancing the hornpipe, or doing something equally socially distressful.

Harry was already withdrawing to find Mrs Whitmore, who had gone to fetch their cloaks and order the carriage, when Alex followed her along the corridor, and stopped her, saying, 'Cousin Harry, a word with you,' in a voice which reminded her of Rule. They were by a glass door, which he held open for her, remarking, 'I would prefer this to be private.'

Harry found herself on a terrace, looking out over a London which was dim under a crescent moon. To the west, flaring gas lights illuminated the streets around Pall Mall. There was a stone bench before a balustrade, and urns full of flowers stood about. Distant music reached their ears from the open windows of another great house near by.

'Is this wise——?' Harry began, only for him to interrupt her, with a look almost of reproof on his face.

'Wise,' he repeated. 'You ask me that? Surely you must know what Nun'ster's reputation is.'

'No,' she replied. 'But I would dare say little worse than that of many I meet.'

'Not so. The man is notorious. He is careless, not only of his own reputation, but of those whom he snares. Every murky scandal of the last twenty years has had Nun'ster at its heart.'

'He hardly seemed such a monster as that,' said Harry, suddenly perverse. Why did she feel a compelling need to withstand Alex when he appeared to have her welfare at heart? 'We engaged in a perfectly rational and proper conversation, distinguished only by its dullness,' she stated firmly. 'More proper than some I have engaged in with other noblemen, I might remind you.'

He ignored this, saying, 'I warn you, Cousin Harry, so that you might protect yourself. But if you are determined to refuse my advice because you think to add the title of Marchioness of Nun'ster to the tally of your triumphs, you are mistaken. He is old enough to be your father, and marriage is not his game.'

Harry suddenly felt light-headed, almost ready to float, her whole body vibrating with she knew not what. She had never experienced such a sensation before, and could not imagine what it was. The lovely calm which she had

sworn to maintain with him flew away. How dared he?
How dared he continue to insult her? She merely had to
talk to a reasonably personable man and Alex saw
conspiracies everywhere, particularly a conspiracy *she*
was promoting.

'Oh, indeed, Cousin Alex,' she said furiously, hardly
recognising her own voice, 'I thank you for your advice.
I am sure you know of what you speak. What was your
game, then, on the stairs at Rule? Better or worse than
his, would you say?'

Alex's colour and his temper rose together. How dared
she fling Rule in his face? Surely she understood how
untypical his behaviour had been, provoked as it was by
her own reckless impudence in virtually cheating him at
chess?

'Oh, madam. . .' Cousin Harry, she noted drily, was
quite forgot '. . . it had slipped my mind what a mistress
of games you are, from chess to the mastery of men. My
warning is not needed, I see, unless, maybe, I should
warn Nun'ster. . . What snares are you laying to trap
him?' Where was his vaunted coolness now as the words
tumbled from him, and his eyes glared at her in the face
of her refusal to bend before his wishes? 'This I must
see. I could almost pity the man. Unless, of course, in
engaging with him you meet your match in wilful guile
at last. Beware, madam; he's an old and seasoned hand
at the game of opportunity.'

Harry could have stamped.

'Oh, how dare you? Nun'ster, at least, has said and
done nothing wrong to me. What right have you to
preach at me? Physician heal thyself.'

With difficulty Alex prevented himself from seizing
her, to silence her, to compel her to. . .to what? His
mind shied away from the consequences of laying hands
on her again. He knew, only too well, what the end of
that would be! But the thought of her with Nun'ster was
almost painful. He knew Nun'ster's way with women,
and to imagine them together. . .! Why he should feel so

strongly about what Cousin Harry did, he could not understand.

He mastered himself sufficiently to say stiffly, 'I merely thought to warn you, madam. I treated you as the innocent you wished to be considered, and not as the siren you are. An innocent to be protected from a man of such ill-repute as Nun'ster. I see I was mistaken.'

They were again in a world of their own as they had been at Rule. A world where Alex was now ashy white, and Harry scarlet with anger. He stepped towards her, and she retreated, saying, 'Coming from the man who virtually assaulted me, this is rich indeed.'

His visible response to this was so strong and angry that she continued her retreat from him until she felt the balustrade at her back, gazing fearfully at his face, his eyes blazing at her, frightened of what he might do, but, despite herself, excited at what she had provoked.

Perhaps a little to the subsequent relief of both of them, for by now they were again beyond reason, and only passion ruled, the glass door suddenly flew open, and Ned appeared.

'Oh, I find you, at last. Mrs Whitmore wondered where you had both vanished to. . .' And then he stopped and looked from one to the other, the very air between them resonating. 'Oh, no, Alex, surely not. You cannot still be teasing Cousin Harry. Whatever next? We are not all your poor lieutenants to be bullied, you know. You are not in the Army now.'

Alex's fury diverted itself from Harry to the luckless Ned.

'By God, it's a good thing for you, Ned, that I am not, and you with me. You would soon find out in what coin you would pay for insolence.'

'And Harry, too, I suppose,' said Ned sturdily. 'Come away, Cousin. If you need protecting, I will protect you.' And, throwing a reproachful glance at his brother, he put an arm around her and led her out.

Alex sank down on the bench. In God's name, why

could he not control himself when he was with her? What unearthly power did the Circe possess that she could excite him so? He had been on the verge of sexually assaulting her again, and this time he could have sworn she had been half provoking him. To what end? And why in the world should she be so attracted to Nun'ster, of all people, unless she wanted his title? How could she treat his well-meant warnings with such cavalier impudence?

Leaning on Ned's arm, Harry was almost ashamed at her own impassioned reactions to Alex, and his doubtless well-meant warnings. It is not like me. I am the cool observer of life as taught by Gilly, not a screaming shrew. And I do believe that if he had fallen on me I would have welcomed him. What in the world can be coming over me that I should behave so?

CHAPTER EIGHT

HERVEY BEAUCLERC, always known by his title of Nun'ster, prepared himself for his visit to Margaret Askham's al fresco party. The weather had been kind, for once, and the company at Askham Court would not have to pretend that sitting indoors, watching the rain, would be the same as enjoying their hostess's beautiful garden in the sun.

Nun'ster had a good mind and a keen understanding, which occasionally, but only occasionally, he realised he had not put to any better use than to follow a life of unrelieved pleasure. In all the years since he had come upon the Town he had only found himself thwarted once, and the thwarting had been so great that in revenge he had acted in such a way as to destroy the happy circle of friends of which he had been a part. But the revenge had been incomplete; the object of it had escaped his grip, and now her daughter had unexpectedly arrived in Society, and his final revenge might be accomplished after all.

If he could not have the mother, then, one way or another, the daughter would be his. Oh, she did not have the incomparable beauty of her lovely mother—that could not be expected—but she had other attributes which might be even better to his purpose: a mind and a will. The pleasure of subduing the one and breaking the other would be exquisite.

It was obvious that she knew nothing of that long-gone, half-forgotten scandal, so that gossip distorted what had actually happened, and he might be able to put that to good use, too. The actors in it were either dead, like her parents, or recluses, like the Duke of Hornsea, or had retreated from life into books, like Adolphus

Harrendene. None of them could or would talk; he might say what he pleased, and there would be none to contradict him.

Oh, he did not wish Henrietta Manners' daughter to marry anyone, let alone Alex Templestowe, that would cut him off from his revenge. The rankling anger which he had carried within him for over twenty years, the bitterness of his defeat, could be wiped away if he could destroy the daughter of the man who had, with the help of powerful friends, deprived him of the only woman he had ever loved. A woman whom he could never have believed would have chosen the poor scholar, John Grey, in preference to himself with all his looks, wealth and talent. She had destroyed him, too, because after her loss he had embarked on his life of furious pleasure to make up for it. With her there had been no height he might not have reached, without her he had become nothing.

Harry found the gardens of Askham Court delightful. They surrounded a small, but beautiful house near the Thames, full of Italian paintings and porcelain collected by Lady Askham's late husband on the Grand Tour over sixty years ago.

On the Duchess's advice she had taken her sketchbook and crayons with her, and soon found her lonely way down to the river, away from the crowd. There she sat quietly sketching, the insupportabilities of life forgotten in the contemplation of paddling waterfowl.

'So, madam, you do not waste the sun or the hour,' said a deep but pleasant voice, and Lord Nun'ster was there, seated on a stone bench, had been there for some time, watching her. 'The nymph of the grove,' he declared, relishing her grave solemnity and the picture which she made against the trees and sky, the Grecian fashions of the day conferring a timelessness on her appearance.

Harry lifted her head from her paper, where Lombardy poplars and cedars, ducks and the ever-changing water were beginning to take shape. 'I had thought myself in Arcady,' she said, smiling. 'Only Pan pipes were needed to complete the illusion.'

'A pity, then,' he said, 'that I merely arrive to call you to tea on the lawn. Had I not come so unapropos, the Gods might have sent one of themselves instead.'

Harry looked at him as he sat there, a handsome man, bantering with her in this supremely civilised fashion, and her bruised heart was soothed a little. She had already forgotten her own first suspicions of Nun'ster under the impact of his seductive charm. He flattered her by addressing her mind. She did not grasp that his designs on her body would come later.

She put down her pencil. 'I suppose even someone the Gods might visit needs sustenance. Ambrosia alone will not do.'

'Ambrosia?' he said. 'The food of the Gods not for mortal men and women, you think? Well, Lady Askham does not provide that, I own, but her fare is better than most. The best there is.'

'You relieve me,' said Harry, rising. 'So far the funeral baked meats of London appear little better than those of Norfolk, if served on grander plates and in grander surroundings among a headier company.'

'Do I detect a touch of world-weariness?' he asked, offering her his arm, after taking her book and little satchel from her to carry himself. 'Is Mrs Ashburn already seeing through the illusions of the world we live in? Do you think my lord and lady in London little better than Hodge at the farm other than in form and ceremony?'

Harry looked at him sharply. 'And if I say yes, will you think me naïve to be so rapid in my conclusions, or would it be naïve to reply that a lengthier consideration might provide a different answer?'

Nun'ster drew a little breath at this. Oh, indeed, a mind worth winning.

'Now, how do I answer that,' he said softly, as they reached the lawn shaded by giant beeches, 'without exposing myself to *your* shafts of wit? Shall I take the lady's usual part, and offer something which turns aside from the truth of the matter with an appearance of sense, without possessing its essence?'

'Ah, my lord,' smiled Harry. 'You are not kind to women after all, since you understand the frailties of our comprehension only too well.'

'Now, Mrs Ashburn,' he said, and what he said was not flattery, although she might take it as such, 'your comprehension possesses little frailty, and Jupiter himself, I think, would have trouble in overcoming it.'

More than one who watched them arrive felt some surprise at the obvious rapport which the two had so rapidly achieved. None with more mixed feelings than Alex Templestowe, who had arrived shortly before the long table had been spread with tea.

He, too, was not accustomed to visit such mild functions, but the knowledge that Harry was to be present had driven him there, as it had driven Nun'ster, but for very different reasons. Seeing the pair of them arrive, heads together, laughing, Harry's face at peace as he had seldom seen it, had the strangest effect on him. The most enormous and unreasoning anger consumed him. So! After all he had said, perhaps *because* of all he had said, madam had seen fit to give him his answer by spending the afternoon tête-à-tête, alone with Nun'ster, and now knew no better than to appear with that disgusting old roué, obviously enchanted by him and his conversation. Knew no better than to allow herself to be flattered by him. What games were they both playing? Which was the hunter? Or was it possible that both were hunting, tiger facing tiger?

An opportunity to speak with her soon came. Margaret Askham annexed Nun'ster; he had been her dead son's friend. Some friend, thought Alex derisively, for he knew the truth of *that* story, but was not surprised that Margaret Askham did not, and it gave him the opportunity to go over to Harry, to help her to tea and cake, and then invite her to stroll with him on the footpath by the river.

Harry would have liked to refuse him, but before all these great ones—for the company was illustrious and had doubtless already dubbed her upstart—she did not like to. There was a look in Alex's eye which she did not care for—a look of high-minded determination to read her some kind of Riot Act for her sins, imaginary and otherwise.

Trapped, she took his arm, and they walked down to the Thames, to watch the ducks again and some rather elegant swans—a shame to liken Arabella to them, she thought. Alex's conversation up to this point was almost determinedly null—an effortless and boring prattle of fine gentleman's platitudes to a lady—most unlike him.

'Indeed, yes,' she said aloud after one stupefyingly dull comment on the season. 'Rain is wet, the cows are in the field, Parliament is sitting. I do believe that converse in Norfolk was livelier than in London, my lord.'

'Cousin Alex,' he reminded her, amused by her despite himself. 'And what, pray, brought that on, Cousin Harry?'

'I was repaying you in kind,' she answered spiritedly.

'That was my prologue,' he insisted, 'delivered before I reach the meat of the matter.' And his expression and voice suddenly became a little severe.

Here it comes, thought Harry irreverently, a reprimand for being with Nun'ster, and daring to enjoy his conversation.

'I thought that you had sense enough to heed my warnings over Hervey Nun'ster,' he began, prompt on cue. 'But I suppose that your Norfolk successes have convinced you that you can repeat them here. It would be an unwise thought. I speak for your good, mind,' he said hastily as he saw her brow grow dark.

'Oh, famous,' Harry replied. 'First I am a siren, full of wiles, and then an innocent to be advised. Neither consistency nor logic appear to be strong points with you, Cousin Alex.'

'Or propriety with you, madam.'

'Oh, Cousin Harry, I beg,' she returned, eyes agleam. 'But all of a piece, I see—inconsistent again.'

By now they were walking along a path where the ground had grown rougher, and was greasy with recent rain. The river was bending before them, and they were out of view of the house. Annoyance at him made Harry a little careless; she was walking along a little above him, so that when she lost her footing, her light pumps sliding on the wet grass, she fell sideways into his arms as she finished her last sentence.

'But you, at least, madam, are consistent,' he said as he caught her to him to break her fall, continuing to hold her after he had done so. 'A fine armful to tempt me, I suppose. Let me answer you in kind. I will at least be consistent in that, if nothing else.' And he kissed her lightly on the mouth. 'There, will that do?'

'And you warn me against Nun'ster!' was her furious reply, as she reluctantly removed her mouth from his— she would not, no, she would not be kissed in contempt.

'Oh, come, Cousin Harry, never say die. You hurled yourself most convincingly at me. What is a poor man to do when he receives such a present? Throw it back like an unwanted fish? Ungallant to say the least.' And he kissed her again, very gently on the cheek this time. 'Tell me, is it Nun'ster you are after? Or are you using him as a bait to catch Templestowe's title as well as Templestowe's lands?' He was pleased to see how much in command of himself he was—little chance that passion would carry him away this time. But, oh, her nearness was temptation itself!

'I slipped,' said Harry stiffly.

'Frequently, one supposes, and always to good purpose, I'm sure,' was his cheerful answer. He was still holding her to him, and this time his kiss found the hollow of her throat, producing in Harry such a *frisson* of delight that she was almost undone.

Oh, the wretch! But she, too, managed to keep her calm control, neither struggling, nor pushing him off, so that this absurd passage of arms between them was conducted with the oddest decorum, as he punctuated their verbal exchanges with butterfly kisses, quite different from the passionate ones of Rule.

They proved, however, far more effective in almost undoing Harry. More flies are caught by honey than by gall, she thought, as now her eyelids received his attentions, and the butterflies were beginning to invade her body, even though all his actions were confined to her face. How could it be that his touch, his lightest touch, could produce such appalling inward sensations, far beyond her imaginings? Her control began to waver. A moment and she would be co-operating with him.

Alex, too, was beginning to find that, to a passionate man who had not indulged himself for some time, dispassion was proving a little hard to maintain. Had they not been in Margaret Askham's gardens, almost within earshot, if not in view of their fellow guests, he might have taken matters to their logical conclusion: pleasured madam, and then given her a firm slap on the rump to show her what he thought of fortune-hunting lightskirts. Bedworthy creatures, all, not persons to whom one handed a Countess's coronet. She might take herself to Nun'ster after that, and see whether a Marchioness's favours could be won more easily—but, no, that would not do at all. Whatever else, he could not endure the thought of Nun'ster's having her.

Perforce, he let her go, smiling a little as she stood back to order herself.

'Be careful you don't slip again, Cousin. But your powers of recuperation are admirable. Such speed, such delightful composure. I congratulate you.'

This vaunted composure was on the verge of being shattered, but, I will not be overset, Harry thought.

'Oh, my lord, it takes more than a couple of snatched kisses to reduce me to hysterics. And I should dearly like to know why a wretch who so continually assaults me should also be so tender of my being mishandled by another.'

Alex would have liked to know the answer to that, too, but could hardly say so.

'If you are quite restored, Cousin Harry, we had best return, or all Margaret Askham's guests will be thinking the worst.'

'Nor would they be far wrong,' said Harry frostily. 'Tell me, my lord, am I the only lady you favour with your attentions, or is no one safe from you? From someone whom I am constantly assured is a man of honour, such conduct hardly stamps you as one.'

'Oh, I treat everyone after the fashion which they deserve, with honour where it is due, Cousin,' he returned lightly.

Unshed tears stung Harry's eyes. Such a reply demonstrated once again his low opinion of his cousin's widow. Oh, Gilly, what must I do, what can I do to remove the stain on my honour? What will ever convince him, or anyone, of my innocence? I, who was only your virgin wife, lovingly rescued by you, am treated as little better than a common slut who walks the streets. I will not cry; no one shall make me. I will not give anyone that satisfaction.

CHAPTER NINE

'HARRY, my dear,' said the Duchess to her, at Hornsea House, in the Strand, on the day before they were going to hear Alex make his maiden speech in the Lords, 'I think that it is my duty to warn you to have a care in your dealing with Hervey Nun'ster. He has a bad reputation so far as women are concerned.' She hesitated, then continued, 'Years ago he was part of the Duke's circle, just before we were married, and your mother and father disappeared into the country.

'There was gossip that he wished to marry your mama, and was distressed when she accepted your father. After that, the Duke's circle suddenly broke up, and the Duke would have nothing more to do with him. I never really knew what happened.' She hesitated again. 'It is only fair to warn you that there was gossip about your mama, too. But I took no heed of it, then or now.'

'He said that he knew my mother,' offered Harry, 'and that she was very beautiful. We agreed that I am not like her. I must say that his conversations with me on the few occasions on which I have met him have been extremely proper.' She hesitated in her turn. 'I must also add that I find him a well-informed and amusing companion. I cannot believe that his interest in me goes beyond that.'

'Perhaps,' said the Duchess. 'But it is well to be forewarned. I know that Alex is worried for you.'

Oh, indeed, thought Harry satirically. And I am far more worried about Alex's dark designs on me than I am about Nun'ster's, but I cannot tell you that, my dear Duchess, for all your many kindnesses. You love your nephew too much for me to criticise him to you.

Aloud, she said, 'It will be a busy day for Alex. In the morning I am to visit his home in Piccadilly for us to

sign the final papers relating to my acquisition of the
Templestowe lands. I find the whole matter odd in the
extreme, but the lawyers assure me that it must be done,
so done it shall be.'

And at least he cannot start kissing me there, before
all those grave and reverend signors; His High
Mightiness would never allow himself to descend to
that—the stairs at Rule and the banks of the Thames
being the proper place for such goings on. I can only
hope that I shall be safe from such assaults at the House
of Lords.

This unruly thought brought on the giggles at the
prospect of Alex Templestowe at one moment solemnly
addressing the highest in the land, and at the next trying
to bring poor Harry Ashburn low. Before or behind the
Woolsack, would it be, where he might choose to undress
her, or kiss her into submission? She turned her giggles
into a suppressed cough, as once before, but not with
such drastic consequences, and the thought of Alex
pursuing her in such august surroundings entertained
her all the way home.

Unfortunately she could not strangle the memory of
this disgraceful fantasy when she and Mrs Whitmore met
Alex in his study on the following morning. He could
not help wondering what had given her complexion such
a pleasant blush, in comparison with her usual ivory
pallor, and what the gleam in her eye meant.

Both Alex's lawyers and her own were present—not
kind Mr Flewitt, for he had surrendered his interest in
her to the eminent London firm who had always repre-
sented the Templestowes. She could not say that she
liked Mr Heriot, whose manner to her was usually faintly
insolent, but she had to endure him.

Alex was waiting for them, and she felt their respective
positions keenly. Part of the problem she had in dealing
with him lay in the fact that she was always aware of
what she had robbed him. Racquette lay between them,
and could not be dismissed or overlooked. She could not

wish her great good fortune away. She was enjoying it
too much for that—far more than she had expected—
but she could wish that she had not acquired it at
someone else's expense, and feel guilty in doing so. What
was worse was that Alex, apart from his dealings with
her, was so completely a conscientious man of honour,
and would have made a good guardian of the house and
lands. She had not even the satisfaction of feeling that
she had rescued it from a wastrel, like many of the men
she had met in London Society. Having run through
their own fortune and property, they were bent on
acquiring hers to do it all over again.

For once, however, Alex was determined to put the
past aside a little. She might have tricked his cousin into
marriage, but she could not have known that she was
going to trick the true heir out of his inheritance. What
exercised him was whether or not she was a worthy
owner. He did not know which distressed him more—
the unlikely thought of Nun'ster's marrying her, and
acquiring Racquette, or of his not marrying her, and
ruining her. Even his cousin's cheating widow did not
deserve *that*.

She looked enchanting, he thought, in lemon-coloured
muslin, and a little chip hat with lemon silk ribbons,
decorated with hand-made lilies of the valley. She was
beginning to acquire a kind of glow, which was the result
of dealing with Alex's baffled harshness, and Nun'ster's
seductive flattery.

She had seen Nun'ster twice more since meeting him
at Askham Court, and he was charm itself.

Talking to her, enjoying the ready wit with which she
responded to all he said, he was suddenly completely
taken with her, so much so that he began to dream of a
delightful change in his plans. Oh, she was far beyond
her mother, and a man of his years wanted more than
mere beauty. What a companion she would make. Might
he not, with Harry by his side, yet do all those things of
which her mother's loss had deprived him? A wife to

help him, a mother to give him brilliant sons. Why waste such a treasure by bedding and then rejecting her? Why, indeed?

Alex saw her eye on a mezzotint. 'I see you are admiring my favourite print. I have always wanted to visit Italy to see the original, and now that the wars are over I may get my wish—although my estates claim me at present. I have been an absentee landlord for far too long.'

He sighed a little, as though he would have liked to continue their conversation in the same style, and she thought, suddenly, that this was the first time since they had met that they had spoken normally together, without antagonism, and without passion. Here was almost the man she had hoped for, had first thought him to be, not the man who despised her for capturing his cousin and his lands.

Almost as though he knew what she was thinking, he smiled at her, observing her sober face, saying cheerfully—and it was the first time that he had commented on her supplanting of him without a note of bitterness in his voice, 'Come, Cousin Harry, it was not you but my grandfather who created this situation. Blame, if blame there be, attaches to him.' As he said this his own lawyer plucked him by the sleeve. But Alex threw the man's hand off, saying impatiently, 'Today I am a soldier, not a diplomat, and a soldier speaks his mind. When all is completed, Mrs Gilbert Ashburn and I will shake hands as a token of good faith. The matter will be over.'

Mrs Whitmore nodded approvingly, and Harry suddenly felt for him, for the first time, something approaching affection—a different feeling from the passion which had overcome her at his lovemaking. She watched him sign the papers put before him, and they were then passed to her.

'And that is that,' he said briskly. 'Your hand, Cousin Harry. Templestowe's lands are yours. It is to be hoped that you will be a good mistress. Wine, gentlemen. Let us toast the future.'

Alex had determined before the meeting that, whatever else, he would not betray the anguish which he felt at losing his inheritance. Harry looked at him with sympathy, knowing the pain that his cheerful manner cloaked. She would repay him in kind. Instead of answering him directly, she said, a trifle shyly, 'Cousin Alex, I understand that you are to address the House of Lords this afternoon, and that it will be your maiden speech. Sarah tells me that there is a gallery where ladies may watch, and I should like of all things to be present— that is, if you have no objections.'

Alex laughed. 'I shall have a good audience upstairs, at least. I am told that the Chamber is sometimes deserted. But you must promise not to create a riot if what I say does not please. I am told that some great ladies did precisely that fifty years ago.'

'Oh, no,' she said gravely, 'no such thing. I might shake my head a little, and look sad, but no more. Perhaps if you forewarned me, I could come prepared to say Tut, Tut, occasionally.'

'We shall be debating the condition of the Midland counties, which is where my main estates lie. It is in the centres where Luddism was rife, and disaffection is still present. Lord Byron spoke on these matters once, urging mercy, and I must perforce follow him. Although he is not a man I greatly care for, no one can deny his courage. There was, and is, great misery there, although my own tenants are more fortunate than most. Blagg, my bailiff, is a good man. I shall urge that if necessary we import corn to reduce its price. That should earn me the scorn of my fellow landowners, but would reduce the chance of riot if implemented. No one will listen to me, and I may even be shouted down.'

'Oh, I hope not,' said Harry, pressing her hands together, and looking anxiously at him. However harshly he had treated her, she could not wish a man so considerate of his poor tenants to be badly treated. She remembered the starving children she had seen in Norfolk, and shivered. Her own nearness to total destitution could never be forgotten, even in her new splendours.

'You must not worry for me,' he replied gaily. 'I have seen much worse; it will not be like the Peninsular War, you know. They are not proposing to shoot at me—at least, not yet.'

The more Harry saw of him, the more of a paradox he was. The man who lost no opportunity to persecute her and pursue her was also the man whose honour, she was so often informed, was stainless, and who was now showing a compassion for the poor and lowly which she had not so far met among London Society. From what she had already heard she knew that a speech of the kind he proposed to make would not be popular. This did not seem to trouble him, and, as though he knew what she was thinking, he added, 'One must do one's duty as one sees it, Cousin Harry, and damn the consequences. War taught me that. Its lessons are not wholly bad, you know, even though ladies like to think so—that is, those who do not see it as all plumes and fine uniforms and martial music.'

'Gilly said that once,' she replied, struck by how often he echoed his cousin's thoughts. The likeness between them was not confined to red hair and a somewhat stern profile. His humour was not so wry as Gilly's, but it was there, and was more often in evidence as she came to know him better. Oh, if only he would show her this man more often, and not the one who saw her as lightskirt and siren. This was the man she could care for, not the one he so often was when they were alone.

'I will see you afterwards,' he said, as they parted, 'so that I may thank my claque in the gallery. Emily Hornsea will be going, so you will not lack for a friend.'

In the midst of all the frivolity of the London Season Harry's visit to the House of Lords to hear Alex speak made a welcome change. Not that the Lords seemed a very serious body. Most of the great gentlemen sprawled about the Chamber seemed half asleep, although Alex's speech certainly woke them up.

Harry was not surprised to find that he cut a good figure, speaking well, with a certain disarming modesty, but his proposals and the firmness with which he made them had little effect on his hearers. One or two of the great Whig peers present made their approval known, but there was a hiss of voices, like angry geese, when he spoke of importing corn, and none of his eloquence about the poverty of the Midland counties and the plight of the framework knitters cut much ice with the well-fed gentlemen anxious to adjourn soon to their dinners.

'So those are our great legislators,' said Harry to Emily Hornsea, for several of Lord Liverpool's cabinet who sat in the Lords were there, and had shown their derision for a young man's folly as they saw it.

The rest of the business after Alex had spoken was extremely boring, with several dull gentlemen droning away into their chests, so that nothing could be heard of their great thoughts. At least every word of what Alex had said was plainly audible, as she told him afterwards.

He looked at her with something of her own demure naughtiness in his expression.

'Perhaps it would have been better for me had I been inaudible,' he answered, 'and then no one would have taken exception to what I said, and Lord Liverpool might have made me a junior minister at the very least. As it is, they will think me in league with Ned Ludd. Colonel Ashburn at his service.'

It was one of the times when he reminded her of Gilly, and this, on top of the humanity of his speech, made her regret the fantasies she had spun of his attacking her in the Lords. His respect for the place in which they had met was evident.

While they were talking, Nun'ster strolled towards them. He had been present for Alex's speech; indeed, on hearing that he was to speak had made his own presence certain. He was sure that Harry would be present, too, and that this would be an opportunity to speak to her.

As usual, his manners were perfect when they went through the ritual politeness demanded. 'Your servant, Templestowe. I must congratulate you on the manner of your speech, my dear fellow, but not on its content. You will have every dirty peasant in the countryside at your throat if you as much as give them anything, let alone all that they demand.'

Nun'ster saw at once by Harry's expression that where she was concerned he had sounded a false note. He cursed himself a little, but to retrieve it was impossible. Best to take all in his stride.

Alex was not pleased either. 'I'm not his dear fellow, and I dislike him exceedingly,' he said to Emily and Harry when Nun'ster had gone, but, while he was there, contented himself by saying, 'It grieves me, sir, to see English countrymen living in no better condition than the poor Spanish peasants I saw in the Peninsula. Anything I can do to mitigate their condition. . .'

'Oh, a little benevolent despotism might help,' said Nun'ster coolly, hoping by saying this to mend his mistake with Harry. 'I am sure you agree, Mrs Ashburn. They are hardly fit to govern themselves.'

'Oh, I don't think that they want that,' replied Harry, equally coolly. 'All they want is something to eat and not to see their babies starve.'

'Your compassion is admirable,' said Nun'ster, bowing to her. 'It does you credit. But we must remember that whatever we do we must not bring about a 1789 here. Revolution would benefit no one, least of all the peasantry themselves.'

There was little either of his hearers could say to that, as neither of them wanted such an outcome. After a few more pleasantries Nun'ster bowed, and moved away, confident that he had restored himself a little with Harry.

Alex looked after him with something like murder in his heart. He had seen the pleasure on Harry's face when

Nun'ster had arrived and, watching him, he had a sudden vision of Harry doing something unspeakable with Nun'ster. Damn it, he thought suddenly and honestly, if she is going to do anything unspeakable with anyone, she had better do it with me!

CHAPTER TEN

'ALEX, I want a word with you.' Ned Ashburn, dressed with more elegance than his usual country carelessness, entered the small study at Alex's Town home off Piccadilly where his brother sat reading.

Alex looked up, not best pleased at being interrupted. He had spent the earlier part of the afternoon going over accounts, and had forgone a ride in Hyde Park with Ned, Cousin Harry and the Duchess. Duty had called, and, as usual, he had answered it. After his work was over he had picked up Captain Cook's account of his voyage to the Pacific, and was engrossed in it before Ned's abrupt arrival.

'Really, Ned, is one never to have a moment to oneself? You know I do not like interruption when I am in here.'

Ned looked at his brother impatiently. 'I would not have troubled you, Alex, but the matter is important to me, and urgent. I have been in the Park with Cousin Harry, and every coxcomb in London was there, paying her compliments, including that swine, Nun'ster.'

'So?' said Alex, whose heart sank on hearing Nun'ster's name. Was she still trifling with him? Would she never learn? 'But that is what one expects, surely. Racquette and the Templestowe estates are a great prize to be won, as all the world knows. Why should we waste our time discussing *that*?'

'Because. . .because I value your opinion,' admitted Ned impulsively. 'You are the steadiest man I know, and always give one good advice. Tell me, what is your opinion on how a fellow should go about proposing marriage to a girl who is older than he is? If one proposes, is it *de rigueur* to ask her to wait until one is older, or would it be more the thing to marry her immediately before she becomes even older?'

Alex nearly dropped his book; fortunately for him he retrieved it before it fell. Its descent would have ruined its binding and his feet.

'What are you at, Ned? You cannot mean to propose to Cousin Harry?'

'And why not?' flashed Ned. 'And it is not for Racquette, either; you are not to think that. I love her, and if I go on waiting some fool who only wants Racquette will snatch her up, and I am nearly nineteen——'

'Just eighteen,' interjected his brother accurately, but unpleasantly.

'Well, eighteen, then, and I know that I shall never meet anyone I shall love half as much as Harry, and you are not to look at me like that, either. Why should I not make her Mrs Ned instead of Mrs Gilbert Ashburn? She is good and kind, the jolliest person I know, and will make me a splendid wife. Oh, and I'm sure she cares for me too; she's always pleased to see me, I can tell. Why should I not ask her? She might even say yes, and then you would look stupid for trying to put me off. Anyone would think that you didn't want me settled. We are not all like you, you know—first racketing about, and then mooning over Arabella, and now living like a mad priest.' He finally ran out of breath.

Alex was suddenly stricken. To his horror, one emotion, and one only, filled his mind as he stared at Ned, and that was the blackest jealousy towards the younger brother he had always loved and protected. Could Cousin Harry really care for Ned that way? And how serious was the young fool? The whole thing was preposterous, wasn't it? Ned was a child.

But it wasn't preposterous. He remembered himself at Ned's age, and he had been far from a child, and far more experienced than he knew Ned to be.

Ned's face, eager and beseeching, brought him back

to the present, away from that early Alex Ashburn, who was neither the youngest Colonel in the British Army, nor the seventh Earl of Templestowe, but a happy adventurer both in and out of bed. Life, war and Arabella had killed that light-hearted boy stone dead. He must go easy with Ned; the lad was serious, and Harry was only three years older than he was, after all.

'It's not usual,' he said, picking his words with care, 'for men to marry women who are older than they are. It is, in fact, the custom for them to take younger women to wife.'

'I know all that,' replied Ned angrily. 'Really, Alex, you do prose on sometimes. I want advice on how to ask her, not on the general state of marriage. It would mean that I couldn't go to Oxford, of course. But I don't mind that. You'd have to give your consent, you know, as my guardian, if we married now, instead of waiting until I'm twenty-one.'

'I don't think that Harry sees you as a possible husband, Ned.'

'Whyever not? I'm not deformed, or a pauper, or a fortune-hunter. I've a competence of my own, or shall have when I'm twenty-one. And we deal so well together.'

'There's more to marriage than that.'

'Well, if you mean bed, of course there is,' said Ned sturdily. 'I've not kissed her yet, but I don't think that she'd mind. I'd go gently in that direction at first, you know; I'm not a brute.'

It was hopeless, thought Alex. And I can't give him the real reason for my reservations, which is, dammit, something which this ridiculous conversation has brought to a head: that I want to take to bed the woman I think of as a harpy, myself. That must be the only reason why I feel such wild resentment towards the poor lad, and all the coxcombs he has been speaking of.

'And Nun'ster's after her, I know,' continued Ned, beginning to prowl, 'and he only wants to ruin her, I'm sure; but if he genuinely wants to marry her, then I hate, just hate, the thought of him having Racquette. Nun'ster, of all people! It cannot be borne.'

Nun'ster to marry Cousin Harry? Yes, it was not to be borne. Alex had a sudden dreadful vision of Harry with Nun'ster again. 'I think that I should wait a little,' he said desperately. 'You might meet someone younger than you are who'd attract you.'

'Like Louisa Lansden, you mean?' said Ned derisively. 'No, thank you. Dull as ditchwater, the lot of them—not a laugh between them. Well, if you won't help me, then I shall have to help myself.' And he stormed out of the room.

Alex put Cook's *Journals* away; he'd lost all desire to read them. There was nothing like clarifying a man's mind over a woman to find out that another man was after her. He didn't think that Cousin Harry saw Ned as a possible husband, but he could well be wrong. He hoped that he was.

He sprang to his feet and began to prowl the way Ned had done. He had been continent for nearly a year, had lived like a monk—the mad priest of Ned's taunt, not at all like the man he had once been. Perhaps that was why he felt so strongly about Harry. Oh, but it wasn't that, and he knew it. He could be in the same room as Lousia Lansden, alone with her, even, and he wouldn't feel a thing, would have difficulty in laying a hand on her— something he couldn't tell Emily when his aunt was touting Louisa as a possible Countess for him.

Now, with Harry, it was all quite different. It was becoming impossible for him to dance with her, or even be too near her, because he had to touch her, and God help him when he did. It was worse than the stairs at Rule, because now he was ready for it, and still could not control himself. Self-control only stretched so far. The other day, in the Park, when he had been in the carriage with her, and the Duchess, and Mrs Whitmore, he had

experienced this mad impulse to kiss her, there, in front
of everyone.

She had turned and said something to him, with that
slight lift in her voice which spoke of her amusement,
and what she said he hardly heard for watching her. How
in the world had he arrived at this position, that the
harpy who had seduced his cousin should now be seducing *him*? All he knew was that he wanted her, and that
Ned had clarified his thoughts for him. He had only one
thought in his head—that no one else must have her. If
she wanted a lover, then, by God, it must be Alex
Ashburn she took, not that old roué Nun'ster. Whenever
he thought of her with Nun'ster he felt almost sick with
rage and jealousy.

Worse and worse, he thought. I am now as bad as a
green boy, as bad as Ned himself, faced with the love of
his life for the first time, only, unlike Ned, he desired
her with all the passion of the hard-living man he had
once been.

Ned had said that it was not to be borne. And, indeed,
it was not. How had she done it? What unearthly magic
had she exercised on him to reduce him to this?
Racquette, which had dominated his thoughts for
months, was not the thing at all. Its presence merely
made it difficult for him to decide what his own true
feelings were for her. Was it simply that her attraction
for him was that, by gaining her, he gained Racquette?

He shook his head. Why deceive himself? It was Harry
he wanted; damn Racquette, damn everybody. He had
thought something like that on the stairs at Rule, and
that was the truth. Bewitched by an ivory face, great
dark eyes, and a delicate wit. True, he hated the thought
of anyone else possessing Racquette, but no, it wasn't
that which drew him to her, not that at all.

Throughout the Season, moving from ball to ball, from
picnic to boating party, when the weather eased a little,
visiting the Academy, and the Tower of London, Harry

had been proposed to on a number of occasions by the
sensible she met, as well as the silly, the honest as well
as the fortune-hunters.

She had begun to recognise the signs, and, talking to
Ned, had suddenly realised that he was beginning to feel
more for her than the jolly companionship of a friend.
This was a little dismaying. The last thing that she
wished to do was hurt him, for he was a friend to her, no
more, and, for the first time at Lady Leominster's vast
reception on the evening of the day on which Ned had
consulted Alex about her, she was careful not to say or
do anything which might serve to encourage him, or
anyone else, for that matter.

Years afterwards Harry was to remember that drowned
summer—for the radiant weather changed suddenly, and
it began to rain and would not stop—as being a series of
great balls given by hostesses whose names were to enter
history: the one at Almack's where she had entered
Society for the first time, Lady Jersey's, where the great
world cut Lord Byron after his wife had left him, taking
their baby daughter with her, and Arabella Harrendene's
magnificent affair, where wine had flowed in the foun-
tains, and Arabella had worn a peacock dress of such
glory that Harry had felt more like a housemaid than
ever in pink and cream.

And Lady Cowper's, where Emily Cowper herself had
gone out of her way to make a fuss of her, saying, 'So,
you are the Templestowe cousin who is all the rage, and
who has Nun'ster at your feet, behaving himself for
once,' and had introduced her to her own cavalier, Lord
Palmerston, nicknamed 'Cupid', who was always to be
found near his Emily, but who had a smile for Harry, as
he had for all pretty women.

Harry was a success—not in a raging, knock-me-down
fashion, but in a gentle way, rather like herself, as one of
her admirers said to her that night. She was never sure
how many of her entourage were attracted by herself.
She was shrewd enough to know that no one would have

given the poor Miss Minster she had once been a second
glance. And there were few who realised what a hard
head and resolute will her pretty voice and gentle manners concealed. Like her sharp wit, they were cloaked by
the charm which she partly owed to Gilly's training.
Only the Duchess, and Mrs Whitmore, had come to
understand the nature of their charge, and that the years
spent in the Norfolk wilderness had not been wasted.

'The husband must have been a remarkable young
man if half she says of him is true,' said the Duchess to
Alex.

Alex nodded. 'I'm sorry I never met him, although I
often think how much I would have resented him if he
had turned up fit and strong to take Racquette from me.'

'And Harry?' queried the Duchess. Alex looked over
to where she sat with Ned, eating iced strawberries.

'Oh, I don't know,' he said restlessly. 'Don't ask me
difficult questions, Emily. You know the Latin saying,
Odi et amo. I hate and I love. I began by hating the very
thought of her. But now. . .' And he let his sentence
remain unfinished. He was still in turmoil, and the eyes
he turned on Ned were not kind. Moments later they
were even less kind. Ned had gone for some iced
champagne for himself and Harry, and Nun'ster had
taken his chair in his absence, was bending towards her,
an expression on his face which Society had rarely seen—
a true and respectful attentiveness to a woman.

Alex could not prevent himself. With a muttered,
'Excuse me, Emily,' he moved towards them. They both
looked up at him as he arrived. Nun'ster rose. They
glared at one another as politely as they could, to Harry's
fascinated delight. 'I see you favour such dull occasions
with your presence these days, Nun'ster. Not usual for
you.'

'But the company is so delightful,' smiled Nun'ster at
the man who he was suddenly sure was his rival. 'And
you, too, rarely honour Society's functions with your
presence.'

Pawn takes pawn, thought Harry.

'But then,' said Alex, 'I have been heavily occupied elsewhere these last few seasons.'

Pawn takes Knight.

'Oh, indeed,' returned Nun'ster idly. 'I agree. The soldier's trade hardly trains one for ballrooms, and handing iced drinks about to ladies.'

Bishop takes pawn, and if I do not stop this soon they will come to blows shortly, which will entertain everyone mightily, but will add one more count against the little Ashburn, which will not do at all, thought Harry.

'Oh, dear,' she said, rising gracefully, and swooshing her fan like Arabella, although hers was rather too small to be effective, she thought critically. 'I really am feeling very faint of a sudden. It must be the heat.'

Both men, who had assumed aggressive postures, and had almost forgotten the cause of their anger, turned together.

'Cousin Harry, you are not ill, I trust? Allow me,' and, 'Mrs Ashburn, you are not ill, I trust? Allow me,' was the response, which unfortunately merely served to change the direction of their mutual anger, so she closed her eyes, flapped her fan artistically, and said,

'If Cousin Alex would be so kind as to fetch Sarah for me, and Lord Nun'ster would be good enough to escort me to the nearest open window. . .' And she leaned gracefully against him.

'Hervey,' he said. 'Call me Hervey, I beg of you.'

Alex was close to striking him. Worse, he did not think Cousin Harry was near to fainting at all. She raised her eyes pathetically to him. Alex drowned in them—oh, the witch! the witch!—but said thickly, 'A moment,' and was gone, leaving her to that cur Nun'ster. How dared she?

He turned at the door to see Nun'ster gallantly supporting her, Ned running up with their glasses of champagne, and Mrs Whitmore coming towards him, saying, 'What is amiss, my lord?' with the Duchess behind her.

What a to-do, what regal fantods, thought Harry amusedly, while all this was going on. And I am fixed with this deception now. Oh, dear, I dare not confess that I am not unwell after all.

She allowed Sarah to remove her from Nun'ster's cherishing arm, saw Alex's furious face over Ned's shoulder, as Ned said, anxiously, 'Oh, Cousin Harry, do try to drink this, I beg of you,' and tenderly helped Sarah to assist her to a chair, Nun'ster taking her fan and gently flapping it at her.

Well, she thought, this is a great stupid pother, but it is better than allowing them to come to fisticuffs over me. What can be wrong with Alex? He cannot allow anyone to pay me any attentions at all, let alone assault me as he chooses to do. And Nun'ster is nearly as bad. Can it possibly be that both men are obsessed with me? Oh, dear, if ever I thought this was exciting in a novel. . . And then, Can it really be true that Alex cares for me, after all, despite himself? And she smiled involuntarily, causing the Duchess, who had been watching her sharply, to say, 'You are feeling a little better, I think, my dear.'

It seemed politic after that to wilt a little, to exclaim faintly, and to hang on to Ned's arm, rather than Nun'ster's. Ned, indeed, was all gallantry, saying reproachfully to his brother, who had returned to the scene, convinced that madam was at her tricks again, but now a little amused also at the way in which the artful minx had separated him and Nun'ster, 'What have you done to distress her, Alex?'

Before Alex could turn to Ned, Harry looked at Ned, and said, 'Oh, Ned, it is the heat, nothing else,' and affected a die-away expression which deceived everyone but Alex, even the Duchess now being convinced that Harry's fit of the vapours was genuine.

She was exclaimed over, her cloak fetched, her carriage summoned a little earlier than had been intended, the Duchess kissing her, and telling her to take care of herself, Alex, Ned and Nun'ster all concern, Harry herself paying limp respects to Lady Leominster, who commiserated with her over her malaise, footmen and servants hovering, even her coachman looking earnest and worried, and she could not help remembering, with some amusement, the little girl she had so lately been, who, even when married to Gilly, had done so much for herself, with none to help her.

Mrs Gilbert Ashburn, the Templestowe heiress, was such a grand person that she could not even feel a little ill without a score of persons dancing attendance on her. In deference to everyone's care for her, she reclined against Sarah Whitmore all the way home, and was content to say nothing, but to reflect instead on the behaviour of Ned, Alex, and Nun'ster, and try to understand exactly how the woman she now was would deal with them all.

Particularly Alex. The others, although she cared for Ned as a young friend, were nothing—even Nun'ster, who was, she thought, merely an older, amusing man to talk to; but Alex? She must face what she really felt for him. If she were honest, however badly he treated her, however much of the siren he thought her to be, and in consequence was harsh to her, she must admit that her feelings for him were deep and passionate, and had been since the night he had awoken her slumbering senses at Rule. Possibly, even, since the day she had landed at his feet in the rose-garden—and how symbolic that was, if she thought about it dispassionately.

Honesty, Gilly had said once, begins with oneself.

CHAPTER ELEVEN

ALEX fought his passion for Harry. It is not right, he thought angrily, I do not want this. I cannot fall in love with such a creature; but he had. She has lured me into her toils as successfully as she did my cousin; how I do not know. I only know that, at one glance of those fine eyes, I am undone. I was never like this with Arabella or any of the other women. What I felt for them is pale before the feelings I have now.

And, dammit, she is unworthy. What can have come over me? For I do not only want to bed her, though, God knows, I am frantic for *that*, but I also want her with me to talk to, to be my companion, trickster though she is. And she was at her tricks last night; I know she was.

And it is not only Nun'ster who is after her. There are a dozen such, and Emily says that she has had a royal Duke in tow—for Racquette, one supposes, seeing that Sussex has little enough of his own, and one morganatic wife already. She cannot really wish to be a royal Duke's. . .or can she? What a crowning end to a career beginning out of nowhere in Norfolk. To marry me would be nothing beside it.

He passed a sleepless night, rising to dress himself with care, and take himself to Templestowe House, his old London home, which he had vowed never to enter with the harpy in it.

He had to know that she was recovered, even if he was reasonably certain that she had feigned illness to separate him and Nun'ster—another cheating trick. But what composure; reluctantly he had to admire it.

Waiting for her in the drawing-room he knew so well, he saw signs of her everywhere—her canvas-work, her books, an open blank folio in which she had been writing

119

on a lectern near the fireplace. She had touched nothing in the room; it was as he remembered it, except that a small portrait of his cousin Gilbert's father as a boy had been moved to a position near the armchair, which was obviously hers, so that she could see it.

The door opened behind him as he studied it, and she came in alone, without Sarah Whitmore, for once. She was wearing dove-grey, with a small pleated ruff of white linen, and similar small ruffs at the end of her long sleeves. Her hair was simply dressed and her eyes were huge in her pale face.

'Cousin Alex,' she said, holding out her hand.

He took it, kissed the back of it gravely, and, as she indicated an armchair opposite to her own, sat down in it. If he admired her Quakerlike gown, she thought his skin-tight black coat, cream hessian breeches and mirror-bright black boots superb. His cravat was a dream—his valet had persuaded him to consent to an artistic creation for once—and his red hair was admirably wind-blown.

'You are recovered this morning, Cousin Harry, I trust?'

'Oh, indeed—a passing failing, no more. It is Sarah who is a little unwell, today.'

'You must give her my wishes for a swift recovery.'

They were so decorous, he thought, it was unbelievable.

'Thank you. She will value that.'

They both fell silent together. Harry smiled suddenly, and said, 'You will take some sherry, Cousin Alex?' And, as he assented, rang for it. 'I believe that we are breaching all canons of etiquette,' she commented, face serene, 'by my receiving you alone. But we are cousins, are we not? And you will remember that I was overset last night, and do nothing that might bring faintness on again.'

He drew his breath in, could not resist the riposte, 'Do you challenge me, Cousin Harry?'

The butler saved her from an answer. He arrived with a footman, carrying a salver with glasses and a decanter.

He served them—a small amount for Harry, without asking her, a bumper for Alex, and then they withdrew.

'You have them well trained, I see.'

'Oh, that is Sarah,' said Harry. 'You must not offer me praise which I do not deserve.' There were small plain biscuits with the sherry, and she offered him one. Equally gravely, he accepted. Conversation languished again. Yes, it was so unlike their previous meetings, it was laughable.

Alex made a sudden decision. 'I have trained a new pair for my curricle, Cousin Harry. I would take it as a favour if you would accompany me to the Park this afternoon for their first outing, to show them to the world,' and wondered what her response would be.

'I could not refuse such a splendid offer,' she replied, quite simply. 'You may call for me.' Inwardly she was greatly surprised—for him to take her to the Park would be to make some sort of declaration, but of what?

They spoke of this and that, at arm's length, until at last Alex rose to go, astonished at the constraint which suddenly existed between them. Perhaps he was mistaken, his passion was a dream, an illusion, and then as he took her hand, to kiss it farewell, their eyes met—and he knew that it was not, most definitely not.

Alex lifted his hands to take her gently by the shoulders to transfer the kiss from her palm, not to her lips, but to her eyelids, for her eyes had closed as he grasped her. She made no resistance, nor did she co-operate with him, until his kisses travelled down her cheek to her mouth.

Alex could feel her trembling under his hands, even as she returned his kiss, and the strange mixture of feelings he now had for her overwhelmed him again. Nothing would have pleased him more than to continue his lovemaking, alone and uninterrupted as they would be, but for the first time he felt a little shame at his handling of her. Harpy she might be, but he ought not to be beginning to make impetuous love to her in her own drawing-room.

He dropped his hands and stood back, saying gently, 'I should not have done that, Cousin Harry.'

'No,' she said, 'that is true, Cousin Alex.' But for the first time, despite the wild beating of her heart, and regret—could it be regret?—that he had stopped, she was able to reply to him without distress.

'And you will still drive with me this afternoon?'

'Of course.'

Alex left her, with the memory of her face in his mind. Harpy she might be, seductress she undoubtedly was, for she had captured him, as well as his cousin, but what of that? He was not Ned, not a child; he would teach madam who was master, take the risk of the tricks which she might play on him. Whatever she was, he now knew that he could not endure the thought of her falling to Nun'ster—or anyone else for that matter.

Hyde Park was as crowded as usual in the late afternoon. Society went there to see and be seen. The delicious news travelled around the fashionable crowd assembled on horseback, on foot and in carriages of every description. Alex Templestowe had a new pair for his curricle, but, more important than that, was the lady he had chosen to ride with him to display them for the first time—none other than his usurping cousin's widow, the little Ashburn. The woman of all women he might have been expected to endure, rather than celebrate—unless, of course, he was chasing her to get his lands back. Hyde Park buzzed.

Ned rode over to where Alex had drawn up, a few of Harry's suitors on horseback around them, loud judgements on the effectiveness of his pair being offered by each young sprig of fashion, as though they were the ultimate judges of bloodstock, instead of young gentlemen not long down from University. He leaned over to greet them.

'Wondered where you were skulking off to, Alex.

Don't let him trouble you, Harry. Bit of a public place to read the Riot Act to her, ain't it, Alex?'

Both of them surveyed Ned's honest, indignant face. They had been quiet together since Alex had collected her earlier; she had admired his turn-out, the curricle with its wheels and body picked out in cream and scarlet, the two splendid blacks.

'I know little of horseflesh,' she had said admiringly. 'But these creatures are beautiful—so sleek and graceful.'

Alex had smiled at that. 'You may not know about horseflesh, but you seem to know the right thing to say.'

He was quite aware that his comment was ambiguous, as ambiguous as his feelings for her. Harry had glanced sharply at him, but took no offence, merely gave him a small smile, holding tight to her reticule and hoping that the slight breeze would not displace her pretty little top hat with its saucy cockade. She was still wondering why he had asked her to drive with him, and as they drew into the Park was well aware of the excitement their presence was causing. For the present she was content to enjoy the afternoon, and the truce which he seemed to have declared, although how long it would last was problematical.

Alex looked at her, quiet and sensible beside him, not chattering, not passing absurd comments, as though every moment had to be filled with words. Was that how she had won his cousin? And what was this odd feeling of pride he was experiencing, as she sat there, high, beside him, in her own admirable turn-out: leaf-green, with the little black top hat, and cream and green cockade? Let them all see her with him, particularly Nun'ster—that should confound the wretched cur, and Arabella, too; it might stop the languishing glances and the hints of their amorous past, and the non-stop clever-silly chatter. Ned, as well; he didn't want to hurt his brother but, dammit, he, Alex, had his rights, and, after plodding up and down the Spanish Peninsula with

Welleseley's Army all those years, was entitled to a little
fun of his own.

But Ned could not see what was in front of his eyes,
judging by what he was saying, for he went on to add, 'If
he troubles you, Cousin Harry, tell me.'

'Really, Ned,' said Alex stiffly. 'You make me sound a
positive ogre.'

'Well, you are a little,' replied Ned helpfully. 'Don't
know how strong you come on, do you?'

'Lessons from children, I can do without,' Alex began
angrily, only to have Harry put her hand gently on his
arm, and say, a little severely,

'Come now, Ned, be good. Alex is not prosing at me.
We are enjoying the sun which has come out for once,
and I promise not to be overset even if I do receive a
lecture—which is not likely.'

It was at this moment that Arabella and her husband
saw Alex and Harry, having been enlightened by another
kind friend. Harrendene had his own reasons for wanting
Alex and Harry to come together, and his wish that
Arabella should free herself from her old love was only
one of them. He saw her face change at the news, the
dark eyes glitter, and the lips tighten. She immediately
spurred her horse to ride over to the curricle, her
husband following with a sigh.

'Oh, famous!' she exclaimed as she drew level. 'As
usual, Alex, your taste in horseflesh is impeccable.' She
feigned not to see Harry, until, after giving the blacks
her full attention, cooing and ahing at them, she said,
patronisingly, 'Oh, is that you, Mrs Ashburn? Forgive
my lack of manners, but I am always quite on my high
ropes where the animal kingdom is concerned.'

Myself not being part of it, was Harry's instant and
inward mental response, but saying aloud, 'Oh, I am well
aware, Lady Harrendene, that I cannot compete in interest
with handsome curricles drawn by ineffable horses. My
own turn of speed is greatly inferior.' Ned gave a great
guffaw, and Alex, whose response was outwardly more

gentlemanly, looked at Harry's grave and smiling face as
she spoke, and thought, Oh, yes, madam siren, I must
never forget what a cool and cunning piece you are.

Arabella flushed unbecomingly. It was she who handed
out the satire in the polite world, and she was not
accustomed to be its target. She glanced angrily at
impolite Ned, and at her husband, whose face had
twitched imperceptibly. How dared they? 'Oh, indeed!'
she exclaimed shrilly. 'I suppose May Day games on the
village green were not the best preparation for the polite
world.'

'Oh, I wouldn't exactly say that,' replied Harry. 'Kiss
in the Ring, Hunt the Slipper and Gathering Nuts in
May would prepare anyone for anything. Society most of
all, from what I have seen of it.'

It was hopeless; the wretched creature would not be
set down. And she was sitting there beside Alex as
though it were her place in life, and he, too, was
laughing.

'Come, Arabella,' he said, and his voice was hardly
kind. 'You have ruled the roost these many years. Cry
quits with Cousin Harry and have done.'

She could have killed him, stone dead. Her desire to
have him again, and to destroy this smiling upstart, was
suddenly so great that it was to spur her into action of
the most unwise kind. Her husband looked at her
expression, and his heart sank. He knew his Arabella,
and knew that the little Ashburn had just made an
enemy, and, worse, that Arabella would not rest until
she had brought about some kind of humiliation on
someone who had taken her on at her own game and
beaten her.

'We must move on, Arabella,' he said gently. 'You
have admired Alex's cattle long enough; they have
names, I suppose, Templestowe?'

'Not very original,' replied Alex. 'Romulus and
Remus. I did think of the heavenly twins, Castor and
Pollux, but I heard that the Regent had just named one

of his pairs after them. I had no wish to appear to challenge or approve him.'

Harrendene laughed. 'A true diplomat, would you not say, Mrs Ashburn?' His glance at her was kind. 'I understand that you will be at Lady Hertford's ball. We hope to see you there.' His glance took in Alex and Ned. 'Come, Arabella,' he said to her, as she sat, fuming at what she judged humiliation. 'There are others here to whom we must pay our respects.' And he rode off, impolite for once in his determination to master her, if only a little, so that she had perforce to follow him.

Ned's expression was approving. He did not like Arabella. 'So, the old man is making her behave a little for once. That was famous of you, Cousin Harry. She uses her nasty tongue on everyone; I don't think she will bait you again.'

Arabella was remonstrating angrily with her husband, with whom she had caught up. 'That was highly inconsiderate of you, Dolly. You knew I wished to speak to Alex.'

'And you know, Arabella, that I have told you to leave Alex Templestowe alone, and Mrs Ashburn, too. I have no objection to your meeting them, providing you behave yourself. I ask little of you, but I do ask this. Oblige me by obliging me. I am tolerant of your behaviour in general, but you must not try me over-much.'

This was intolerable to her, after the recent unfortunate passage, and her determination to be revenged on Harry and regain Alex was redoubled.

Well, at least, thought Harry on the way home, after exchanging friendly words with Emily and succeeding in outfacing the great world, I have fully arrived at last. A royal Duke in the distance, accepted by the Templestowes without a quibble now, and I have put down Arabella Harrendene, whom I must admit overawed me a little when I first met her. Whether I was wise to do so is another matter, but she did ask for it. I wonder what Alex really thought, and was it politic of

me to exercise before him the wit which Gilly encouraged
me to use? I suppose he will think it is the siren's song
again, designed to lure him on. Oh, dear, but Gilly
would want me to be myself, I know.

And, of course, Alex did think so, but, as he sat with
her, looking at her charming but beautiful profile—the
best part of her, he was beginning to think, because
unexpected—he also decided that, siren or not, he was
now prepared to pursue her in earnest, while accepting
what she was.

'So,' he said, as they sat outside Templestowe House,
before he helped her down, 'you chose to cross swords
with Arabella, at last. I was wondering how long it would
be before she was impaled, like poor Honoria Lansden.
I suppose it is the contrast between your demure appearance and the sharpness of your mind which is so devas-
tating to men and women alike.'

'I don't think they actually impale with swords,'
returned Harry thoughtfully. 'Something called a ganch
is what the Turks used in their executions, I believe,
although I never cared to enquire over-much into the
details. Too painful.'

'Now you are doing it to me,' said Alex, delighted by
the mixture of pedantry and sly humour she was display-
ing. 'Tell me, Mrs Ashburn, was it before or after you
met my Cousin Gilbert that you learned to do this? Or
was it how you——?'

'Snared him?' she cut in swiftly, as he paused to find
the right word—one that would say what he meant, but
the offence in it oblique, rather than direct. 'Oh, I leave
you to guess that for yourself, Cousin Alex. To give away
all my secrets would deprive me of. . .allure, would you
say?' For the first time she consciously used the power
which she suddenly knew she possessed—the power to
attract men. Let him think she had always known she
had it, and, what was more, had used it to trap Gilly,
and perhaps others. If he chose to think the worst of her,
then why not oblige him? Why not, indeed?

'You are hardly original, you know,' she said, and her smile was even more mocking than she knew. 'You are not, after all, the first to make such a comment.' And she thought of some of the things Nun'ster and others had said to her—even fat Sussex, who had bellowed at her wit, and called her a pretty witch, and she had not even encouraged *him*. No need to, since, like all the royal Dukes, he required no incentive to pursue a rich and pretty woman.

'What a pity,' said Alex softly, 'that we are perched up here, in full public view, so that I may not give you what you richly deserve.'

Oh, so I am safe, am I? thought Harry. 'Indeed, Cousin Alex, pray what is that? I am all agog for presents these days. Unwrapping them is one of my delights.' Her smile, again, was more potent than she knew.

If this goes on much longer, thought Alex, looking at the wicked little twist of her lips, I am in danger of seizing her, jumping down, and running into the house to give madam a present she wouldn't forget in a hurry. 'Well, now, Cousin Harry,' he drawled, 'what would you like? Something straightforward, or would that be a dead bore? Something richly baroque, perhaps, upside-down, like a Turkish impaling only a great deal more pleasant for both of us, I promise.'

Well, she had asked for that, had she not? And now must deal with it.

'No trial, so no execution,' she said promptly. 'Fetch me your judge and jury, Cousin Alex, or otherwise—nothing.'

'But I am all the judge and jury needed in my own curricle, Cousin Harry. I find you guilty as charged. Why delay the carrying out of the sentence?' And his face was soft with desire.

Yes, I believe you wouldn't delay, was Harry's silent response, half excited, half frightened by what she was provoking. But, for the life of her, she could not stop playing with fire.

'Not now,' she answered, yawning prettily behind an elegantly gloved hand. 'I am a little fatigued. Too much excitement, Cousin Alex.'

'Or not enough,' he countered. Oh, it would be a pleasure to bed her. Would she be as witty there, with her body, as she was with her mind? He would dare swear she would, and how he longed to find out. She must have driven his cousin mad—and what did the Norfolk bumpkins make of her? What execution had she done among *them*, if she affected hardened denizens of Society so? Yes, this must stop.

Harry thought so too. They were entering deep waters, and she was not sure how well she would swim in them. For the first time she passionately wished that her marriage to Gilly had been a true one. Then she might really know how to deal with an athletic and experienced man whose look told even her own inexperienced self how desperately he needed to engage with her on the field, not of warring minds, but of willing bodies.

She had a sudden vision of herself in his arms, sinking beneath him. Oh, this would not do at all. She was trembling. 'If you do not help me down soon, Cousin Alex,' she said, her voice a little shaky, 'my neighbours will wonder at us. What Parliamentary bill can we be planning, that we should engage in such long and earnest conversation?'

'A bill to promote Cousin Harry to a place where I can show her what she would most like to see,' he replied, as he handed her down. '*Au revoir*, my witty Circe; we shall engage again at Lady Hertford's.'

CHAPTER TWELVE

NUN'STER had heard of, but not seen, Alex and Harry together in Hyde Park, but the hearing was enough. He had noted the expression on Alex Templestowe's face when he had been with Harry at Lady Leominster's ball, and was shrewd enough to know that, quite suddenly, Templestowe was pursuing the usurping cousin, although to what end Nun'ster was not sure. It could be bed—remembering Templestowe as he had last been some years ago—or his lands recovered through marriage, or just Harry, herself, that he wanted as his wife. All that was immaterial, other than that it meant Nun'ster must move before Templestowe did, and that it must be sooner than he had wished.

He dressed for Lady Hertford's ball with even more care than usual. He would ask her this evening. A Marchioness's coronet and himself—what more could a woman on the make want, particularly a woman as clever as he knew Harry to be? They had met and talked happily all summer, he had been careful to say and do nothing which would spoil the picture of an earnest and serious man of culture whom the world had seriously misrepresented. He knew the great world's gossip—that Nun'ster had been hooked by a trickster as cunning as himself—but he only knew that he wanted her. As once before, his hard heart was touched.

Harry dressed in expectation too. She was suddenly deliciously aware of the joys of being a success, and aware of her new powers as a woman as never before. Gilly had told her, not long before he died, that if ever she found herself in the great world of Society she would succeed there, and she had laughed at him a little. But, as so often, he had been right. The face she saw in her

mirror these days was radiantly attractive, if not beautiful, and tonight the white crêpe gown, with its crystal
decorations, the small wreath of matching carnations
perched on her black curls, a new fan decorated with
tiny porcelain Chinese faces, and the pearl pendant which
fitted her turn-out perfectly, all complemented herself
and the occasion.

Her entry was a little triumphant. Lady Hertford
grunted at her, 'Ah, the female Jacobin, supporting her
sans-culotte cousin' and then, slyly, having heard the latest
gossip, 'How far does your defence of him go now, eh,
madam?' And, had she been a fat farmer's wife, instead of
a fat peeress, would have poked me in the ribs, thought
Harry, amusedly. Released, she was instantly surrounded,
and in her new confidence could deal as lightly with all the
pretenders to her hand as she wished.

Ned had arrived early. He had engaged Harry to dance
the Quadrille, early on, and when they met, immediately
before it, he said to her, taking her hand and looking
deep into her eyes, 'You look absolutely splendid
tonight, Cousin Harry—bewitching, indeed. Why waste
our time dancing? I have something to say to you which
cannot wait. Something important.'

Oh, dear, thought Harry, here it comes, and I can no
longer hold him off. Best to let him make his offer.
Sooner or later, I must hurt him.

She allowed him to lead her through one of the glass
doors opening on to a terrace which overlooked a small
garden, the scent of roses heavy about them, even though
London's roar was not far away. A white-painted bench
stood between two small statues, each holding a horn of
flowers. Ned seated her on the bench, and then stood
before her.

His sudden rush of confidence had disappeared; his
eyes were fixed on her in almost agonised supplication.

'Oh, Cousin Harry, I hardly know how to begin.' He
was half stammering between entreaty and embarrass-
ment. 'I know you're older than I am, and that some

fools would see that as a bar, but it makes no matter to me.' He stopped at that, suddenly thinking that this was, perhaps, not the most tactful way to start.

He was then silent for so long that Harry almost felt that she had to prompt him. 'What an ass I am,' he said impulsively, 'thinking of clever things to say to you when I am not clever, and all I really need to say is that I love you dearly, that we are such jolly good friends, that I want you to be more than that, and will you marry me, even if we have to wait for that ass Alex to give his consent when he thinks I have reached years of discretion, which I already have if I have had the good sense to fall in love with such a trump as you? Oh, please say yes, I beg of you, dear Cousin Harry; don't break my heart, for I shall never get over you.'

He looked at her so beseechingly that it almost broke Harry's heart to have to turn him down.

Before she could speak, he started again. 'It's not Racquette, you know; never think that. It's you, truly you. We can give Racquette away if you want.'

This gave Harry her opportunity to answer him. 'No, Ned,' she said gently. 'I know it's not Racquette. You're not the man to propose to me for my property. And, oh, how I wish I could say yes to you. But I can't. I love you as I would love a dear brother, and I can't offer you a greater honour than that; I only wish I could. And your age has nothing to do with it. If I wanted you as a husband I would say yes if you were eighteen or eighty, rest assured of that. I'm sure you'll find a pretty girl who does love you, one day.'

'No,' he said, his face clouding at her every word. 'No, I'm sure I won't. I never met a girl like you before. I don't think there are many. But I had to ask. I hope I haven't distressed you.'

'Oh, no,' she assured him. 'I can't be distressed by being honoured. And you have honoured me, be sure of that.'

'I can't say that I'm not disappointed,' he said slowly.

'I hope that when you do marry it will be to someone who loves and appreciates you as much as I do. I can't say fairer than that.'

She took his hand, and pressed it, saying gently, 'I know it will be hard for you, but in the end you will see that it was for the best.'

But he shook his head mutely at her, insisting earnestly, 'Oh, no, I can't believe that. But I won't distress you, Cousin Harry, by pushing my claim further than I should—that would not be an honourable thing to do at all.' He lifted her hand to his lips and added, 'We may be friends, I know. And if you ever need anyone to protect you, why, I shall always be there.'

Harry looked at his disappointed face, and thought how manly was the fashion in which he bore his disappointment. She could no longer think of him as a boy. 'Friends, always,' she agreed, pressing the hand she still held. 'And now you had better return me to the ballroom, before our disappearance causes even more gossip.'

So, it was a bitter-sweet evening after all, Harry thought wryly, and that is surely enough excitement for one night—which just goes to show, she decided later, that I really ought not to set up as a prophet, being so completely unable to foresee the future!

Ned's proposal did not so much upset her as make her thoughtful, and rather impatient with the heedless gaiety going on about her—she knew how deeply he felt. When there was a pause in the dancing, she avoided all invitations to be taken in to supper, in order to avoid the company. Instead she made for a little drawing-room-cum-study which opened off one of the reception-rooms, and found her way there alone, hoping that her absence might not be noted in the mob which pressed through to the food and drink. It was the largest crowd which she had yet seen at a ball or reception.

Alone, she had time to admire the room and its

treasures, including some packed bookshelves, where she found and pulled down for inspection an elegant calf-bound edition of Bloomfield's *Farmer's Boy* embellished with Bewick's charming woodcuts of men and animals. She was engrossed in it, hardly hearing the door open behind her, until a man's deep and pleasant voice said, 'Ah, Mrs Ashburn; I thought that I saw you retreating from the hurly-burly.'

It was Nun'ster. She turned, the book in her hand, and replied, 'Yes, I was suddenly tired of the heat and the noise. This room is charming and the bookshelves better.' She placed the book down. 'I doubt whether Lady Hertford would approve of my preference for solitude rather than her company at the ball.'

'Lady Hertford might not, but I do.' He thought that the picture she presented was delightful, and the occasion completely apropos to his purpose. 'May I enquire what you found to command your interest so?'

'Oh, Bloomfield and Bewick. A talented pair. I was admiring the pig.'

'Excellent indeed. Pray be seated, madam. Let us talk together. I, too, am weary of over-much prancing. Why, I wonder, does dancing, one of the few pastimes we share with savages, please us so?'

'It is natural, I suppose,' she answered, remembering Gilly saying something of the sort, once, and then he had added, a little sadly, as she had rearranged his pillows for him, 'I suppose I resent it because it is one of things I may never do with you.' How strange to think of him now.

'Oh, but we have progressed beyond nature, have we not?' he returned, smiling at her. 'Except. . .' And he hesitated.

'Except?' she said, prompting him.

'Except that I wish to say something completely natural to you. . .' And he paused again.

Harry had no idea what was coming. She saw Nun'ster only as a pleasant older friend with whom she was delighted to talk of matters which interested her and seemed to interest him. A more suave and experienced Gilly, a kind of friendly uncle, someone whose bad reputation seemed to have been unfairly earned, since he had been more proper with her than many. To that extent he had succeeded in impressing her, but he would have been horrified to know that his appeal to her was so entirely sexless.

'You surely know what I am about to say,' he said, rising suddenly, and pacing about the little room, before returning to where she sat and bending over to address her more intimately. 'My dear Mrs Ashburn, although I hope you will allow me to address you as Harriet. . . My very dear Harriet, we share so many things, you and I—books, music, ideas and earnest conversation on those topics which matter, all this——' and he waved a hand to take in the lovely room '—I can offer you so much more than this, even. We deal so well together, why not let us deal so for life? I offer you the world in all its variety, myself, my hand, and a Marchioness's coronet, to boot, although I know that that bauble will not move you so much as the rest. Marry me, my dear Harriet, and finally make of me the man I ought to be, and give me a noble mother for my children.' And there he was, improbably on one knee before her, by his manner and expression totally confident that she would accept him.

Oh, she did not want this. He was a friend, an impersonal uncle, not a lover or a husband. Indeed not a lover. If she knew anything at all, she knew that. His nearness oppressed her, as did his sudden declaration of affection. He stupefied her, so that she drew back a little, and tried to regain the hand he had trapped in his.

Harry saw Nun'ster's face change at her slight recoil, and knew she must go carefully. As with Ned, she must do nothing to hurt him. What she did not know was that nothing she could say or do would soften the dreadful blow to his pride which he was about to receive. For so long he had fascinated, mesmerised and controlled the women whom he had favoured that he half assumed that he had only to ask and she would be his. He forgot that the mind which he had admired as much as her body might be his undoing.

'You do me great honour, my lord——' she began.

'Oh, Hervey,' he said swiftly, 'call me Hervey.'

'You do me great honour, Hervey,' she repeated, 'and I am most mindful of that. It is not every day that one is offered a Marchioness's coronet and the love of a man of such distinction as yourself. I grant that we deal well together, but I cannot accept your noble and gracious offer. I say this with the greatest regret, for your company pleases me, as I am sure you know. But I care for you as a friend, not at all as a lover. As a friend I treasure you, and it would be wrong of me to accept your offer without love.'

'You refuse me?' he said, in a tone of complete disbelief, his face growing dark with anger and disappointment as he spoke.

'With the greatest respect,' said Harry earnestly. 'But we may remain friends, I hope.'

'Friends?' His face changed even more, grew ugly. '*Friends*? You prate at me, madam. I do not want you as a *friend*.' And he almost spat the word at her. 'Consider what I offer you. That which I have only offered to one other.'

'I have considered,' replied Harry, suddenly desperate for this to be over. He was showing her a face so different from the one she thought she knew. His grip on her hand had tightened intolerably. Oh, those who had told her to beware of him had been so right. She was becoming almost frightened of him, so hard and cruel had his expression grown in the last few minutes. 'It would be wrong of me, most wrong, to accept you without the proper affection which marriage demands.'

'Wrong? No proper affection?' His expression was murderous. His tone was jeering; he rose to his feet, flinging her hand away from him. 'Oh, this is unsupportable. Not to be borne. Are you like your mother, then? Conferring the charms of your person on everyone but myself? Is it only Alex Templestowe who is allowed to rifle your treasure, or do you consent to his baby brother's pleasuring you as well, or any man who pleases you? You bring a bad reputation from Norfolk with you, madam. Twice. That I should be refused twice, and by such creatures as your mother and yourself.'

'No,' said Harry, suddenly white and trembling, standing, ready to fly as her recent pleasant and charming companion showed her the face of hate and derision, and frustrated lust, for even in her inexperience she recognised *that*, as he spat venom at her. 'You have no right to speak to me so. No right at all. My refusal had nothing to do with anyone else. My affections are not engaged elsewhere, and my life is stainless.'

'Not engaged elsewhere! Stainless! You are as big a liar and whore as most of your sex. I have seen your face when you have been with him. Oh, like your mother, indeed. I wonder Society receives you, knowing what she was. And you wear the badge of her shame around your neck. Why do you think Hornsea gave her his pendant?'

'I must leave you,' said Harry, moving towards the door, hanging on to her own control as best she could, and appalled at what she had unwittingly precipitated. 'I am sorry that you are so distressed, that we may not be friends. I thought that our minds agreed so well.'

'Our minds! Oh, yes. Our minds. That was a stroke of fortune I had not planned on. But, believe me, your body was always my target, and you reserve that, I suppose, for everyone but me.'

'Oh, unworthy!' exclaimed Harry, now safely by the door. 'You will excuse me if I leave,' she said, a little wildly, wondering what etiquette governed this situation. 'You cannot really wish me to remain.'

'Oh, yes, go by all means, madam. But do not flatter yourself that I shall forget you, or that you may not yet give Hervey Nun'ster that which he deserves. I have not done with you yet, my fine madam. Do not forget that, I beg of you,' were the last words she heard as she fled the room.

CHAPTER THIRTEEN

ALEX had not intended to be a latecomer at Lady Hertford's ball. But he was delayed by the arrival of a message from his agent which needed an immediate reply, and, Duty always being his first mistress, he obeyed her call before going off to his pleasure.

He arrived halfway through supper, and looked about him for Harry, avoiding Arabella and the claims of others. He found Sarah Whitmore, but Harry was not with her, and she said, 'Oh, she was with Ned when last I saw her; she surely cannot be far away.' But she was not with Ned.

And then he saw her, coming out of a small drawing-room off one of the reception-rooms. She was alone, and even at some distance he thought that she looked a little perturbed, not at all her usual cool and charming self. He was about to go forward to speak to her, when the door opened again and Nun'ster emerged, looking around him, and then strode purposefully away down the room.

Alex was suddenly full of the gravest suspicions. So, madam was up to her tricks again! Secret assignations with Hervey Nun'ster after all the warnings which he and Sarah and the Duchess had given her. And, by her manner, the meeting had not pleased her. No Marchioness's coronet offered after all, perhaps? Well, that might make her more amenable towards Alex Templestowe, who, despite this fresh evidence of madam's true nature, was still trapped by her siren song. He raged inwardly at himself as he saw her, still alone, walking a little despondently towards the supper-room, and, as Harry thought, safety.

He caught her up, reaching her to say, 'So, madam, I

139

find you, at last. What have you been doing that none of your friends might know where you were?'

Oh, dear, thought Harry, gazing at his grim face. Is there to be no end to demanding men this evening? What can a poor girl do to avoid unwanted proposals of marriage, and equally unwanted sermons on her conduct from an angry nobleman who imagines me committing all kinds of crime? What can he think I have been doing this time?

At least Alex's appearance, looking nearly as thunderous as Nun'ster himself, had the merit of rousing her out of the lassitude which Nun'ster's sudden revelation of himself, as being all and more than she had been warned he was, had brought on.

'I thank you for your concern,' she said, and her calm was dangerous, 'but I really do not need policing every five minutes. This is Lady Hertford's ball, after all, and not some East End slum where I might be in danger on every corner.'

'Oh, you have a clever answer for everything, Cousin Harry—I should have known that by now; but even you, I suppose, may sometimes be wrong and mistake your man.'

'Oh, indeed,' she replied, suddenly scarlet, where before she had been pale. 'And you may apply that to yourself, Cousin Alex. Conceive that you, too, might be wrong, if the mere idea is not beyond you.'

'I know my duty, madam, and what Society requires of me, and I sometimes wonder if you are always in the same condition.'

Anger made her handsome—or he was more besotted than ever, he thought.

'Let me be plain, Cousin Alex. I do not find Society's manners admirable. With few exceptions the men I meet seem to me to have only one idea in their heads, and that is to deprive women of any honour which they possess. As for the women, they seem equally fixed on the men, and their morals match those of the men, too.

If you call Town a jungle you would not be far wrong. Now, you may oblige me by taking me in to supper. I warn you that in my present condition if I were a man I should wish to get royally drunk, but, being a woman, I must content myself with holding my tongue and hoping that I do not explode before morning. Kindly fetch me a glass of champagne as well as a plate of cold meats. In my present mood I shall likely retire to a corner and worry at them on the floor like a wounded lioness.'

Alex could not prevent himself from laughing out loud. Suddenly all the anger he had felt with her had evaporated in the face of her exasperating and determined wit. Had they been alone he would have taken her in his arms, and made the declaration that was trembling on his tongue.

As it was, he said, 'Oh, Cousin Harry, I forgive you. Of course, I will fetch your food, and plenty of it, provided you promise to retain your admirable appearance, and not rival our hostess in girth.'

'Well, that would be difficult in one evening,' asserted Harry, relieved that the tensions between them had relaxed, and they were nearer to the rapport of the day before. 'But I should really like to know for what I am forgiven and why.' But then, putting her hand up, 'No, pray. Do not enlighten me; I am sure I should not like it, and we are being almost civil to one another. Someone should run up the Union flag to mark this astonishing occasion.'

'Yes,' he said, gently for him, 'and, of course, you are right. London is empty and shallow, a perpetual chase after pleasure. A thunderous place.' His reply was an olive-branch, and she took it as such as they strolled to the supper-room.

'Thunderous,' she repeated, looking at the strong face, admiring its stern lines, so different from the soft, untried charm of most of the men she met. 'What a good word. Norfolk, now, was like a placid shower of rain on a fine day.'

'You miss your country retreat?' There was doubt in his voice.

'Yes and no. I must be honest. I would not for the world have missed what leaving it in such a strange fashion has brought me. To see the places of which I only knew by report: to visit Parliament, even if, with respect to you and your fellow peers, it was far from the noble and serious place I thought it to be. And to meet the great ones of this world—*that* must be something. Together with all the lovely things which I now own, and which I could only have dreamed of seeing for a few moments as a visitor to a great house on a summer's afternoon while being patronised by the housekeeper. And now they surround me everywhere.'

He surveyed her eager face thoughtfully. Every word she said, and the manner of the saying, could only increase his respect for her understanding.

'But,' he said, bantering her a little.

'But?' she queried.

'There is a "but" implicit in your tone. All the things you have gained—but something is lost?'

'Oh, yes,' she said, smiling up at him. 'Yes, I see. The "but" is the loss of Arcady, rural innocence. It may be boring, but it is innocent as London is not.' And she thought for a moment of Nun'ster, whose conduct had appalled her so. 'We are all so knowing. Even I am beginning to ignore the beauties and treasures which surround me, am guilty of taking them for granted. That must have been a thing for you in Spain. Nothing to be taken for granted, I suppose, in war.'

Alex was struck. Enchanted by her ready understanding. No woman had ever spoken to him so sensibly of such things before. He had to grant her that.

'Yes, indeed. I could not bear it when I returned and those I met dismissed it as mere adventure. There was adventure, true, but more than that. I know it changed me greatly, and I cannot chatter idly of my time there. It is easy to speak of honour and duty when to live up to them is easy. The challenge comes when to know what they are is hard. And sometimes, in Spain, honour and duty were in conflict; one could only choose the greater good, or more often choose to do the thing which created the least harm.'

Every word he uttered served only to increase Harry's respect for him, and her regret that such a man should be so wary of her. He had said once that he was only a simple soldier, but there was nothing simple about him. He thought and felt deeply. Gilly would have liked him, and would have been sad at his low opinion of her.

She accepted her food and drink from him, and the rest of the evening passed in a lower key. She was relieved not to see Nun'ster again, and judged, correctly, that he had left after her refusal of him, and, fortunately for her temper, Alex chose to be pleasant to her, and ignored Ned's glowering at them both. Ned was suddenly aware, for the first time, that Alex's manner to her had changed its nature.

There was one other strange occurrence, things going in fours, not threes, tonight, being her private comment. Dolly Harrendene came up to her between dances, sat beside her and talked briefly of nothing. Then he had looked at her with more determination than he usually showed, and had told her that he'd known her mother. 'A most beautiful woman,' he said. 'The loveliest of her generation. Your father was my friend, as she was.' He had paused, then said gently, without undue emphasis, 'If *you* should ever need a friend, my dear, you ought to know that you have one in Adolphus Harrendene. For her sake, as well as your own, I would not like to see you hurt, or injured. I am always at your service.'

He had gone on to talk of other things again, leaving her a little surprised. He is disassociating himself from Arabella, was her conclusion. He must know how much she dislikes me—because of Alex—and felt touched that someone should say such a kind word in the middle of the barren wasteland which she sometimes felt Society was.

By the time she visited Vauxhall, Harry had recovered from the shock of Nun'ster's proposals, but not from the unpleasant slurs he had cast on her own and her mother's reputations. To some extent she could ignore them because she knew that what he had said about herself was not true. What hurt was the knowledge that others felt as he did, and Alex's conduct towards her was explained, if explanation were needed, for he had made his opinion of her plain, too.

She had not seen Nun'ster since Lady Hertford's ball. He had disappeared from Society's more respectable functions as rapidly as he had reappeared at them. She hoped that his last furious words, thrown at her as she left, were merely the exaggerations of a disappointed man.

Harry had told no one in Society of his proposal—not even Duchess Emily or Sarah Whitmore, who were her guardians. In some strange way she thought that it might rebound against her. But she had to tell someone, and it was her servant Hannah, dear, kind, but rough Hannah, who had cared for her since childhood, and whom she knew would not talk, whom she chose to confide in, dealing lightly with Nun'ster's threats, after her refusal.

Hannah did not like what she had heard of Nun'ster— the servants' grapevine was more reliable even than Harry's information, but then, she did not like any of the new people in Miss Harry's life. None of them was good enough for her. She knew of her mistress's unfair reputation, and this roused her to anger when she defended her to her fellow servants—only to meet their scepticism and amusement. A great pity that Mr Gilly had not lived, was her verdict. He was the proper person to care for Miss Harry. He'd appreciated her.

Ned almost passed Hannah's muster, but his older brother Alex, who obviously had no understanding of

Miss Harry's true worth, enraged her, and if she were able to give him a piece of her mind one day she would. Handsome is as handsome does, she thought more than once.

She helped Harry to dress for Vauxhall, insisting on slightly stouter shoes than the light slippers Harry usually wore for evenings. 'You are to be careful, mind,' she said sternly. 'The servants say that Vauxhall is in danger of becoming not quite the thing these days. More low people there than is wise.'

'Oh, dear, Hannah,' replied Harry, amused, 'we are not living among Barbary corsairs,' and laughed inwardly at the improbable notion that Alex and Hannah were alike in their absurd care for her, and the criticism which accompanied it. 'I shall be in a large party, you know, not on my own.'

'Large party of ninnies,' said Hannah. 'I know 'em. Not worth two-pennorth of any man's money, any of 'em. Pity Mr Gilly is not still with us, and then you wouldn't be capering about with fools.'

'So you often say,' was Harry's somewhat exasperated reply. 'You're sure you wouldn't like to buy a pair of handcuffs and fasten me to you for the rest of the Season?'

Hannah's disapproving glare at this sally stayed with Harry and was responsible for her slightly amused expression as the Duchess collected herself and Sarah Whitmore that evening.

'You grow more in looks every day, my dear,' was the Duchess's approving comment as she surveyed Harry and her turn-out. 'You will rival your mother yet.'

'Oh, I would need a pantomine transformation scene for that,' returned Harry, but she was pleased, all the same, and equally flattered by the response of all the gentlemen she met, including Alex, who was apparently prepared to be not completely disapproving this evening, and to whom the Duchess handed her over—to Ned's disappointment—saying, 'I place your cousin in your care, Alex, tonight.'

Even the presence of Arabella, stately as a galleon in a dress of far too great magnificence, quite inappropriate for an evening outdoor party in summer, thought Harry critically, could not dampen her spirits. Nun'ster and his slander and threats seemed far away and unimportant.

Vauxhall, when they reached it, proved to be more like Hannah's misgivings had suggested than Harry had been prepared to believe. There was a tawdry air about it, as though it had seen better days and was aware of it. The ladies in the party were advised to stay together, and not to become detached from their male escorts. The box into which they were shown was heavily gilded, but was slightly soiled. They were promised singers, tumblers, and later a firework display.

The Duchess looked about her, and said in her gentle voice, after they had made a short promenade around the gardens, 'You expressed some reservations about coming here, Alex, and I fear that you are right. There are a large number of low persons present. It will soon not be worth the visit.'

Harry thought, however, that walking in the gardens was preferable to being in the box. Under the soft lights the grass and flowers looked rather romantic than otherwise. Alex said to her, as they seated themselves again, 'You are in looks tonight, Cousin Harry. Tell me, is it nature, or art, which gives you this air of command? Or did you possess it in Norfolk, and have only slowly treated us to it here?'

'Oh, I did many things in Norfolk,' replied Harry, who found her supposed career of crime before she married Gilly a constant source of amusement to herself, if no one else, its contrast with the mundane and chaste reality being so great. 'You must understand, of course, that I needed to adapt certain aspects of my conduct to the greater challenge I found here, and naturally that took some little time.'

'Naturally,' said Alex, with a grin. 'I quite understand you. But you are in full control of the situation now, you think? Or would you like me to test that assumption, to see whether it is well grounded or no?'

This really must not go too far, thought Harry, saying aloud, 'Oh, no. Not tonight. Not here.'

'Some other time, then? You must inform me when. I should not care to disappoint you.'

'Oh, I am sure you would never do that,' said Harry, laughing up into his face, still full of her new-found confidence in her powers, and determined to give his haughty lordship a good run for his money, since he was so evidently enjoying the chase—as, she was compelled to admit, she was enjoying being pursued—So long, of course, as I am not caught! Dangerous it might be. Heady it was.

Arabella's eyes were on them. She could see the growing rapport between them, knew nothing of the war going on between Alex's head and his heart. The head which mistrusted Cousin Harry, the heart which had come to feel for her what he had never thought that he could feel for a woman again. Oh, let him enjoy his bumpkin while he could, for she knew something which neither Alex nor Harry did, and her thoughts were malicious as she watched them together, saw him take Harry's hand—not knowing that he did it almost against his will—and saw Harry's face as she looked at him.

Enjoy yourselves together while you may, she thought, unaware that her expression was such that her husband was shocked at it, for you may not have much more time to do so.

Food was brought to them. Vauxhall had once been famed for it, but, even in the days of its glory, the joke had always been that the ham was cut so thin that you could read a book through it—'And that has certainly not changed with the years,' said Ned, eyeing his share dubiously.

Harry thought that Vauxhall was rather like London—

wonderful on first sight, but closer inspection revealed
the grime behind the façade. She ate her food, and joined
in the banter, but her heart and mind were with Alex,
who managed to sit by her, until Arabella thrust between
them, and demanded that they make another promenade.

'Later,' said the Duchess, noting Alex's icy annoyance
at Arabella's intrusion.

'Your pardon, madam,' replied Arabella, 'but if we
leave it much later we shall not return here in time for a
good view of the fireworks.'

'You're not usually so intent on exercise, my dear,'
remarked Harrendene to his wife, who turned her
shoulder to him, saying,

'Really, Dolly, you seem determined to thwart me
these days. Mrs Ashburn and I are fixed on taking
another stroll. I hear that you are a famous walker, my
dear. You must take a turn with me.'

'Not on your own,' asserted Alex coldly. 'Vauxhall is
not safe for ladies without escorts.'

'No, indeed,' said Arabella cordially. 'You may take
us, Alex, and the rest may join us as well. The more the
merrier.' The pointed lack of reference to her husband
did not go unnoticed by her hearers.

Inevitably, with such a large group, it became strung
out. Ned came over to escort Harry, but was sent away
by Arabella, who hung on to Harry's arm—a favour
which she could have well done without. 'No, no, Ned,'
she said determinedly. 'We ladies occasionally like to
prose together without the men being present.' And good
manners, perforce, constrained him to leave them
together.

Harry would have preferred to be with Ned, and found
Arabella's walking rather slow and stately, and they fell
further and further behind the others. Indeed, as the
crowds jostled around them, the two women became
isolated, something which they had been warned against
repeatedly.

At first, Arabella took no notice of this, even stopping

at one point to draw Harry's attention to the beauty of a small vista. Harry gradually became perturbed. Her relatively slight stature, compared with Arabella's, meant that she was pushed about and rudely handled, and when the group in front disappeared almost completely from view she said, 'I think that we ought to rejoin the others before we become lost.'

'Oh, my dear,' replied Arabella, 'how thoughtless of me. You are right. Come.' And, seizing Harry by the wrist, began to drag her along to catch their party up, annoying the people through whom she was thrusting so incontinently.

They reached a cross-path where the crowd was at its thickest, and included persons by no means of the first flight—indeed, Harry thought, of no flight at all, appearing positively subterranean, and two elegant ladies of fashion on their own were beginning to attract unwanted attention.

One young fellow tried to seize Harry by the arm. But this was by no means the worst, which was to follow. For, emerging from the side path, a group of burly and ill-dressed men suddenly surrounded her, wrenching her away from Arabella's grasp. The leader caught Harry to him, held her intimately for a moment, his vile breath hot on her face, before throwing her to his friend, shouting, 'Here, Bart—a pretty doxy for you to hold.'

Harry found herself brutally passed from one foul-smelling ruffian to another, who grasped her wrist cruelly, and began to run her away from Arabella. She tried to protest, shouting, 'No, no, release me at once,' and when that had no effect, 'Help me, help me,' which proved useless also.

She was lost! In a moment everything which she knew was swept away. Arabella, Alex, the Duchess and the rest were all gone, as she was rushed through the swirling crowd, a helpless captive.

CHAPTER FOURTEEN

THE people around Harry took no notice of her. Some even laughed, one man shouting drunkenly as she was swept by him, 'Look after yourself, mistress.' She had a last glimpse of Arabella, standing, shocked, mouth open in a scream which she could not hear in the bedlam of the crowd through which she was being dragged.

The nightmare continued as the men—they numbered three—pulled her along in the direction of the main gate. One of them swore as she panted and struggled, but he had no wish to pick her up and run off with her—that was his easiest option—because to do so would have attracted unwanted attention. As it was, most who saw them thought it a cruel form of horseplay: a woman being jollied along, rather than kidnapped. Harry's fine clothes meant nothing. Most whores wore as fine.

Harry continued to shout for help, which appeared to attract amusement rather than pity. Even in her fear and distress she tried to think rationally, to avoid panic. Resistance appeared not to help; she was merely collecting bruises, being dragged along the faster, and her wrist was ever more cruelly held.

Guile, guile is the thing, Gilly had often said to her when they were playing chess. But what guile could she use here? Something else he had said once—that unexpected cessation of resistance could be effective—came back to her. She kicked at the ankles of the ruffian pulling her along, gave a great scream, then, without warning, suddenly relaxed her whole body and collapsed, losing her feet and becoming a dead weight.

Surprised, her captor momentarily lost his grip. She had fallen against a small pavilion near the gates. Harry grasped with both hands at one of its stanchions, cast iron painted to look like marble, and hung on for dear life, screaming at the top of her voice. The spectacle of a helpless female lying on the ground, clutching the pillar of an empty pavilion, created more mirth than concern among the spectators, who saw it as yet another splendid show put on for their entertainment.

Fortunately for Harry her captors did not want to attract too much attention. One interested group of soberly dressed tradesmen and their women, seeing an otherwise respectable female behaving in so disorderly a manner, stopped to enquire what the fuss was about, thus delaying the kidnappers long enough, she hoped breathlessly, for help to arrive.

She attempted to shout to them for assistance, but the largest ruffian informed them that the gal was his run-away wife who had left him to go on the game, and that he was returning her home with the help of his friends.

'No, no. He lies. They are stealing me away; please help me,' she cried desperately, only to be ignored. No one was prepared to come between man and wife, and they moved on with a laugh for her captors, and shouted advice to her to behave herself in future.

Panting, she held on for dear life, but the leader now knelt beside her and began to prise her loose. Enraged, she dropped her head to bite his hand, and he let out a yell, gazing into her angry, scarlet face with something approaching respect.

'Damn you, you hellcat, you,' he growled. 'If it weren't that we'd been told not to damage the goods, I'd give you a lesson in good behaviour before I handed you over. You're the rowdiest fine lady I've come across in many a long year. "Little, and won't offer much resist-ance". A likely tale.' And he pinched her wrist cruelly.

'And damn you, too,' she said defiantly, but facing the inevitable as she was slowly dragged away. I will not resign myself to this, I will not, she thought.

Arabella's scream coincided with the main party's realisation that they had become separated from the two

women. Alex had already turned back to pick them up,
when he saw Arabella standing alone, face white, mouth
open, her distress at what had happened to Harry
genuine, even though she had manoeuvred her for the
ruffians to take.

'What is it?' said Alex, his own face suddenly white,
the others behind him also becoming aware for the first
time that disaster had struck. 'Where is Harry?'

'They took her,' sobbed Arabella vaguely. 'Men came
and dragged her away.' She was in such a state of shock
that she was hardly able to describe them or say which
way Harry had been taken. 'Over there—that way, I
think; I'm not sure,' she choked, pointing first in the
direction where she had last seen the kidnappers with
their victim, and then in another.

She clutched at Alex, delaying him, as he began to
make for the path to the gates. Ned glared at her, and
said unkindly, 'Oh, do give over, Arabella. Try to pull
yourself together. At least give us some idea of what
happened.'

Harrendene came over to take her arm. He had been
far ahead when the brouhaha began, and now said coldly
to his wife, 'It is not like you, Arabella, to lose your
head. Calm yourself.'

'Oh, leave that,' said Alex almost rudely in his distress.
'Come with me towards the main gate, Ned. And
Harrendene, you'd best take the opposite direction. They
cannot have gone forwards, or we should have seen them,
and backwards would merely trap them in the gardens.
Gerald——' for Gerald Illingworth, the Duke's heir, was
part of the Duchess's company '——you had better escort
the ladies back to the box for safety.'

For by now the whole party had assembled to learn
the unpleasant news. Alex, almost without thinking, had
taken command, as though he were back with his
regiment; the habit of leadership was strong in him.
Inwardly, he was on fire at Harry's disappearance, and,
if he had not already known, his horror at what might be

happening to her would have told him how much his cousin's despised wife had come to mean to him.

He and Ned ran towards the entrance, making as good speed as they could, sworn at by the crowd as they pushed through them roughly in their eagerness to recover Harry. They caught up with her as she was slowly being worked loose from the stanchion to which she clung so grimly.

In their eagerness they almost ran by her, until Alex grasped that the small crowd which was laughing at the antics of three men and a woman on the ground was being amused by poor Harry's plight. The leader had just managed to prise her loose, lift her up, and place a large, smelly hand over her mouth to prevent her cries as Alex caught up with him, shouting, in his best parade-ground bellow, and with all the authority of the great gentleman he was, 'Let her go at once, damn you.' He could see Harry's eyes, wild above her captor's cruel hand, and the sight enraged him.

The leading ruffian stared at him, at his clothes, his patent authority, everything about him proclaiming his standing. And worse, he was the kind of aristocrat who could give Gentleman Jackson a good fight, too. He had his orders. If things went wrong, he was to abandon the enterprise and escape. There was to be no chance of any of them being caught and questioned, and the man who had hired them to take Harry, with Arabella's conniv-ance, being traced.

'Stow that,' he said, dropping her roughly to the ground, he and his fellows making for the gates at full speed, Ned giving fruitless chase behind them. For drawn up outside the gates was a waiting coach, plain black, with no identifying marks upon it, into which they all piled and were driven smartly off. Ned was left standing helpless in the road, watching them go.

Alex bent over Harry, who was struggling up, scarlet with rage and fear, relief at her salvation suddenly upon her. Her clothes were torn and her face grimy. The

defiance which had sustained her began to ooze away, as
she fully understood what had almost happened to her,
and she leaned against Alex, shaking in sudden shock.

He picked her up, and held her to him. 'Thank God;
thank God you are safe. How came you on the ground?'

Harry found speech difficult. 'I was trying to hinder
them, to give you time. . .' She stopped.

'So brave,' he told her, and swung her off her feet to
carry her, ignoring curious stares. He began to walk with
her, back to their box. She thought that she felt his lips
brush her cheek, not harshly and in passion, as so often
before, but gently, and this affected her more than all his
previous wild lovemaking had done. He was reassuring
her, cradling and petting her as though she were a child
again, and the thought was sweet.

But the memory of the assault, and of how near she
had come to losing everything, swept over her, so that
she suddenly started up, and said with a wild cry, 'Oh,
Alex, I thought I was lost. Oh, I thank God, too, that
you came. I fell down to try to stop them taking me
away, and I held on to something, I hardly remember
what. But I could not have held on much longer. Why
should they take me? Why?'

The firework display began as she choked this out.
Ribbons of light and glittering stars burst in the sky to
the accompaniment of the occasional thunderclap. Alex
could give no sensible answer to Harry's question. He
could only say, 'Sometimes young girls are taken in these
places. Please, Cousin Harry, try to forget what has
happened to you.' And what a stupid thing to say to her,
he thought despairingly, but all words are stupid at such
a time. He could only try to reassure her by holding her
to him.

Harry, in his arms, her head against his shoulder,
feeling all the hard strength of him, his warm breath on
her cheek, hearing the broken sounds of love and encour-
agement he was making, knew, beyond a doubt, that
whatever she had ever felt for Alex was quite different

from anything she had ever felt for anyone else—even Gilly. She was in the right place, it was as though she had come home, and she would be sorry when at last he came to put her down.

Never mind his scorn for her, his contempt; all that paled if only she could remain where she was, if words and thought were not needed, if only the mundane world would not need to come between them, when he would again remember who and what she was—or what he thought she was.

Ned came running up, breathlessly. 'She's not hurt? Say she's not hurt, Alex.'

Harry looked at him across Alex's arm. 'Not hurt,' she managed. 'Only frightened.'

'I'd have killed them if I'd caught them,' he declared fiercely, and Harry gave him a weak smile.

'My two cavaliers,' she said. 'And if I am to be brave, then you must put me down, Alex. I think I could manage to walk now.'

He would have argued with her, but, seeing the resolution on her face, he stood her gently on her feet, saying, 'Only if you promise to tell me if you feel faint, and will take my arm tightly. I must not lose you again.'

With his gentle assistance—she wished that she could think it loving—Harry walked back to their box. She was shivering, but looked gallantly at him, and tried to smile. He could not but admire her spirit, and the fight which she had put up to try to foil her attackers. Never mind what she was, what she had done. Here was a woman worth the winning. And he wondered ruefully if that was what his cousin had thought, and had he taken her despite her character, as he, Alex, was now prepared to do?

Ned took Harry's other arm, exclaiming over its bruises. Arabella gave a great scream when she saw Harry approaching, and generally, commented Ned rather acidly afterwards, made more fuss than the poor victim, who said bravely, 'A glass of wine will help, I think,' and sank into a chair, before being ministered to by everyone, except Arabella, who needed a great deal of ministering herself.

'But what a mystery,' said the Duchess, as they waited for the two women to recover themselves before leaving for home. 'Why in the world should anyone try to carry off poor Harry?'

'Well, they do carry off dogs and demand payment,' said Gerald. 'I suppose some enterprising thief thought he could carry Mrs Ashburn off and demand a ransom note for her safe return. She is, after all, an extremely wealthy young woman. There is no doubt that the attack was carefully planned.'

'Yes,' agreed Ned. 'There was a waiting coach, and Harry thinks that she might have been followed for some time. She remembers seeing the leading villain before he carried her off. He was watching the Punch and Judy show, and she thinks he might have been watching the box as well.'

'Good God, what a cool-headed young lady she is, to be sure,' remarked Gerald, looking at Harry, who was fast recovering, and refusing to be treated as an invalid. 'To retain her composure so admirably.'

'Yes,' said Alex, 'and a good thing she did. If they had taken her straight off, we should never have caught them up. She saved herself.'

CHAPTER FIFTEEN

THE Season was rapidly drawing to a close. The attempted kidnap of the little Ashburn was a nine days' wonder, and like such wonders was soon forgotten by all except those who were most engaged in it. Alex now knew that he must make a decision over Harry soon. If not, there were others who might fix themselves on her, and she might accept one of them.

His conflict was resolved when he heard that Sussex, fat Sussex of all people, intended to propose to her. That was not to be borne. Ned had told him, and watched his brother's face as he did so. Yes, Alex was his rival after the fact, no doubt of it.

It was exactly a week since the attack at Vauxhall; she would surely be recovered from it by now, and he would make his offer on the morrow. Arabella was dreadfully sure that he was going to propose to Harry. Worse, after the attack at Vauxhall, whenever they met, which was not often, he was even colder to her than he had been before. She had done so little to help herself or Hervey, and her apparent loss of control had contrasted badly with Harry's own resolution when faced with disaster.

She must do something, she must. She had nearly lost him, perhaps had lost him. Desperate, that morning, she waited for her husband to leave for his club before entering his study. She hated him, too, these days. He had reprimanded her for being unkind about the little Ashburn; it would serve him right if she used his own possessions to gain her own way.

His study was a room she rarely visited, and she was not surprised to find everything there in splendid order, letters and papers neatly sorted, tied together with tape, and classified.

Impatience almost made her a little careless, but at last she found, away from the rest of his personal papers, a plain box, with a trick catch, which she finally mastered. Inside was what she wanted: at the bottom of the box there were two letters to Dolly signed by Henrietta Grey, the name of the milkmaid's mother, which she read avidly, eyes widening as she did so.

Well, that should settle the little Ashburn when she saw them, she thought, as she abstracted the letters, carefully replacing everything else. She would visit her this very morning before Alex or anyone else spoke to her. She rang for her maid and her carriage.

Harry was feeling particularly at one with life when Arabella called. For the first time since arriving in London she felt in control of herself, no longer besieged, finally accepted. The Magistrate and the Runners had been informed of the kidnap, had made enquiries, but had found nothing. They concluded that any well-dressed lady of obvious fashion who looked vulnerable might have been taken, and the waiting coach was for whomsoever they found.

She was surprised to find Arabella visiting her. She was working with Mrs Whitmore on her correspondence, in the little study, and Sarah offered to accompany her when Arabella was announced; she did not trust her with Harry.

'Not necessary, but thank you, all the same. I wonder what she can want?'

'A courtesy call?' replied Sarah, and Harry left to find Arabella looking magnificent as usual, in the large drawing-room at the back of the house which overlooked a lawn and formal flower-beds.

'So pleasant to see all this again,' sighed Arabella. 'I positively lived here once. Such happy memories.' And her look was sentimental in the extreme.

She asked after Harry, 'Are you recovered from Vauxhall?' and made idle small talk until Harry wondered what the point of the visit was. She was sure that there was a point.

'Such a success as you have been——' Arabella was fulsome, quite unlike her usual dismissive manner towards the little Ashburn, Harry thought '—one is sure, knowing you, that you would only ever want to do that which is proper. One does not wish to distress you, but I found these, quite by accident. I thought that you should see them. You would not wish to say or do the wrong thing.'

'And what wrong thing is that?' said Harry, intrigued by Arabella's sudden care for her reputation.

'Oh, your strange situation, and your involvement with Alex; one sees that he is taken with you a little, but bearing all things in mind, and knowing his sense of honour—quite Spanish, my dear—your true situation must irk you.'

What can she be at? thought Harry irreverently.

'My true situation?' she said aloud.

'Well,' drawled Arabella, 'you must, I'm sure, always have a doubt in your mind—you having so good an understanding—that Alex really wants you, and not his lands and home back. He was quite broken, you know, when he lost Racquette. Quite broken. He has never been the same since. How splendid for him that you seem so attracted to his somewhat rough charm.'

She obviously expected an answer. Harry did not give her one. Did she think Alex was after Racquette? It was perhaps something which she ought to consider more seriously. It might account for the slight change in his manner towards her. But she let none of this show on her face before Arabella. Was Arabella saying something which everyone knew but herself?

'And your own dubious position. Marrying his cousin so strangely, and your parentage, your mama.'

'My mother?' Another question, and she watched as Arabella took some papers from her reticule and offered them to her.

'Yes, my dear. Perhaps you should read these. Your mother seems strangely lavish with her favours in them. All this must make you ask yourself whether you are a proper wife for Alex—a man so conscious of the duties of his position, and with such an exquisite sense of fitness that it is almost uncomfortable for those around him.'

Afterwards Harry was to reproach herself. She should not have read the letters, or, having done so, she should not have accepted Arabella's interpretation of them. But at the time she was mesmerised. Nun'ster's hints, Arabella's confidence, and her public statement of several things which had been troubling Harry, all led her to take Arabella's reading of them as true, even if she could not believe Arabella's confident assertion that Alex was about to offer for her. Surely not! He had made his disapproval and doubts about her quite plain.

She opened the first letter slowly. Both were addressed to Lord Harrendene, and had obviously been written many years ago. There was no date on the first, but the paper was yellow with age, and it was undoubtedly her mother's hand.

Both began, 'My dearest Dolly'. At first there was nothing to trouble her. The writer assured dear Dolly that she was well, settled in a small village, not named, and the letters were being forwarded from the nearest town.

> You know only too well my dreadful circumstances, and only the memory of our affection for one another, and for the Duke, has made my seclusion acceptable. Dear John has been so understanding of our arrangements, and fully accepts the need for secrecy. Even the Duchess must not know of what passed between us, lest others come to learn of my retreat. *He* must never know. Your discretion, I already know, is absolute, and must remain so.

The second letter, dated some years later, said much the same. The writer assured her reader that she was happy and settled with John, although his health remained frail. They had long hoped for a child, and after their early disappointment had waited for years, and suddenly a child was on the way at last. Harry assumed by the date that she was the long-awaited baby. The letter again referred to close relationships between them all. The writer begged that the Duchess be informed of the child, but not of their whereabouts—that would never do.

The implication of all this was plain, as Arabella's triumphant face assured her, when Harry looked up after reading them.

'You see, my dear? What a charming little set. The Devonshires had nothing on them, but were not so discreet. And married off to your father to avoid scandal, one supposes.'

'There could be other explanations,' said Harry desperately.

'Come, we are not children.' Arabella was all honey. 'What other explanations, indeed? Pray, what? And the Duchess not to be informed, you note.'

'The Duchess has never breathed a word against my mother,' Harry protested.

'Naturally not. Such discretion disarms suspicion,' drawled Arabella, 'but not a secret after all. Others knew, and have talked.'

Harry thought of what Nun'ster had hinted of her mother, of overheard gossip since she had come to Town. Could it be that he had been telling the truth? There was one comfort. At least there was no doubt about her own parentage.

'It is for you,' said Arabella, stowing the letters away to return them to the cabinet from whence she had stolen them, 'to decide where your honour and duty lie after reading them.'

Harry would have liked to have read them again. Where, indeed, did her duty lie? Would a possible scandal, well over twenty years old, put a stain on her forever? Worse was done every day. Arabella had mentioned the Devonshires' set. Everyone knew that the Devonshire House nurseries had been full of the 'mistakes' of the Duke, his wife, her sister and the Duke's mistress, Lady Elizabeth Foster, whom he had later married, but not until after many years of *ménage à trois* with the Duchess. But none of that had seemed to matter. The children had all grown up to make respectable marriages, if not the best. But Harry Ashburn was not a member of a great ducal house; she was a nobody, already suspect because of the strange nature of her marriage, and her consequent inheritance.

What Arabella had done by showing her the letters was to undermine her newly found self-confidence. It lay in ruins. She remembered only too well Alex's strong sense of honour, and the Duchess—the friend who had been so kind to her, without whom, she well knew, Society would never have accepted her—what would she have said if she had read the letters?

After Arabella had gone, trailing clouds of morality and duplicity behind her—for how, thought Harry, could she have obtained the letters honestly?—she did not return to her study and Mrs Whitmore. She needed to be alone, now that all her certainties had disappeared. To whom could she turn? Not the Duchess, that was sure. If only Gilly were with her. She was sure that he would have known what to say and do. But then, her common sense said, if he were here, he would be my husband, and no one would be proposing to me, and Arabella would have had no need to show me the letters. For, she thought, one thing is plain: she is motivated by jealousy over Alex; it is not care for me that brought her here today. Far from it. And if he asks me now, what must my answer be? That might depend on the manner of his asking, or even if he asks at all, and I cannot take that for granted, given the manner in which he has always treated me, whatever Arabella thinks.

* * *

Alex dressed himself that afternoon with some care, pleasing Forbes for once, who usually complained that his master did not take enough thought over his appearance. But a man going to propose to a woman for the first time in nearly ten years must make a good show when he did so.

By the time Forbes had finished with him, from the top of his red head, curls subdued and brushed into the wind-swept style which fashion demanded, his cravat a veritable work of art, as Harry had once said, satisfying Forbes's thwarted artistic soul, to the tip of his polished boots, so shiny that they might have served as mirrors, he was a credit to his country, his class and the efforts of his tailor, shirtmaker, hosier, breeches supplier, bootmaker, and everything that was his, as he said to his happy servant.

'And if I am damned uncomfortable in all this, you dog, then I have the satisfaction, I suppose, of knowing that I have made you a happy man for the first time in years.'

'Since you went to Spain, to be exact, my lord,' confirmed Forbes, bowing and grinning.

'Now, do you think my waistcoat sufficiently artistic?' said Alex, staring at it in his glass. 'A little too chaste, is it? Something with monkeys carrying parasols on it, do you think, or a pair of mating peacocks, would be more the thing, perhaps?'

'You are pleased to engage in funning, my lord,' said Forbes severely. 'You are completely to the point as you are. Were you always to be turned out so, I should be a happy man.'

'And that is the aim of my life, I suppose,' replied Alex, laughing. 'What a coxcomb I must have been before I was a soldier. Doubtless you want that man back?'

'No, my lord,' said Forbes judiciously. 'A little more leaning in that direction, perhaps. Less fly-away, and rural, shall we say? Take what you are now as a model, and all will be well.'

Alex was still laughing as he went downstairs. He felt as he had not done for years.

He met Ned as he was leaving. Ned stared at him. 'Good God, Alex, I can't remember when I last saw you so fine. If it were not that you look so robust I should wonder at your state of mind.'

'You are no more flattering than Forbes in your assessment of my usual condition,' said Alex, pulling on a pair of super-fine gloves, so close-fitting that help was almost needed with them. 'But at least I have made him a happy man.'

'Well, I can't say you make me feel happy,' said Ned frankly. 'I suppose you are done up like a maypole in full fig because you are off to propose to Harry or some such. I suppose I shall have to wish you luck, but, judging by the way she looked at you at Vauxhall, t'other night, I don't think you need it. Your luck is made. Though why it should be, after the way you have treated her, I can't imagine.'

Alex drove through the streets of Mayfair, his hat at a jaunty angle, and more than one who knew him stared at young Alex Ashburn come back to life again.

And, of course, thought Harry, afterwards, it was the very worst time for him to come a-courting, as Hannah would have said. I hardly knew whether I was up or down when the butler came in and said that Lord Templestowe had arrived—'I have put him in the Chinese drawing-room, and he would like to speak to you at your pleasure, madam.'

So, Arabella had been right, after all, and here she was, dressed in her old tan, shabby as you please, not in any kind of glory. But, of course, she might be wrong, and he merely wished to speak with her of other things, but of what?

Harry was not to know that Alex thought that she looked enchanting in her severe tan, so much better than the frippery most women covered themselves in. He was standing in the window as she entered, and turned to greet her.

How splendid he looked! She had never seen him in the full uniform of the dandy set before. The skin-tight clothing showed off his powerful physique, and took off the severe edge of his looks. He was, indeed, a little overpowering. The breathlessness she was so often overcome with in his presence was worse than usual, and her own sense of worthlessness seemed greater than ever.

Alex had no notion of this. Harry seemed to be her normal cool, controlled self. He hardly knew how to begin. The careless ease with which he had conducted his earlier courtship of Arabella seemed to have disappeared forever. His own ambivalent feelings about Harry, the belief that she might be aiming for an even higher prize than himself, his need to convince her—and himself—that by proposing to her he was not merely acting to regain his lost inheritance, all served to make it extremely difficult for him to know exactly how to phrase his offer.

'Mrs Ashburn—Cousin Harry,' he began. 'You must surely know what I am about to say.'

This had unfortunate overtones of Nun'ster, who had said virtually the same thing, and she replied somewhat wildly, 'No, indeed, not at all,' which she knew, the moment that she had said it, was far from the truth, and that he must surely know that.

'Oh, come,' he said, smiling a little, in an attempt to reassure her, 'you are cleverer than that. Never say that you do not know how completely you have succeeded in winning me over.'

After Arabella's revelations, and the fear that her mother's reputation as a temptress was known to all, as well as the scandal about herself, this, again, was unfortunate. Harry's eyes glittered dangerously. 'Winning you over? To what, my lord?' No Cousin Alex here, he noted. This was not going quite as it should.

'Why, my dear Cousin Harry, to my asking you something I once would not have thought possible.' And that was the wrong thing to say, he knew at once, the moment it was out, and it was too late to recall it.

'Oh, indeed. And what did you not think possible? Am I permitted to know?'

Alex hesitated. He seemed to be wading deeper into the mire with every word. 'Perhaps I might put that a little more fortunately. Cousin Harry, I no longer wish you to be my cousin, I wish you to be my wife. Will you marry me?' There, it was out, blunt and a little ungracious-sounding, but out.

Harry's colour was high. Such condescension! Such an offer, so palpably hedged about with reservations, to one probably considered unworthy of it. Her own feelings of unworthiness were redoubled—adding to her anger at the tone of what he was saying. 'An offer to be treasured, my lord,' she replied frostily. 'Once not thought possible, I note, but "won over", and now probably regretted, by your manner. Are you sure that you wish to make it at all?'

Harry had never thought to respond to a proposal of marriage from him in such a fashion, but everything he had said flicked her on the raw. Nun'ster's behaviour, Arabella's hints, Society's sneers about her own supposed reputation, and the dubious nature of the letters which she had read earlier, were not the best preparation for receiving so ungracious an offer. 'Cleverer than that', indeed! She found that she was shaking.

'Come madam——' he was now a little angry too '—I have made you a noble offer, not an ignoble one. My hand and my name. To be Templestowe's Countess, no less. It is not as though I had proposed. . .'

'To bed me without marriage,' she finished for him, before she could stop herself, adding, 'But that would not restore you Racquette, however much it might pleasure you otherwise.' So, she thought bitterly, as this flew out, quite without her meaning to say it, Arabella's hints that his lost lands were behind his pursuit of me found their mark and hurt me, after all.

Alex's face darkened. 'By God, madam. Racquette I might gain, but that is not it, not it at all. Little though it pleases me in my more rational moments, it is you I want. Bed and board and conversation and companionship, too. Dammit, I love you to distraction, and how that has happened I do not know, and, despite that, you, of all people, have the impudence to throw Racquette in my face. Damn Racquette, and damn the grandfather who deprived me of it, and made it difficult for me to offer for you.'

By now they were standing face to face again, furious eyes locked, colour high, two highly intelligent and passionate souls, each carrying the burden of a great hurt, each consumed by love for the other, almost against their will. Star-crossed lovers, who had met only because of an old man's wicked desire to wound, and the echo of what he had done and everything which had sprung from it reverberated between them, tainting all their intercourse, preventing them from coming together as they should have done.

'Most gracious, my lord, most gracious!' exclaimed Harry fiercely. 'And what do you feel for me in your "more rational moments"?' She flung his words back at him. 'It is hardly love, or admiration, one supposes, for myself "of all people", as you so kindly said. Did you expect Arabella's milkmaid, your and Gilly's temptress, to throw herself at your feet, full of undying gratitude for being made such a magnificent offer in so insulting a manner—that you were willing to overlook mine and my mother's murky past, and reluctantly compel yourself to make me your wife, instead of your mistress?'

'No, indeed. I expected an answer commensurate with the worth of what I offered you.' This came out between clenched teeth, and Alex's expression was murderous, between rage and baffled desire.

'I thought that that was what I gave you, Lord

Templestowe. Your nobility in wishing to offer for such a creature as myself beggars belief. But no, I am not worthy. Your "more rational self" should have expected such an answer. I do not love you, and you are correct to think, as you doubtless do, that even to be Templestowe's Countess is not now enough for me. I aim for a far greater prize.'

'By God,' said Alex, lost to everything, 'if it is Nun'ster you are after, rest assured *he* will never propose, and what Sussex might offer you is not worth having, and, as for not loving me, I do not believe a word of what you say to me about that. What I have seen of you recently convinces me of quite the opposite.' And, before he could prevent himself, the beloved object was in his arms, where, dammit, she belonged, and he was showering kisses on her face and on her beautiful eyes, caressing her body with his urgent hands, first gently, and then with increasing passion.

Oh, thought Harry, it was not like Nun'ster at all! Everything in her responded to him, but, 'I will not be loved in contempt, to be despised in your "more rational moments". Consider, my lord, I am not worthy, and marrying me is surely too high a price for you to pay for Racquette. For shame!' And she pulled away with such force, after her first betraying co-operation, that she was free of him. 'Are you all mad in Society, that I cannot refuse a man without being assaulted by words and deeds? I think that you had better leave before you commit an act you may later regret—in your more rational moments!'

Dammit, as usual she was right. And what an unholy botch of it he had made. One would never have thought that he had once been a diplomat, and to end by assaulting her again! Was there no end to his folly? What could have happened to the man who loved them and left them? The man Arabella had created. The man who lately had not wanted them at all, and now wanted this prize so desperately he was beyond reason. Oh, she was

a witch, a very witch, and it was his own fault for falling
in love with her; it had deprived him of honour and
sense. For a man of his years and experience to be so
headlong in his desire was deplorable, and no wonder
that his unruly tongue had run away with him. Even
now, he could not prevent himself from saying, 'You will
not reconsider?'

'No. Not at all. Go away. Assume your more rational
self. That should douse all fires.'

Oh, and what a tongue she had! It should extinguish
him, but didn't. Quite the contrary, with each word he
was more on fire for her than ever, but in shame, or
honour, he did not know which, he must leave at once.
He looked wryly at her. Harry had never looked more
desirable, cheeks aflame, eyes shining like dark stars,
and the brilliant mind which informed them served only
to make her more of a prize.

'Yes,' he said slowly. 'I will go. I was wrong and
careless in what I said to you. Wrong to take you in my
arms against your will—if against your will it truly was—
but I do not accept your refusal. I will not give you up.
Rightly or wrongly I believe that you are the woman for
me, and that we are well matched. I will not trouble you
further today, but I hope to convince you in the future
that you are mistaken.'

He had gone. Harry sank down on to the sofa and
broke into a passion of weeping. Regret, thwarted love,
hurt pride, and her own fierce integrity all combined to
bring her almost to despair. Oh, yes, she loved him, no
doubt of that, but she would not be treated in such a
fashion. He must come to her in unreserved love and
affection, or not at all. Without that, even his caresses,
however physically sweet, were anathema, and their love
would be shameful, because founded on lies and misun-
derstandings, and not ennobling, as it ought to be.

CHAPTER SIXTEEN

ALEX left Harry in a state of ferment. As Ned would have said, his head was on fire. He had gone to see Harry, sure—well, almost sure of his reception, and for the third time in his life his expectations were totally confounded. He hardly knew what he was doing. He could not immediately return home to Ned and Forbes.

Instead, he drove to Jackson's gym, stripped off and sparred a few rounds with the gentleman himself. He hardly knew who or what he was striking at—Harry, or himself for his own folly in supposing that life, after all, was on his side.

'You needed that, my lord,' was all the gentleman said, quietly, when the session was over. 'Sometimes action is the only restorative.' And that was true enough, he thought ruefully, as he took his bruised face and damaged knuckles home.

One thing struck him as he remembered and relived the conversation with her. 'I am not worthy!' She had said this more than once, and her expression when she'd said it had been such a strange mixture of regret and pain that for the first time—why, he did not know—he questioned the reputation which she had brought with her from Norfolk.

Nothing she had said to him should cause him to question it. Indeed, she had almost taken pleasure in throwing it in his face. He remembered her saying that she had married his cousin for his mansion and broad acres. She had implicitly agreed with him when he had taunted her with her siren's career in Norfolk, suggested that she was after still greater prizes in London, and in this last conversation she had held her head high, and

170

said, nay insisted, that she was after a greater prize than any he could offer her.

Yes, she had consistently mocked him with her past, and then he thought of the wit with which she had mocked others occasionally, a wry turning back on them of their own follies, and for the first time it occurred to him that he, like others, had taken at face value her words about herself; but was she, perhaps, subtly amusing herself, by misdirecting others' thoughts and prejudices?

Alex sprang to his feet and paced the room. Thought of the pride which lay beneath the gentle manner with which Harry faced the world. Why should he suppose that this pride was any less than his own? That Harry was less complex than himself? He suddenly knew that he could no longer continue to speculate on what Harry really was.

Was she as good and true as her manner proclaimed? Or was that a cloak for a mind not only subtle, but mercenary and calculating? He would get to the bottom of this, and there was only one way. He knew at once what he would do. The Season was virtually over, he had promised himself to leave for his home at Allerton as soon as he could—the home whose lands marched with the Duke of Hornsea's estate at Oldheath Priory where Harry was due to visit the Duchess shortly. Before he went there, he would go to Norfolk, to Netherdene, the village where his cousin Gilbert and Harry had lived their short married life together, and find out the truth.

He set off again, jauntiness gone, this time to Heriot, the Templestowe solicitor, who stared at him when Alex entered his office in Lincoln's Inn, and asked him abruptly for the name of Harry's man of business in Netherdene, and stared again when he noted down Mr Flewitt's address. He would go there at once. Pointless to stay in London—he was sick of the place anyway; he would send his servants, including Forbes, to Allerton in south Nottinghamshire to await him there, and take Evans, his old sergeant and now his man in charge of his

stables, with him. It would be like old times again—only
the campaign would be in Norfolk, not Spain.

Action always relieved him, as Jackson had rightly
said, and it was good to be going post haste to East
Anglia—a county which he had never visited—with
Evans, who had smiled grimly at poor Forbes when told
of the Colonel's plans, and had thought that his master
had come to his senses again. It would be like the war
come back, to go on the road with him, with the
advantage that you were not going to be shot at.

Alex was drily amused at Evans's quiet satisfaction on
the journey, which fortunately for both of them was
undertaken in one of the few sunny breaks in that dismal
summer. Riding through the flat fields and the high skies
of East Anglia was as different from riding in Spain as
peace was different from war.

The great houses of the district were plainly visible
from the rough road, largely treeless, which they followed to Netherdene. Drawing near to his goal, Alex
wondered which of those he passed was the mansion to
which his dying cousin had taken his bride. Well, he
would know soon enough, and Harry's secret, too. He
was not sure whether he wanted to know the truth, if the
truth were unpleasant.

He left Evans unpacking at Netherdene's most
comfortable inn while he set off to find Mr Flewitt's
office. Netherdene, as he walked through it, was what he
had expected it to be: a pretty backwater lost in the
emptiness of the vast East Anglian plain. A village street,
lined with cottages, and the odd, slightly larger gentlemen's houses, ran through the middle, some lanes and
closes leading from it. The church was huge, obviously
built for better times and a larger population. The
Parsonage was as big as a barracks, but in good condition. Money had recently been spent on it.

He wondered in which of the modest homes his cousin
Harry had lived, and how she had managed the transition
to wealth after she had married his cousin. Mr Flewitt's

office was in a pretty but small building, bow windows facing the street.

The solicitor was happy to receive Lord Templestowe, and wondered why he was so favoured by such a magnate's visit. He was immediately struck by my lord's face and bearing, but did not show it. Alex filled his small office with his presence, and, the preliminaries over, said, 'Let me be blunt, sir. I have little time to waste. Is there any reason why anyone should think that Mrs Gilbert Ashburn's marriage to my cousin was in any way disgraceful or unworthy?'

Mr Flewitt gave a short exclamation, and then threw down the quill pen which he had picked up. 'I suppose it is Frith again,' he said angrily. 'For a man of the cloth he is sadly lacking in Christian charity.'

'No,' replied Alex, 'not at all. I have spoken to no one of this—not even to Mrs Ashburn herself, and I need clarification. Let me be plain again: the gossip is that she tricked him into marriage for his fortune.'

'Let *me* be plain, my lord,' said Mr Flewitt severely. 'Out of *his* Christian charity, although I believe that he claimed no religion, your cousin Gilbert, who was slowly dying at the time, offered marriage to Miss Harriet Grey, known as Minster, his childhood friend, because she had been left penniless on her stepfather's death, and did not possess so much as a home. Miss Minster accepted his offer, and cared for him devotedly until his death. After it, she was completely broken for some time. I feared for her, but, as you may have discovered, she is a most resilient and brave young woman, and recovered to live a quiet life here. The conduct of both was exemplary. Your young cousin, sir, was a remarkable person, and his wife no less so. I can offer them nothing but honour. Frith, the Rector here, behaved badly to both of them, and his word cannot be trusted.'

Alex surveyed him numbly. Everything he heard carried the ring of truth.

'I should like to believe that,' he said simply.

'Believe it, my lord, believe it,' insisted Mr Flewitt. He removed his half-moon spectacles. 'I may add, because it seems necessary, that your cousin informed me, that, as he had expected, Miss Minster needed some little persuasion before she consented to marry him. The marriage, of course, was a white one. Mr Ashburn was paralysed, and too ill to consummate it. He loved her devotedly, my lord, and it grieved him that he could not be her true husband. He had always loved her, but I believe that she felt for him only as a brother, which was why she was hesitant to marry him, even to be his wife in name only.'

What the lawyer had just told him struck Alex almost physically. It was a hammer-blow.

'A white marriage?' he repeated, stunned.

'It could not be otherwise,' said Mr Flewitt. 'By then, Mr Ashburn was helpless, and his condition declined daily.'

An unconsummated marriage, a virgin bride and a virgin wife and widow. Alex thought of the stairs at Rule, of his own assault on her, the great drowned eyes; the marks of maidenly modesty, which he had thought assumed, were only too real. And he had treated her as he would have treated a whore. He closed his eyes in pain against the memory. Every cruel, taunting word, every sexual innuendo, carelessly uttered, which he had directed at her, came back to reproach him. A pure young girl, and he, what had he said and done to her?

The coolly innocent manner. The ironic and gentle candour, all of which he had thought of as guile, the deceits of a siren put on to delude men, were only too true. The outward and visible signs of an inward virtue. He could feel only the most scalding shame, and it was no wonder to him that she had rejected his suit, the patronising half-contemptuous offer which he had made to her.

Mr Flewitt's eyes were hard on his face.

'You thought quite otherwise, my lord.'

'Yes,' admitted Alex, his voice stifled. 'Rumour lied, as usual. And I have to confess that I have behaved shamefully.'

'It is an honourable man who can make such a confession,' stated Mr Flewitt simply.

Alex shook his head. 'In defence,' he said numbly, 'I can only offer that she, herself, said that she married my cousin for his mansion and his broad acres.'

'Yes,' said Mr Flewitt. 'I can imagine her saying that. She has an acute mind, as I expect you know. But her reputation, my lord, is spotless, and I would have thought that her modesty spoke for itself. Frith, as I said, lied by inference, and gossip leaped upon it. And you, my lord, suffered by the marriage, if indirectly. Mr and Mrs Gilbert Ashburn knew nothing of the inheritance when they married, or the manner in which they unwittingly deprived you.'

It was almost a rebuke, and a rebuke which he deserved.

'Come,' said Mr Flewitt, rising. 'I think that there is something which you should see. I assume that you are remaining here tonight, and do not leave until tomorrow?'

'Yes, I leave for my Midlands home in the morning.'

Mr Flewitt pulled open a drawer and fetched out a key. 'Then I shall take you to Dene House, the luxurious mansion and broad acres which Mrs Ashburn acquired by her fortunate marriage.' And his eyes twinkled mockingly as he said it. He pointed Alex to the door.

'You have a carriage?' enquired Alex. 'I fear that I cannot offer you mine. The matter was so urgent to me that I came here on horseback with only my old sergeant for company.'

'Oh, no carriage is needed,' said Mr Flewitt airily, his expression inscrutable. 'We have only a short walk, my lord.'

Curious glances followed the tall and elegant stranger

as he and Mr Flewitt walked along Netherdene's main street.

Mr Flewitt stopped before one of the small gentlemen's homes along it—not the smallest of all, but by no means the largest. It was set back from the road with a tiny carefully tended garden before it. Mr Flewitt opened a white painted gate, and with a shock Alex saw fastened to it a small board with the words 'Dene House' painted on it in black.

The old solicitor saw his look, and said with a smile, 'Yes, my lord, this is the mansion and these are the broad acres for which Miss Minster married your cousin Gilbert. The garden was her special pride; she was always at work in it. There is a kitchen plot at the back. Both the house and gardens are kept in good condition at her wish. They were not sold, she was happy here, and she left Netherdene with regret. But great wealth brings duties, and her husband would have wished her to behave properly, she said.'

Mr Flewitt was no fool, and noted how subdued my lord's manner had become. Alex's thoughts were whirling. All his beliefs and suppositions concerning Harry lay in ruins about him. 'This was my cousin's only home?' he asked, his voice hollow.

'Indeed, yes,' confirmed Mr Flewitt, repressively. 'Your cousin Gilbert's father married a shopkeeper's daughter, his only child, and improved her little fortune by his own hard work, and was able to leave a modest competence to Mr Gilbert—which was fortunate since he became an invalid so young. Mrs Gilbert Ashburn—Miss Minster—inherited that modest competence, and his house, no more.'

They were at the front door, Alex still in a state resembling shock, but there was more to come. They entered the house by a small hall, just big enough for the two of them to stand in. Alex seemed even larger than he was in this doll's house, for, compared with everything he was used to, the place seemed little more.

Mr Flewitt smiled drily to himself at the expression on my lord's face. So, he had believed poor Harriet an adventuress, swallowed the unpleasant lies which Frith had started on their way, and which had doubtless been magnified in the repeated telling.

They were now in a largish dark room. Mr Flewitt drew the curtains covering the glass doors which opened on to a small lawn and a shrubbery, and the kitchen garden beyond them. Alex looked curiously around the pretty but shabby room, wondering what he was doing in it. But he soon saw why the lawyer had brought him.

On the wall facing the window was a portrait of himself at eighteen—eager face, red hair, incipient strong body, everything. Even the tilt of the head, and the slightly satiric twist of the mouth was his.

Mr Flewitt watched him. Saw the shock of self-recognition.

'Surprising, is it not? That is your cousin, my lord, before illness destroyed him. That is the man Miss Minster married in his last days. I knew you and who you must be when you walked into my office. You even have his voice.'

What could he say? Harry's refusal seemed the more surprising, unless, of course, she thought his likeness to his cousin Gilbert an affront to the memory of the dead man, considering the dreadful way in which he, Alex, had treated her. He looked around the room's simple furnishings, at the chess set laid out on an occasional table, ready for play, except that the black King and the white Queen were missing.

To Mr Flewitt it was plain that what he had seen had disturbed my lord profoundly.

Alex picked up one of the chess men. He stared blindly at it. He was playing chess at Rule again, patronising her with every word he said—that was when he was not treating her with ill-deserved contempt. He was on the stairs at Rule. . . The memory was almost unbearable.

He hardly heard what Mr Flewitt was saying to him, followed him out, sick at heart, conscious of only one thing—that somehow he must be alone and come to terms with all that he had said and done to Harry, the woman who had selflessly tended a dying man, an untried and innocent girl whom he had handled, and to whom he had spoken, as though she were a Haymarket lightskirt.

Mr Flewitt was a tactful man. He was well aware of my lord's distress at what he had seen and heard, and was able to guess, a little, at the reason for it. He remained silent as they walked back to his office. Alex stopped at the door, and said, almost fiercely, 'This is the truth that you are telling me, sir?'

Mr Flewitt nodded his head. 'I was Mr Gilbert Ashburn's confidant, and Mrs Ashburn's adviser. Everything which I have told you is the truth to my certain knowledge.' He did not say that he was aware of my lord's distress, but added gently, 'My lord, it may be impertinent, but I do not think that you ought to be alone this evening. I should be honoured if you would dine with me. I think, with respect, that you are like your cousin in more than looks, and it would give me great pleasure to spend the evening with you.'

Alex was almost ready to refuse, but suddenly his own self was unbearable to him. To dine with the old man would delay the time when he had to come face to face with how he had behaved to Harry, and what he must do to make amends, if any amends were possible.

Before he left Netherdene, Mr Flewitt took him to the church where Gilly's name was on a wall-plaque. An urn full of fresh flowers stood before it, kept constantly renewed at Mrs Ashburn's wish, Mr Flewitt said.

Well, Alex had discovered the truth, and much good it did him. The enormity of his own behaviour, and that of others, was brought home to him not only by what the old man said, but as much by the manner of his saying it. How to repair what he had done, and how to approach her again, occupied him all the way to Allerton, and Evans thought his master more dour than he had ever been, even in the dark days when that nasty creature, Arabella Temple, had distressed him so.

CHAPTER SEVENTEEN

THE Season was over, and Society left Town. It could hardly end soon enough for Harry after the débâcle of Alex's proposal. She was sorry that she had promised to go to Oldheath, where she was sure to see him again, but, in honour, there was no way she could cry off.

She was glad to see the last of London. The Duchess had left before her, and, bowling along the winding drive to Oldheath Priory in Nottinghamshire, reached after several days' travel from London, Harry felt a sense of relief, even though the journey had been accomplished in the sort of pomp that plain Harriet Minster could never have hoped to enjoy.

The Priory, glimpsed through the trees, was like an engraving from a Gothic novel. One wall of the old church was left, with the giant west window, its glass gone. Behind it were the woods of the Duke's vast estate which stretched for miles into the neighbouring county of Derbyshire.

Her coach passed through a series of ornamental gardens, to draw up in front of a small door—the main entrance to the Priory was in the Duke's wing, where he lived as in seclusion, and to which no visitors had access. In the splendid hall which led from it, the Duchess and Alex were waiting to greet her before a giant hearth, where a fire had been lit, for the room was cold, even on a warm afternoon in late August.

Harry was not sure whether she was glad or sorry to see Alex again. Involuntarily, she began to tremble a little, but his greeting was as warm as the Duchess's. I suppose that he has decided to forgive me, she could not help thinking. More magnanimity for which I am expected to feel grateful!

'The other guests have all gone over to Welbeck, to visit the Portlands,' explained the Duchess, after kissing her warmly on the cheek, and showing her the tea and collation waiting for her by the fire. 'But we decided to greet you in style, did we not, Alex?'

He nodded assent. 'Now, you must not expect to see the Duke, my dear,' continued Emily, as they drank tea. 'He never sees visitors, and only leaves his quarters to use the library, and that when no one else is there. He stays away from us all, and his heir and nephew, Gerald Illingworth, acts as host here—at his wish.'

I shall never cease to be surprised at the habits of these great people, thought Harry, but her smile for the Duchess was warm, although she avoided Alex's eye. Doubtless the Duchess was matchmaking—and what a bad joke that was! Still matchmaking, she asked Alex to show Harry round the gardens once she had seen her room, and Harry had no alternative but to assent. She was further disturbed to hear that not only were Adolphus and Arabella Harrendene to arrive shortly, but that Gerald had insisted on inviting Nun'ster, who was an old boon companion of his—'Though what the Duke will say,' sighed the Duchess, 'I can't think. He cannot abide the man.'

So there was Alex waiting for her in the Great Hall when she came down again, refreshed and changed, and wearing a pair of stout shoes, for the rain had been heavy and the grounds would be waterlogged. 'You feel sufficiently recovered from your journey to walk with me?' he began.

To her horror her voice came out almost as a squeak, but he appeared not to notice, and made no sort of reference to their last meeting. And altogether, she thought, a little dazed, one would have thought that we had parted on the best of terms.

He must have thought that she looked tired, for he did not take her very far, finally sitting her down on a stone bench among the exotic chrysanthemums and the more prosaic Michaelmas daisies. A spaniel came over and lay at Alex's feet. He scratched the dog's ears. 'Plato,' he said. 'The Duchess will not have him in London. He is a country dog, she says.'

Harry suddenly thought that Alex was a country person. He was dressed easily, without a cravat; only a loose black silk scarf, à la Byron, was tied in a bow inside an open-necked white shirt, and, seated beside her, long legs stretched out, he looked more at ease than she had ever seen him. The scents of the garden, heightened by a recent shower, were strong in their nostrils.

'You will be tired from your journey,' he said.

'A little. But country air revives me.'

'Your presence revives me,' he returned quietly.

'Even after. . . London?' she ventured, remembering the rage and passion in which they had parted, surprised by the difference in his manner.

'Oh, I hope to change that soon,' he said, his eyes brilliant upon her, nothing of the frustrated man who had rounded on her so fiercely left in him.

'But——' she began.

'Shh. . . I know,' he said, and put a finger gently on her lips, and the light touch shocked them both. 'Do not say it. Your mind is made up, you think. I shall unmake it.'

'Not now. Not here,' she asserted nervously.

'Oh, no,' he replied, removing the finger. 'Not now. Soon.' And his look was a challenge. 'I never retreat, or, rather, if I do, it is to attack again. I learned that from the Great Duke as we toiled across Spain. You are smaller than Spain.'

She knew that he meant Wellington.

'And did he always win?'

'Oh, always. Defeat was not in his dictionary. I warn you, it is not in mine.'

'But I have a dictionary, too. It may be different from yours.'

'Indeed you have. You are a learned lady, I know,

even if you wear it lightly. I think that your dictionary is the same as mine, though.'

'Well, we shall see.' She was almost shocked by the difference in his speech to her. Nothing of the faint derision with which, even in their happier moments, he had always used with her.

'In time,' he said, and plucked one of the daisies to give to her. 'Wear my favour a little, madam. It is a country flower, and none the worse for that.'

Harry took the daisy, and if he wanted to play at words with her she would oblige him.

'What is your motto, Sir Knight? For a motto must always accompany a favour.'

'*Amor vincit omnia*. Love conquers all; what else?'

Now, what could she say to that? The last word was his, after all, and his eyes on her held triumph—but, what was most surprising, love as well.

'You see,' he said. 'I can flirt, too. I was too heavy with you in London. We shall remedy that here. Beware, Mrs Ashburn. I was a diplomat as well as a soldier.' And then he took her hand and kissed it, his eyes never leaving her. And again, his manner and tone were as different from the way in which he had previously dealt with her as it was possible to be.

Surprisingly she felt tears almost upon her. She was not used to such gentleness, and was almost frightened. If she softened towards him in return, would he attack her again? She did not think that she could bear it. She had been too bruised in the wars of love between them to joust with him lightly now, and realised with a shock that she could have better dealt with harshness from him than this sudden surprising consideration. She turned her head away from him, and Alex flinched a little at the sight, realising that she was a little afraid of him, and what he might do.

And no wonder, he thought, shame overwhelming him again, when my actions to her must have seemed as bad as rape. I must go carefully, or she will run from me like a frightened bird, so greatly have I damaged any rapport which might have existed between us; if only I had used my common sense and not listened to the voice of rumour.

'Never fear,' he said softly, 'I shall not do anything to distress you. I only know that, as always, your tongue says one thing, and your eyes tell me another; I shall remember that. Now we must return, or Emily will think that the Priory ghost has made away with us. It always walks and wails around this time of year.'

'Monks and a ghost and a ruined arch,' she remarked, as she rose, recovering her spirits a little, but still wondering what had caused this change in him, suspicious of it still. '*Udolpho*, indeed. And are there villains lurking here?'

'No,' he said, suddenly sober, 'and if any should come, I shall drive them away for you. That I promise.'

The next two days were as happy as any Harry could remember. Alex's manner to her remained so kind and considerate that she gradually came to lose her fear of him a little—the fear that their last encounter had left with her, when he had shown that, despite all, he still saw her as an adventuress. Ned was with them and was still her knight, although his intervention was little needed. The only cloud was the coming presence of Arabella.

Ned, indeed, watched them with sad eyes, but his brother's happiness was patent, and the Duchess said to him one afternoon as Harry and Alex played chess on the lawn—for the drowned summer had been succeeded by a warm and sunny autumn—and it was obvious that their minds were anywhere but on the game, 'I don't suppose, Ned, that you remember Alex as he was before he went to Spain and Arabella married Adolphus Harrendene? You would be too young, but he was such a light-hearted and happy young man. Never frivolous, I admit, but not as stern as he is now. Losing Racquette didn't help him to recover his old easy ways, either.'

'That does surprise me,' replied Ned. 'I do remember that he used to laugh a lot, and he's not laughed much lately. Harry's changed him, though, hasn't she?' he finished painfully.

'Yes,' said the Duchess. 'You do know that she's not for you, don't you, Ned?' And as he turned scarlet she added kindly, 'You need someone to protect, and, for all her gentleness, Harry is strong. She doesn't need protection, and she'll stand up to Alex. You'll find someone who does need you, one day, you see.'

Alex watched her in some pain. The damage he had done to their relationship as a consequence of his mistaken belief in her bad reputation was plain to see. He was still uncertain how to approach her. Should he tell her of his trip to Netherdene and what he had found there? Was she not likely to say, 'And did it need *that* to convince you that I was pure and true? What self did I show you to make you think otherwise—from our very first encounter? Will doubting Thomas ever believe the truth—even when shown the wounds?'

No, he would not tell her, but try, with his altered manner, to convince her that he had changed completely, and truly wanted her for his wife—without reservations, and that Racquette had nothing to do with it. And that might be difficult—given her maidenly fear of him, which he, himself, had provoked. But he would lay siege to her as subtly as he could.

Like most gentlemen of his class, Alex was sexually experienced, and he had no doubt that, despite her fear, despite her rejection of his proposal, Harry Ashburn was strongly attracted to him, however much she denied it. He must somehow convince her of the depth of his love for her, without his advances ending as they had done so often in the past, in pain and confrontation. He would be gentle and considerate in his lovemaking, and leave no doubt in her mind of his profound respect for her—which, given all that had previously passed between them, might be difficult.

Alex knew that she had refused to go over to Matcham with the other guests to bring Adolphus and Arabella Harrendene back with them, pleading tiredness. He, too, went to Duchess Emily and cried off on some concocted excuse. He saw her sceptical eye on him as he spoke. He thought that she knew what he was about, and had no intention of stopping him from trying to win Harry over.

He made sure that she was alone in the Duchess's little garden-room, where no one would disturb them. All the guests were safely away at Matcham, and it was more than a servant's position was worth to enter a room without being sent for, or otherwise interrupt or accost his or her betters. He found Harry reclining on a sofa before open glass doors; a book was in her hand, but she was doing little reading.

She had seldom looked more charming, wearing a simple cream muslin dress with a low neck, and her hair was even shorter than it had been—dressed like a boy's, her curls framing her face.

'Oh, Cousin Harry, there you are. A turn in the garden, perhaps? The recent shower is over.'

'No,' she replied as she shook her head. She did not want to be too near him, particularly with no other guests about. Paradoxically, since he had ceased to assault or taunt her, by word or deed, she had found herself the more fearful, and, of course, the more powerfully attracted to him. Whether it was being in the country, or whether her senses had been heightened, not only through her previous physical contacts with him, but because she was now living in the same house, and was always aware of his presence, she did not know, but she was more than ever drawn to him.

He pulled up a chair to sit opposite her—a little, but only a little, nearer to her than etiquette demanded, and she now had no means of retreat. Colour mantled her cheeks. She put down her book.

'You are enjoying life here at Oldheath, I think?' His tone was purposefully idle, designed to put her at her ease. This time he would not try to storm the citadel, but would conquer it by using loving guile.

'Indeed,' replied Harry. 'The Duchess is an easy companion.'

'Yes, and she invites pleasant company.' He leaned forward, his grey eyes compelling. 'You are looking well today, Cousin Harry. Simplicity becomes you. I cannot say that of many women.'

He was at last using the formal language of courtship to her, which he had never done before. Again, she hardly knew how to answer him. Her flush grew and her breathing shortened at his nearness, at the scent and presence of the essential Alex. He was now gazing ardently at her. He had never looked more like Gilly as he did so, except that his face was sterner and harder— as Gilly's might have been had he lived. Oh, but she had never felt like this with Gilly!

He picked up the hand which lay nearest to him. 'You will allow me. You have beautiful hands, Cousin Harry. They are one of the features I admire most in a woman.' And he gently kissed the one he was holding, his eyes still on her.

Harry found that she was trembling. 'One?' she said faintly. She found his nearness and his loving words alternately frightening and desirable. She was immediately aware that, if she had wished to deter him, this was not the way to do it.

'There are others.' He was beginning to understand that she was powerless against his irresistible gentleness, whereas his previous approaches, made under his misapprehension of her true nature, had armed her against him.

He tightened his grasp on her hand a little, saying, 'For example, a soft, blushing cheek.' However he had managed it, she did not know, but he was now beside her on the sofa, and it was not her cheek only which received his salutation. In order to kiss it, he had relinquished her hand, taken her, oh, so gently, by the shoulders, and, saying almost under his breath, 'And soft lips,' he was kissing them.

Anything more unlike his previous treatment of her she could not imagine. Her senses reeled, and before she could prevent herself Harry discovered that she was responding strongly to his caresses. The kissing became prolonged and, from being butterflies, which played about her face, soon involved other parts of her person. But her own kisses, first offered in response to the mouth which pleasured her own, took in his warm cheek, and then ran along his jaw, delighting in the faint harshness of his shaven beard, so strong a contrast to her own feminine smoothness. His arms were now around her, her eyes closed, and she was embracing him as passionately as he fondled her.

Meantime, the butterflies travelled down her neck, celebrated the hollows of her throat, and, as Alex found no resistance to his gentle urgency, but rather, willing co-operation, his own passion mounted. He had begun by wishing to initiate her to a little restrained love-making, suited to an untried girl, but her response fuelled his passion, and he was now beyond reason, beyond caution, only aware that he had in his arms the woman he had always wanted, but had never thought he would ever meet. The woman whose mind and body alike complemented his.

He slipped the light dress from her shoulders to reveal her beautiful unbound breasts, and began to kiss them. On the stairs at Rule only his hand had stroked them, through her confining clothes, but now his lips and tongue caressed them, rousing her slumbering senses. 'Oh, delectable,' he said, his voice muffled. 'Oh, delectable—roses drowned in cream.' And she hardly knew what he was saying as she gasped with pleasure. Even more delectable to Harry were the sensations he was producing in her. Reason had flown, and bodily delight was all.

Harry's lovemaking became as active as Alex's. She

had a burning urgency to please the body which was so busy pleasing her, and somehow they arrived on the floor—how, she never quite knew, or how a cushion had found itself under her head.

And her clothes—what had happened to them? Nothing, but nothing, mattered, only that he was now above her, and was murmuring, 'Oh, my love, my love, my pure white lily, my day star.' They were not only exchanging kisses, but his hands were everywhere— above, around, about, below, in the words of a poem she had once read.

Particularly below. For he was touching her there— there, in her most secret parts, where no man had ever been. For Alex was now quite lost, since gentle and loving affection had brought to him what exasperated, resentful desire could never bring—a willing, passionate woman in his arms, on fire as he was for the final consummation of what had lain between them since their first meeting in the rose-garden at Rule. 'Oh,' she cried, as he stroked and fondled her in the very gate of love, 'oh.' And she was overcome with wave after wave of pleasure. Oh, what is he doing to me—and what can I do for him? she thought desperately.

And what was she doing, for and to him? For was it not Cousin Harry who had undone his cravat, unbuttoned his shirt to put her hands and arms and her own body against *him*, not his clothes? To feel the strength of him, the muscles hidden by his needless clothes, the body, hardened by war and exercise, so ready and fit to be the instrument to pleasure her. His mouth on her breast, her breast in his mouth, her child and her lover at one and the same time. 'Oh, please,' she cried, 'oh, please.' And what was she asking for, but him, to accept him fully, to be one with him? And she cried, 'Oh, please,' again, arching her body so that his questing hands might quest more easily.

And her own questing hands, which had learned to make love without ever having been taught—for she was as witty in the erotic arts as ever he could have hoped she would be—found the core of him at last, and knew that he was ready for her, that this was what she had been born to do—every loving woman's destiny. . .except that then, at the very last moment, as she lay open and willing for him to take her—only then, reason gasped suddenly in her ear, as it lay dying, almost dead, killed by passion, What are you doing? You are a virgin; how will he feel when he discovers that? For he thinks quite otherwise, and in your wantonness you have done nothing to undeceive him. And, more prosaically, What will it do to the carpet? How to explain *that*? A thought of such stunning and dreadful anticlimax that her gasps of passion became gasps of something else, even as she simultaneously thought, Oh, but I want him, I do, I do, but not here, not now, not like this. What shall we both feel afterwards, all rules of conduct broken, passion spent? and, pulling away, she said, 'No, Alex, no. We must stop.'

'Too late,' he replied thickly. 'I love you and want you so much, my darling. Too late now.' And he readied himself to take her, but she wrenched away, pushing against his chest, compelling him to look, lost in passion though he was, into her eyes.

'Oh, no, Alex, you must stop at once; however much we want each other now, we shall regret this afterwards. Only consider, I was never truly a wife.' And her reasoned words, so different from the murmured and wild endearments of a moment ago, restored him to reason, too, reminding him that he was seducing, for seduction it was, a young and innocent girl, however much his own lovemaking had helped to transform her into his willing partner in passion.

'Oh, God,' he moaned, rolling away from her, almost in pain from desire, frustrated at the very last fence of all. 'How did I bring us both to this? I only meant to show you that you loved me, not dishonour you as I so nearly did. Not force you. . .'

'No force,' said Harry, sitting up, her mouth swollen
with passion, trying to pull her discarded clothes about
her, suddenly conscious of her semi-nakedness. 'I was
your willing accomplice. Oh, I am as wanton as they say
my mother was, for I still want you most desperately,
and how I wish I had not stopped you.' And she began
to cry, her own frustrated body taking its revenge.

Alex hardly heard what she said. Whatever he had
intended, it was not this.

He, too, ordered himself, cursing mutely at buttons
and straps, and all the impedimenta of living, turning at
last to her as she, too, sat restored to order on the sofa.

Impetuously, he knelt down beside her, put a loving
arm around her shoulders, and murmured, 'Oh, do not
distress yourself, my darling. Forgive me, forgive me, if
you can, for all that I have said and done to you since we
first met. No excuse which I can offer you can lessen my
offence, or my own share in your unhappiness, for, as I
have come to love you, I should have known that you
were what you appeared to be, and not what others said
you were. I can only hope that what I said and did then,
and just now, will not prevent you from accepting me—
for surely you cannot now refuse to marry me, my own
love. All the ties of affection, and closeness of mind and
body, bring us together. That, you can hardly deny after
this afternoon. Oh, Harry, be my wife, I beg of you.
Good and true as you are, you are all I want.'

'Good and true,' she repeated, almost bitterly, looking
away. 'Oh, you were right to doubt me, when I am so
wanton that you have merely to kiss me, and I was
willing to be your mistress on the instant. You cannot
want such a creature.'

'I know now that what was said of you and my cousin
was a lie,' he replied, voice impassioned. 'Oh, Harry,
you only behaved as you did because you truly love me,
as I know I now love you. Oh, why do you hesitate?'

'Because I fear that, once married, I might as easily

dishonour you. You know what they say of my mother. I fear I may be the same.'

He took her hand. 'I know what they said of you, and I went to Norfolk and discovered they were wrong. Oh, Harry, I know the true story of your marriage to my cousin Gilbert. I have no fear of you.'

The tears ran down her face. 'Oh, how I wish I could say yes to you. You must let me think, Alex, give me a little time for me to find out what I truly am. I wish to be sure that I am fit to be your wife.'

'But if I have no doubts now, whatever I said before. . .' he began.

She put her finger on his lips. 'Oh, hush, my darling——' and the endearment nearly unmanned him '—forget the past. You have offered for me and spoken to me in honour, at last, and I, too, must behave honourably. I cannot answer you now, but I will do so as soon as I may. Grant me that.' And in honour he was compelled to agree.

The man who had once wished to shame the woman he had thought a Circe and a temptress was now the man who wished to convince her of her innocence, of her fitness to be his wife. 'I cannot think,' he said, 'that the old scandal matters, or that it can possibly affect you, and I also know that I am partly responsible, by my behaviour since I met you, for your self-doubts. I will give you the time that you need. Tomorrow I leave for Allerton. You must visit me there. I shall not compel you, my darling. I shall always remain your humble and faithful lover, whatever you decide, but I pray that you will decide for me. See my home, before you make your final decision.' He paused, and added, 'I must know. It is not because I remind you painfully of my cousin Gilbert, I trust? I understand that I look very like him, which makes my recent behaviour to you seem even worse.'

'Oh, no,' said Harry, glad to reassure him over something, however small. 'You are like Gilly, but that is an advantage, you know. He was so good and true.'

Well, he had to be content with that when he had hoped for more. But he was not sure that he even deserved that, and he left her in the garden-room, their battleground of love and renunciation.

CHAPTER EIGHTEEN

HERVEY NUN'STER walked down to dinner, on the evening of the day on which Alex proposed to Harry, well pleased with himself. He had persuaded Gerald Illingworth to invite him to Oldheath when he knew Harry Ashburn would be there, and he hoped that when he finally moved against her he would not fail as his men had failed him at Vauxhall.

He had arrived at about the time that Arabella and her husband had come from Matcham, and there had been no sign of Harry. At dinner he thought that she looked rather pale, and wondered what was troubling her. He watched as first Arabella and then Alex Templestowe approached her in the drawing-room after dinner, Arabella drawling at her, 'Are you quite well, Mrs Ashburn? You look a little wan.' She was on her highest ropes, and Harry was well aware that she was not looking her best.

Alex's intervention, and his quiet concern for her, touched her, particularly the way in which he protected her from Arabella, and later from Nun'ster, who came up, all obsequious attention.

Duchess Emily's shrewd eyes were on her, too, and she whispered briefly to Harry, 'Come to my room for a tisane before you retire, child. You look in need of a restorative.'

Well, at least, she thought wryly, my looks today are such that they will not attract Nun'ster. But she was wrong there. He had suddenly discovered a strange desire to protect her—at the same time that he was plotting to ravish her.

Alex went to his room that night in some mental and physical distress. He disliked himself for his treatment of Harry. He had begun his lovemaking lightly enough. He had certainly not had any intention of seducing her, but, once he'd had her in his arms, and had received her ardent response, his feelings for her, coupled with his own starved senses, had nearly betrayed them both. The sight of her face at dinner had been almost more disturbing than her demeanour after his conduct of the afternoon. Worse, he had created in himself a strong physical desire for her which could not be satisfied. He wanted her for the companion he had always hoped a wife might be, but now he also wanted her in his bed, and knew by the passion that she had displayed that she reciprocated both sets of his feelings, even though she had refused his proposal.

He had earlier dismissed Forbes for the night, telling his valet that he would manage for himself—he did not want company—and he began to undress by the light of the one candelabra on the tall chest of drawers by the door. He pulled off his elaborate cravat, and tossed it on the chair near the window. His shirt followed, and as he drew it over his head he thought that he heard a slight noise from the curtained bed.

Surprised, he turned, and, the noise coming again, he walked over, and pulled back the curtains. Arabella lay there, propped up against the pillows, hair streaming over them. The sheet was up to her chin. She smiled at him provocatively, and then slowly lowered the sheet to reveal herself as naked, and her magnificent body had seldom looked more desirable.

Alex stood there, his own torso remarkable in the candle-light. Despite himself the sight of her, displayed for his taking, roused him. To his disgust and shame he knew that only by the strongest exercise of will could he prevent himself from going over to her and doing with her exactly what she wished.

And it would be an exercise of the coldest lust, the satisfaction of an appetite, an itch, partly created by his experience of the afternoon, mere sexual gymnastics—

for he felt for her no love or affection, not even friendship, but an active dislike, compounded by this
behaviour.

Her whole expression changed. 'Oh, yes,' she said
triumphantly. 'Not so saintly after all, Alex. Yes, you
may come to me.' And her eyes devoured him.

'No,' he stated, and rage replaced desire. 'I don't want
you. Go. You have a husband down the corridor.'

'In a separate room,' she said. 'And never tell me that
you didn't want me when you saw me. I know better.'

'No,' he conceded, staring at her, face inimical, 'you
are right. But I don't bed in lust with whores, Arabella.
And your price is too high. I won't pay you with my
honour.'

'Your honour, Alex?' Her smile was ugly. 'Never tell
me you haven't had your share of women.'

'Any I had were mine because I chose them, and joyed
in and with them. To come to you, feeling nothing for
you, would be a betrayal. You compel me to say this to
you, Arabella. It gives me no pleasure. Now go.'

'I will not,' she said. 'I intend to stay. Damn you for a
high-minded prig, and damn her, too, for coming
between us.'

'There has been nothing to come between these many
years, and you know it. If you will not go, Arabella, I
shall ring for Forbes, and wake the house. You must
accept what follows as I shall. I do not think that you
want an open scandal.'

'You would not dare,' she said.

'Then try me.' He walked to the bell-pull. 'I shall not
like being Joseph, and you will not enjoy being
Potiphar's wife, but, unless you leave, those are the parts
we shall play.' And he made to pull it.

She knew that he meant what he said. Rage and
desolation swept through her. She dared not be ruined.

'Oh, damn you, damn you. Why do you always deny
me?' And she bent down and began to pull on the bed-
gown she had abandoned on the floor.

'I did not deny you, Arabella. You denied me when you betrayed our betrothal to marry Harrendene. You lost me then, and you must accept it.'

'I accept nothing.' She was at the door. 'You hear me, Alex? Nothing. As for Harrendene, he does not care what I do.'

'I think that you are mistaken. There are some things he draws the line at, and you would do well not to cross that line.'

The look she gave him as she left was pure malignance, and he shuddered at it.

Harry went to Duchess Emily's room before retiring to her own. The Duchess had asked her to share her nightly tisane with her—the herbal drink designed to help her to sleep. The two women sat talking together, the Duchess shrewdly trying to put Harry at her ease. She had no clue to what had passed between her and Alex, but she knew that something had occurred to distress them both. Despite the difference between their ages, the two women were good companions. Feeling a little calmer, Harry finally rose, taking up her candle. 'I must go,' she said reluctantly. 'Hannah will be tired.'

The Duchess kissed her on the cheek. 'I know,' she replied, 'I keep you too long. But you are the daughter I never had. Sleep well. I am sorry that Arabella is here to tease you, but the Duke is an old friend of Harrendene's, and wants him at Oldheath, even if he rarely comes out to see him! You see what an odd life we live. He makes so few demands on me, I feel that I have to satisfy this one, little though I like her.'

The candle threw strange shadows along the corridor as Harry walked towards her room. On the way she had to pass Alex's room, but, before she reached it, the door opened, and Arabella emerged, hair tumbled, bed-gown clutched around her, feet bare, an abandoned picture of disarray.

Harry stared at her, aghast. Arabella carefully shut the

door behind her, and walked towards her, eyes glittering triumphantly.

'Well met,' she drawled. 'I know that you are discreet and will say nothing. Alex and I must have our meetings, you know. Harrendene is a dead bore in bed and out of it. Alex now. . .' And her smile was a Gorgon's rictus for Harry.

A cold despair, mixed with a profound sense of betrayal, swept over Harry. She said drily, through a closed throat, 'What you and Alex do is nothing to me, Arabella.'

'I thought not. Most happy to hear it,' smiled Arabella, for whom this meeting had come pat on the hour. Let his saintly lordship wonder why his jumped-up house-maid refused to smile on him tomorrow. He might be glad of Arabella's company yet.

'Goodnight,' she said, and her smile was sweet poison. 'Sleep well. I know that I shall.' And she gave a lascivious yawn.

Well, thought Harry, as she watched Arabella go, true love and eternal devotion, indeed. That didn't last many hours, did it, Alex? What an exciting day you had. You nearly convinced me of your sincerity this afternoon. But that was this afternoon. By night you were ready for Arabella again. I told her the truth; you are nothing to me. But she knew that she lied, and, once in her bed, sleep was long in coming. For could it be that Racquette was what he really wanted, and that Arabella was still, after all, his true love?

For Alex, too, sleep was a luxury he could not achieve. He almost regretted refusing Arabella. He could have used that lovely body and then pitched her out of his room; it was all that she deserved. But to have done so would have broken every rule of life which he had laid down for himself. Besides that, the thought of Harry, as he had seen her that day, her face in pleasure with him, and in distress at him, demanded that he keep his

honour, however much the body's demands urged him
to other courses.

Wearily he sat up, relit the candle, and picked up from
his bedside table the heavy volume of Gibbon's *Decline
and Fall*, which he had borrowed from the Duke's
library, and which he had begun to read earlier. The
sweeping cadences of the long sentences might lull his
mind to sleep, and would stop him from thinking of the
two women who filled his mind. Opening the book, he
gave a rueful grin. Women had always been on the
periphery of his busy life; it was strange to find them
occupying the centre.

Hannah Pye was laying out Harry's clothes for the
morning on the big table in the window of her bedroom.
Harry was propped up against the pillows drinking tea;
her face was white, and there were purple smudges of
sleeplessness under her eyes.

Hannah was no fool. She had eyes and ears, and knew
what her so-called betters were up to. The relationship
between Alex and Harry was the gossip of the servants'
hall. Forbes, Alex's valet, was of the opinion that his
master was hooked at last. No one could understand why
Mrs Gilly was so adamant in refusing him. Forbes was
sure that he had offered, and that Mrs Gilly had a *tendre*
for him—a statement which Hannah could not deny,
whatever her mistress said. She turned briskly towards
the bed.

'I don't know what you think you're at, Miss
Harry——' Mrs Ashburn and Mrs Gilly did not exist in
Hannah's world '—moping and mooning about as you
are. Lord Templestowe is more than taken with you, and
you care for him. So what's all the to-do about?'

Harry looked brokenly at her. 'You are mistaken. He
cares for Arabella. Arabella says——'

'Arabella says,' scoffed Hannah, rudely breaking in on
her mistress, and derisively echoing her. 'I wouldn't trust
a word that hussy says. If she recited the Lord's Prayer

I'd have to think that there was something wrong with it. She's man-mad, and the man she's maddest for is him. I can't say that I blame her, mind, except that she's such a—no, I can't say the word, Miss Harry, but you surely know what I mean.'

Yes, Miss Harry surely did. And Hannah hadn't seen Arabella coming out of Alex's room looking as though she and Alex had gone several rounds together, reminding her only too strongly of her own behaviour yesterday. She went hot all over.

Hannah came to the bed, bed-gown in hand, stared at her, and exclaimed, 'Oh, Miss Harry, do you have the fever?' placing a large hand on her forehead, and looking at her mistress in some puzzlement. 'You'd best stay in bed.'

'Oh, no!' Harry almost leapt out. Bed was the last place she wanted to be, the very last. Out in the open, on a horse, galloping vigorously, or in the library, trying to construe a really hard piece of Livy, anything to take her mind off its appalling obsession with what old Mr Wentworth had once coyly called 'Cupid's affairs'.

She remembered wistfully how heartily she had laughed at the mere idea of troubling about such unlikely matters, as Hannah turned her about, and made her ready for the day. It must be having so little to do now that she was a fine lady which was causing such dreadful thoughts. Livy, that was it. She had told Gilly in his last illness that she would never neglect the Classics, and she would keep to her word. The library after breakfast. The very thing. Ut with the subjunctive ought to be enough to put out any flame!

Accordingly, after breakfast Harry repaired to the library. Arabella had offered a walk in the grounds, but she had refused, saying gaily, 'Thank you. But I have work to do in the library. You will excuse me. Take Mrs Whitmore instead.' For that lady had no wish to practise scholarship with Harry.

'The library?' Arabella had echoed, as though Harry

had said the madhouse, or the infirmary for poor women. 'Is there such a place?' And she had laughed as though Harry were simple-minded. 'A bluestocking, then. I had not thought that of you. Well, that short-sighted badger who is allowed to share the dining table with us will be pleased. You are welcome to him.'

Short-sighted badger! thought Harry indignantly, as kind Mr Forsythe made her welcome, beaming at her over his half-moon glasses, and taking her to the two large bookcases where the Classics, Greek and Latin, stood row upon row in order behind the latticed doors, which he opened to fetch out a splendid Livy, bound in red morocco, heavily gilt.

'And here is Caesar also,' he said. 'The Duke will be so happy to learn that one of his guests will find pleasure here. Lord Templestowe always borrows from us when he stays, but prefers to work in his room.'

He helped her to carry the book, and a Latin dictionary, over to a table near the fire. The library was in a cold room which the sun rarely entered. 'Deliberately planned,' he explained, 'to avoid fading the bindings.'

Above the fire was a portrait of a handsome young man with a melancholy face, standing before the Priory, dim in the background. Mr Forsythe noticed her gazing at it. 'The Duke when young,' he said, 'by Romney. One of his best. The room is full of treasures, as you see.' And, when Harry expressed interest in them, he took her on a grand tour of the porcelain, cameos, medals, statues, and priceless paintings, which included a Titian, a Tintoretto and a huge Canaletto.

Finally she sat down, opened the Livy and the big commonplace-book Gilly had given her, bound in blue leather, with her name on the first page in Gilly's beautiful script: 'To my dear wife, Harry Ashburn'. She had filled the first twenty pages in her own careful hand with a translation done with him in his last days as he had lain helpless, and now she would continue with it as he had wished, and she had promised.

She was so engrossed that she did not hear someone enter until a shadow crossed her page and she looked up. An unassuming small man was lifting a folio from the big map-case close by her. He was wearing an old blue coat, faded and worn, cream knee-breeches, with darned silk stockings. His hair was long and tied back with a ribbon in the fashion of the last century, and his shoes were shabby and unpolished. For a moment she thought that he was an upper servant or an assistant to Mr Forsythe, who was hovering anxiously, and then she realised that he was a faded and diminished version of the man in the painting over the fire. It was the reclusive Duke, Emily's husband, rarely seen by anyone, even by her.

'You will allow me to share your table?' he said gently.

'With pleasure,' she replied.

He lifted the atlas he had chosen on the table. Before he opened it he came over to her, and, saying, 'With your permission, may I?' he turned the book from which she had been working towards him.

'Livy?' he observed in some surprise, and then looked at her commonplace-book and the translation which she had been writing in it, and at her elegant script. 'A strange choice for a young lady.'

'Not my choice originally,' she admitted, not quite sure how to address him, but he was being agreeably informal with her, and she repaid the compliment. 'But translating from the Latin is a good discipline for the mind, my late husband said.'

'Indeed. A most discerning young man. And you must be Harriet Ashburn, as I suspected.' He still made no effort to introduce himself. 'Most young ladies would prefer Mrs Radcliffe or Miss Clara Reeve.'

'For entertainment,' she replied coolly, although her heart was beating unaccountably fast, 'not for instruction. And even for entertainment I prefer Miss Jane Austen.'

He surveyed her equally coolly. 'You are a remarkable young lady, which does not surprise me. I knew your mother once. A most beautiful woman.'

Still cool, she gave him her usual answer. 'I am not much like her, I fear.'

'No, indeed,' he confirmed, almost idly. 'But beauty is not everything, you know. A good heart, now, and an intellect, last longer than looks. I do not demean your mother. She had great qualities too. And you like my library, Forsythe tells me. That says much for you.'

Harry could not prevent herself from wondering what he would have made of the true reason for her presence. She had the uncomfortable feeling that he would have appreciated it, and even gently applauded it.

He indicated the atlas to which he had returned. 'I think that you would appreciate this, Cousin Harry. I am told that is your sobriquet. I like it. We are, I believe, distantly related.'

'I did not know that,' she said, as she admired a pair of engraved cherubs blowing a gale across the Far Pacific.

'Oh, indeed. You may call me Hornsea, or Cousin Charles, whichever you please. I see you like my folio, too.'

'Yes, Cousin Charles,' she replied, feeling that it would be appropriate to meet his informality with her own. A Duke, no less, claiming to be her cousin. She could not believe it, and wondered why he made the claim.

Coffee was brought in, and they were to take it together, he said. But not before a visitor arrived. It was Alex. He stared at them, a little surprised.

'You sent for me, Charles?'

'I think so,' said Hornsea vaguely. 'Yes, so I did. You know Cousin Harry, I believe. Now I remember. I thought it fit that three book-lovers should come together. You will be careful with my Gibbon,

Templestowe. The author kindly wrote me a message in it.'

'So I saw,' replied Alex, taking his coffee from Mr Forsythe—a happy man, with three people appreciating his work.

'And Cousin Harry is construing Livy,' said the Duke idly. 'A strange occupation for a young lady, but I suppose that she has a reason for it.' And he turned his vague smile on her.

'My cousin Gilbert's influence, I imagine,' commented Alex.

Harry regarded him over her coffee-cup. He did not look as though he had spent part of the night pleasuring Arabella, she had to grant him that. She hurled a dart at him; he looked so pleased with himself.

'Better than our mastering Ovid's *Art of Love*,' she said defiantly. 'But I suppose that is more in your line.'

'Oh, no,' denied the Duke, not at all put out at hearing this rather unladylike remark, although Harry was delighted to see that Alex looked a little miffed. 'Vegetius's *Art of War*, perhaps, seeing that he was a soldier, or even Machiavelli's *Prince*—to celebrate his diplomacy, my dear—would be the most appropriate of all. I'm pleased to note that you have a ready wit. To be too virtuous is not really a virtue at all.' He, too, drank his coffee, talked to them a little, then rose. 'I would wish you to be friends. Pray oblige me. I must leave you. Over-much excitement is bad for me.'

They watched him depart. He looked like a poor clerk, not like one of the richest men in England.

'I suppose we must do as we are told,' smiled Harry.

'Indeed,' said Alex; he seemed to have forgiven her for her poisoned dart, or had he not noticed it? 'Forsythe will tell you that we are both greatly honoured. Is not that so, sir?'

'I cannot remember when the Duke spoke to other than his servants and staff,' said Mr Forsythe, 'and I could not but overhear that he spoke to you, Mrs

Ashburn, as I have not heard him speak to a stranger for
these many years. Lord Templestowe is rare in that the
Duke insists on meeting him for a little whenever he
visits. I think that we can say that you are added to the
few to whom he speaks.'

He bowed himself away.

Harry poured herself and Alex more coffee. They were
awkward with one another, for a variety of reasons.
Unaware of Arabella's lie, Alex was easier than Harry;
he continued to speak of the Duke. 'He expects me to
come to stay at least once a year, and will then perhaps
see me once. Now that he has done so I may return to
Allerton. I am needed there. Absentee landlords are not
good for the tenants. One forgets their needs, and
particularly in hard times such as these.'

Harry thought that Alex was the first 'great one'—for
so she thought of her new companions—the first 'Lord
of Creation', as a wit had once called them, who had ever
acknowledged to her the existence of those who supported their beautiful but idle lives. She, too, must
remember those who supported her, and not stay away
overlong, enjoying herself.

'And you will come to Ailerton, Cousin Harry,' he
said, his eyes warm on her, 'as I asked yesterday. It is an
easy journey from here, and the Duchess will be happy
to escort you. Allerton is a manor house, smaller than
Rule, not grand like the Priory or Racquette, but, of all
my homes, it is my favourite.'

His happy enthusiasm and his care for those who
depended on him softened Harry towards him again.
Useless to repine over him and Arabella, far better to
enjoy his company; he rarely spoke to Arabella in public,
and she felt another wave of heat pass over her as she
wondered of what they talked when they were in bed
together, and for the first time she felt a little doubt as to
what she had really seen the night before. Could it be
true that he had gone straight from his impassioned and
loving words into Arabella's arms? Was he really so

lacking in honour? After all, he had allowed the world's gossips to delude him into believing that she was a harpy and more. Was it equally possible that Arabella was lying and blackening him?

Useless to speculate, to allow suspicion to poison and distress her, when she was already distressed by her own passionate responses, and the whispered gossip of the past. She must solve her own problems before she passed judgement on others. Accordingly, when Alex asked her to ride out with him that afternoon, before he left for Allerton, she agreed, and when they returned, after a companionable hour, spent for once in peace, and he said, holding her hand, 'You will beware of Nun'ster, I hope. I do not like the way he looks at you,' she did not fly at him, or argue, but said, in her gravest manner,

'You may be sure I will be careful, Alex.'

And on his replying, 'And you will give me your answer soon?' his grey eyes steady on her own, she nodded mutely, and for once they parted in amity, and, as he walked away from her, straight-backed, a soldier in mufti, she was half ready to call him back and give him his answer immediately—but the shadow of Arabella still lay a little between them, as well as her own self-doubt.

CHAPTER NINETEEN

ALEX was gone. And life was empty without him.
Distressing to enter a room to find that he was not there,
to walk in the gardens, and not hope to see him,
treacherous Plato, who had deserted the Duchess for
him, trotting always at his heels. Plato, who was desolate,
as Harry was, who roved the house and gardens looking
for him. Seated on the stone bench, she scratched the
dog's ears. 'You miss him, too,' she said softly, and
thought, Well, there is one thing which comforts me. I
do not only want him to love me, to take me to bed, but
I want his companionship—to talk to him, as I used to
talk to Gilly, on equal terms, mind to mind. It is not
only his body I want—but him. All of him. And I am
sure that he feels the same.

She tried to avoid the others, spending long hours in
the library, where Nun'ster never came, which surprised
her, for he had shown himself a man of learning,
interested in things of the mind. He hardly spoke to her,
but when he did his manner was impeccable, grave and
respectful, except once, when they were alone, he said,
quietly—which made it worse—'I hope you do not think
that I have forgot what I said to you—I mean to have
you, you know.' And then was all reserve again.

But something the Duke said revealed why Nun'ster
avoided the library. One morning, as she sat working,
the Duke, who had walked over to the window, uttered
a short, but undistinguishable word, and then said to
her, 'Mrs Ashburn. A word of advice,' his voice mild but
authoritative. 'I see that cur Nun'ster is here. Avoid him.
He should not be in my house. I will speak to
Illingworth. He must be asked to leave as soon as is
decent, and must not be invited here again.'

It was the longest speech he had made for some time, and must have overset him, because he left before coffee arrived, leaving his book open. A thing he rarely did.

She did not tell the others of her unusual relationship with the Duke, nor did she allow herself ever to be alone with Nun'ster. She used Mrs Whitmore as a shield, and that lady was a little surprised to find Harry as dependent on her as she had been in her early days in Society.

She also avoided Arabella, but this was not difficult. Now that Alex had gone, Arabella ceased to tease her, choosing instead to adopt a pleasant manner to her, particularly when the Duchess Emily was about.

One reason why Nun'ster was not allowed to approach her overmuch was that Adolphus Harrendene, who always seemed so vague and indifferent to what was going on around him, took to appearing suddenly whenever Nun'ster attempted to manoeuvre her into a tête-à-tête.

Harrendene would wander into the room where they were, and strike up an idle conversation. Harry wished that she could thank him for his intervention—she was sure that it was deliberate—and it certainly annoyed Nun'ster.

She came to the conclusion that Harrendene must be watching both his wife and Nun'ster—perhaps, remarkably, seeing them as accomplices. Arabella became quite savage with her husband as his usual quiet sufferance of her behaviour changed into something more rigorous. He took to demanding her company with him when he went riding or driving, even on several occasions at night almost ordering that she retire at the same time as he did, although it was an open secret that they occupied separate rooms.

Well, he said that he would protect me, if he could, thought Harry, and it is plain that he means to do as he promised. One evening, shortly after Alex had left, he asked Harry to play chess with him, countermanding Arabella's suggestion that she and Harry stroll together in the Italian garden, where she planned to leave her to Nun'ster.

'You have monopolised Mrs Ashburn long enough, my dear,' he said in his kind, vague way which always reminded Harry of the Duke, 'and Mrs Ashburn is the only person here, now that Alex has gone, who can offer me a reasonable game. You may walk tomorrow; the gardens are at their best during the day, after all.'

One more piece of annoyance to add to the tally Arabella had begun to keep of her husband's offences. What could be the matter with the man? Surely he had not developed a *tendre* for the milkmaid?—all Arabella's demeaning epithets for Harry were now agricultural. Since Alex's departure Dolly had become positively odious, had even reprimanded her for her friendship with Nun'ster, if you please.

'Well, who am I to engage with, then?' she said. 'First I am to avoid the Templestowes, and now Nun'ster incurs your prohibition. Do you wish me a nun?'

'Rather that than your present behaviour. You grow sour, Arabella; it does not become you.'

This was too much like Nun'ster's unpleasant sneers to be comfortable.

'You used not to mind my friends.'

'You used to choose them with a little more discretion.'

He had treated her with such idle kindness and leniency that she had become contemptuous of him— had forgotten what a good mind he possessed. Watching him play chess with Harry, she was consumed with anger at him, an anger which was all too common these days, and was beginning to pull her face into ugly lines.

Nun'ster thought this as he came to sit beside her.

'Why so troubled?' he drawled.

'Oh, does it show?' She tried to be light. 'My wretched husband seeks to choose my friends for me. You and I are too much together, forsooth.'

'He may be right at that,' Nun'ster said coolly. He might use Arabella. He did not have to like her. 'It

would not do for us to be seen as possible conspirators—
we must be more apart in future.'

'And that will be a bore, too,' she moaned, angry
again. 'Who else is there to talk to here who has any wit
or spirit?'

'Oh, you flatter me,' he answered, thinking what a
shrew she was becoming. 'But we must satisfy your
husband if I am to succeed without suspicion. I bid you
good evening, Lady Harrendene.' And he strolled off,
leaving Arabella impotent and angry, nothing going right
any more, anywhere, and all since the cottager's daughter
had come on the scene. Well, Nun'ster willing, she might
be off it soon.

So Harry was a little protected from her tormentor,
but, oh, how she missed Alex! Mind and body both. She
ached, yes, she ached to see him again, and hung on to
the Duchess's promise that they would visit Allerton
soon. She missed Ned, too. Missed his eager puppying
about her, as Plato, the Duchess's spaniel, missed Alex,
still mournfully sniffing around the men's feet in search
of the man he had fixed his heart on.

I am like Plato, but even less dignified, if possible,
thought Harry. What a fool I was to let ridiculous
scruples move me to reject him. The remembered scene
in the garden-room no longer had the power to disturb
her, for it had told her that, whatever her mind and her
reason said and did, her heart and body were telling her
quite another thing. And Alex had been right about that,
and suddenly to throw away such a prospect of fulfilled
and mutual passion with the man she loved because of
misgivings about her own character and her mother's
seemed an offence against nature.

Alex had been gone a week when the Duchess proposed
a visit to Allerton, providing the weather held, she said.
These mid-September days, indeed, were kinder than
summer had been. As soon as Allerton was mentioned
Arabella was in a passion to go. She positively demanded

that the visit take place at the earliest possible opportunity, disregarding her husband's lack of enthusiasm
for it. They led separate lives. On several occasions
Harrendene had entered the library, a little surprised to
find Harry working there, the Duke beside her. At
Harrendene's entrance the Duke always left, despite his
long friendship with him.

As for Arabella, Alex's summary rejection of her had
not diminished her desire for him. It was now mixed
with an equally strong rage to punish both him and
Harry, to make them suffer as she was suffering. He
shall crawl to me yet, she thought, and, as for the
milkmaid, I shall feed her to Nun'ster if I get half a
chance.

Arabella agonised over what to wear to visit Allerton.
Harry dressed herself sensibly in a blue dress of light
wool, buttoned to the neck with a piecrust frill, and
strong stout shoes, rather than her usual kid slippers.
The Duchess put hampers of cold food, meat, fish, game
and poultry, fruit, new baked loaves and a pound cake
into the boot of the Hornsea coach—'For Allerton is
small. Alex will not have prepared for us. He will have
his own wine cellar, and we can either lunch al fresco, or
in his dining-room.'

Only the presence of Nun'ster, fortunately not in her
carriage, by the Duchess's contriving, although Harry
did not know this, cast a shadow on Harry's day. The
journey was pleasant. They drove up a good road to the
north; Arabella had insisted on travelling with Harry,
removing Mrs Whitmore to her husband's carriage, so
that she could be with Gerald Illingworth, whom, failing
Alex, she was determined to charm.

'Harrendene is so slow,' she said, 'he is sure to fall
behind. I like to be in advance of time, don't you?' she
flung at Harry, who, if she had dared, would have left
instead of Mrs Whitmore, had not Arabella made such a
point of wishing her company. Seeing that she spent the
whole journey overtly holding Harry up for ridicule to

the two Lansdens, who travelling with them, Harry wondered at her own patience in the face of such open provocation.

First, Arabella drawled amusement at Harry's strong shoes. 'Are you expecting to speed the plough, Mrs Ashburn?' Then it was her sketch-book and pencil-case which drew her scornful attention. 'Amateur art is so distressing.' And finally, 'Of course, the country is your spiritual home. I suppose that explains all.'

'"All" being?' Harry could not help saying, feeling dangerously near committing some social *bêtise*, such as giving Arabella a firm smack, and telling her to leave off her tantrums. She could only suppose that the proximity of Alex was causing this behaviour.

'Your devotion to the bucolic, to the countryside, Mrs Ashburn.'

'But it is the countryside which keeps us all in ease and idleness,' said Harry.

'Oh, what a quaint notion. Do not so dignify the peasantry, I beg of you, Mrs Ashburn. They need not toil for me.'

In the face of such idiocy, moral and practical, Harry had no answer. She fell silent, and enjoyed the views of the wooded countryside, blotting out Arabella's virtually ceaseless conversation.

They passed through Allerton village, which was charming, an antidote to other villages which they had passed through, which had been full of thin-faced women, idle men, and starving children. With its well-kept cottages, surrounded by pretty gardens, rows of cabbages among the flowers, Allerton was all that one imagined a village ought to be. Beyond it were fields where the perilously late harvest was being gathered. The carriages stopped, at the Duchess's orders, at the edge of a very large field where carts and wagons stood surrounded by men, women and children, carrying food for the men who were scything the corn. Some were binding sheaves, others, in the distance, were hooking

those made earlier on to other waiting carts. Stripped to
the waist, and sweating in the autumn sun, the reapers
advanced in a diagonal line. The leader was singing, and
the scythes swung in time to his song.

It was only as they approached the spot where the
carriages had stopped that the watching gentry realised
that in the middle of the long line, dressed like his
labourers, his red hair a beacon in the sun, Alex
Templestowe was taking part in the work of his farm.
He was so intent on keeping up his rhythm, conscious
that he lacked the practice of his fellows, that unlike
them he was unaware of the spectators.

'Good God, that's surely Templestowe, or one of his
father's mistakes,' drawled Illingworth from his seat on
his carriage's box. 'Yes, Templestowe it is. What a fellow
he is, to be sure.' As the labourers ended their task, and
leaned on their scythes, he put his hands round his
mouth and hallooed through them. 'Templestowe, you
dog. What next? Muck-spreading? We've come to join
you tête-à-tête, not plough the fields and scatter.'

Alex, panting slightly, sweat running down his chest
and shoulders, looked up at the shout. A grin spread
over his face as he walked towards them. He took a towel
from one of the attendant women who were now handing
drinks about, and accepted a tankard of ale himself.

'Thirsty work,' he said, after he had drained it to the
dregs, and wiped his mouth as his men did with the back
of his hand.

Harry was staring at him nearly as hard as Arabella;
the other women looked away. The gentlemen were
amused. So that is what he looks like stripped, thought
Harry, who had never seen men's bodies so plainly
before. They were Greek statues come to life, but
exciting in a way cold marble could never be. Even in
the garden-room she had not seen as much of him as
this.

Alex was pulling a shirt over his head. 'I shall see you

all later when I'm respectable. You know the way to the manor, I'm sure.'

And they all drove off, the men, women, children and barking dogs looking after them, before sitting down to eat their lunch in the kind shadow of the hedge.

'Dear me,' said Harry, in as good an imitation of Arabella's drawl as she could achieve, 'I fear that poor Alex is being most unfashionably bucolic.' And for once Arabella found it difficult to reply, contenting herself with making a moue, thinking savagely, No wonder he prefers the milkmaid if he wishes to be a labourer himself, and then, when they had finally arrived at the manor, patronising the housekeeper and the servants who came out on to the gravel sweep to assist them.

They all sat down to their luncheon, spread out on the great oak table, dating from medieval times, in the main room at Allerton. The room occupied most of the ground floor of the original building, and had not been 'improved' at all by its present owners, but left as it had been for nearly six hundred years. It had been built to be used as the manor's courtroom, and the place where all the family and the servants and the farm workers ate. Now it was merely the dining-room of Alex and his guests, and easily accommodated the Oldheath party, and Alex found them there when, after washing himself at the pump in the stables, and leaving off his labourer's clothes for something more suitable, he came to join them at their meal, red hair dark and sleek from his impromptu bath.

Ned had already welcomed them, but it was Alex whom Plato found—he had travelled with them in the Duchess's carriage—and Emily watched as, after discovering his lost friend, he stretched himself out across Alex's feet as he sat at table.

'Faithless hound!' she exclaimed. 'It was I who was so favoured once. What magic did you exert on him, Alex, to suborn him away?'

'Oh, horses and dogs all like Alex,' said Ned, looking proudly at his brother. 'He never does anything, you know, just walks about being lordly, and the animal kingdom falls at his feet.'

And women, too, thought Harry. Judging by the way in which Arabella and I carry on, and the looks other women give him. And it's true; he doesn't try, like many men. He just is, and that is enough.

It was pleasant, sitting there, in the rather stark room. The living quarters were in a wing added towards the back of the house, and these Harry inspected later. It was, she found, the home of men—shabby and comfortable, full of equipment for the field and the chase, a rack of sporting guns in a small room off the hall. But it was also full of books and smoky old pictures, painted by nobody in particular, a home where children would be happy—not a treasure-house, like the great mansions she had visited so far, although there were treasures in it.

It was plain Ned, as well as Alex, loved Allerton, although he told her during lunch that he, too, had been left a little house and some acres at Thurnby, not far away. 'Nothing remarkable,' he said, 'almost a cottage, but mine, you know. I have been a lucky younger son to have been left anything, but Aunt Emily said my mama insisted that provision was made before I was born. I am learning to farm and how to manage a small estate from Blagg, Alex's man here. I shall go to Oxford next year, because it is expected of me, but I am not a scholar like Cousin Gilbert was, or Alex. He was clever at his books, you know, although you would never guess it. That is not his style.'

He was generous about his brother, Harry thought, unlike many younger sons, who resented the wealth and privileges reserved for the eldest. But then, Alex had been almost a father to him, the fourteen years' difference between them meaning that Alex was already a man when Ned had first become aware of the world.

She felt Alex's eye upon her as she sat between the

Illingworths, as far away from Nun'ster as Emily could put her. When the housekeeper brought in pitchers of new-made lemonade he came over and poured her a glass himself, saying, 'I shall show you around later. The Duchess is my ally, and will manage things for us to be together, away from the others. She would have made a splendid adjutant.'

And so she did. It was the Duchess, indeed, who made certain that Alex was left alone with Harry in the afternoon, by saying briskly after the meal was over, 'Now Alex, you must show your cousin Harry around the manor and the farm. The rest of us are well acquainted with it—a drive to the Three Mile Meadow to view the harvesting there and then a walk in the Far Park will do for the rest of us. You will need to relax a little, Alex, after your strenuous exertions of the morning.'

Arabella concealed her annoyance as best she could. She had not gone to Allerton to be fobbed off with watching rustics while the dairymaid was left with Alex. But, with her husband's eye hard on her, there was little that she could say or do. She tried to leave Mrs Whitmore behind to act as a dragon, until the Duchess said, in her most gentle voice, 'I am sure that you would rather come with us, Sarah. You will not wish to hear Alex prose of scientific farming, and we may all rest assured that Evans will be a better duenna for Alex than ever Sarah would be.'

The general laugh this brought from everyone, well aware that Evans guarded his master with all the devotion of a servant from a fairy-tale looking after his prince, did nothing to please Arabella, particularly when Mrs Whitmore, well aware of the Duchess's ploy, and her determination to see Alex and Harry fixed, come what may, replied, 'I shall be only too happy to keep Lady Harrendene company, and make up for the loss of Mrs Ashburn, which I am sure she will feel deeply. Only too happy,' she repeated again, in her vaguest manner, 'to

be Lady Harrendene's foil,' and she proceeded to drive
Arabella slowly mad by prattling at her with extreme
vacuity on every sight presented to her that afternoon.
'The girls so pretty,' and, 'Pray, what is that instrument
for?' 'Salvator Rosa would so admire this view,' while
secretly hoping that her charge and Alex Templestowe
would come to better terms, back at the manor, with
Arabella safely away from them. Ned had also tried to
attach himself to his brother and Harry, but the Duchess
had soon disposed of him.

'You must sit by me, Master Ned, and tell me about
the sights, and where you birds'-nested last.'

As though I am still only a little lad, he thought
resentfully, as he, too, was dragged along in Emily's
train.

If Harry and Alex realised what the Duchess was at,
neither betrayed it overtly. Alex showed to great advantage, here in his favourite home. He was not dressed
carelessly, but his clothes were country style, without the
starched formality of Town.

Being alone with Alex was not as difficult as she had
feared. To begin with, the strange oppression to her
breathing which she had earlier suffered when near him
had disappeared. It was as though the session in the
garden-room had liberated her. Now the trouble was
that she wanted to touch him, to push back the locks of
his red hair which, drying, had sprung into its usual
loose curls, to take his hand, to. . . I must stop thinking
about this, she thought, because the next thing would
be that she would want *him* to touch *her*, and, once that
began, where would it end again? Decorum must reign
here.

Ned was right about Alex's mental attainments. More
and more over the last weeks, here in the Midlands, she
had come to see him as a healthy and athletic version of
Gilly. Gilly as he would have been without his illness.
He was harder than Gilly, but then, he had been a
soldier, and lived a harder life.

He spoke to her frankly and freely of what he was doing at Allerton, as though she was his equal, not at all as a man condescending to a woman, as most of the men about her, even the kindest, were only too wont to do.

'You see,' he said, 'we are farming scientifically on this estate. I have read the writings of, and corresponded with, both Coke of Norfolk, and the Duke of Bedford, and I intend to follow their line, particularly Coke's. I have no tenant farmers now to provide me with rents. I am the farmer here, and Blagg, my agent, co-operates with me. You will meet him in the estate office by the dairy, which you must see.'

It was obvious when they inspected it that the dairy was Alex's pride. Like the cottages at Allerton and on the estate it was part of the model village which he was creating. Harry admired its tiled white walls and its cleanliness, and the two pretty girls working there, and thought that Alex's cattle fared better than the Duke's tenants.

'And can you milk the cows as well as scythe the fields?' she enquired mischievously.

'Of course, but not in these clothes, Cousin Harry.' And, as they left, he said, 'I am determined, in time, to learn all the tasks performed by my people on the estate. And I'm pleased to see that you arrived suitably shod for inspecting a farm.'

'Why are you so different from the others?' she asked impulsively, walking with him across the paddock towards the barns.

'Am I so different?' he returned wryly. 'Yes, I suppose I am now. I wasn't once. It was the war. You see, when my mother died and I inherited what she had brought to her marriage, I was a mindless boy. And even when I was older I was content to let Stafford, then my agent here, rackrent the tenants. And then I became a soldier, and went to the Peninsula with the Duke—Sir Arthur as he was then. . .' He paused as they reached a gate, and, instead of going through it, he leaned on it, pulled a straw from the ground, put it in the corner of his mouth, and then gravely offered her one, to do the same. Laughing, she imitated him.

'Fellow countrymen,' he said, smiling at her. 'This is better than London, but one has one's duty there, too. Yes. It was the war. When we retreated across Spain, all those long, hard months, I lived as my men did, and shared their sufferings, as a good officer should, and I could not see that I was different from them at all. Shylock, you know: "Hath not a Jew. . .?" And then, had not Evans, my sergeant, and the men, too, cared for me devotedly when I was wounded, I should have died, for all my wealth and title. What was Templestowe's heir but another piece of bleeding earth?

'And while I was at the wars the Luddites struck hard at Allerton, and when I returned I saw that I was no better then the Spanish aristocrats I had met and despised. I was as unfeeling as they. My labourers deserved my care as much as my soldiers. Nay, more, for they were totally mine. So I pensioned off Stafford, brought in Blagg, learned about farming, and left him to begin reforming the estates when I returned to war again. For my duty still lay there then.'

So that explained Evans—and Alex, too.

'That was noble of you,' she said, 'to acknowledge your faults.'

'Oh, do not refine on that over-much,' he replied earnestly. 'For I gain from it, you know. Not only does Allerton pay me back more than my other lands where reform is harder, or impossible, but I escape the worst of the riots, Luddite and otherwise.'

He opened the gate for her, and they moved on to the barns, and to the estate office and the little house where Blagg lived and worked. He was waiting for them there, a squat, strong man, a gentleman's younger son, and they all talked happily together about crop yields, and cattle and water meadows, their presence or lack. Yes, it was like being with Gilly again. Instruction and pleasure

mixed. How could this man have been dishonest with
Arabella?

Harry was thoughtful as they walked back to the
manor house. Yes, this was a man she could marry, and
would surely be happy with, a man of occupation. Gilly
would have approved of him, and would have envied
Alex his superb physique and his athleticism.

Alex offered her his arm on their walk back, and she
could feel the hard power of him, the power she had seen
as he'd scythed in the fields, the muscles on his back and
chest rippling in the sun. Oh, yes, she acknowledged his
physical attractions as well as his mental and moral ones.
Arabella or no Arabella, she was suddenly more than
ready to accept him. Yes, she thought again, I am a fool
to allow vague scruples about a long-dead scandal about
myself, and jealousy of Arabella to deter me.

And Alex, walking beside Harry, admired her silences,
as well as her speech, the practical clothes she had put
on to visit him, and thought that if she graced Racquette
and Oldheath she also fitted in here, and would be only
too willing to discuss his plans for the future with him,
not yawn, and demand to be taken back to London to be
amused. He shuddered at the thought of what his
marriage to Arabella would have been, and, thinking so,
took Harry's hand, turned her towards him, bent his
head and kissed her gently on the lips. Not a passionless
kiss, nor a passionate one, but a kiss which held promises
in it.

'Do not give me your answer today,' he said. 'I would
not coerce you. I shall come to ask you again before you
leave Oldheath. Reflect on all that we obviously mean to
one another, and ask yourself if you can continue to
refuse me. I offer you all that is mine, including Allerton,
and I see by your face that the offer pleases you. No, do
not answer me now. My impatience is over; I do not
wish to coerce you in any way. I wish you to come in
love, freely given, or not at all.'

CHAPTER TWENTY

HARRY took the memory of Alex and Allerton back with her to the Priory; Arabella suddenly seemed to have lost the power to wound, and Nun'ster—why, Nun'ster, she thought—mistakenly—for all his threats, was nothing. Arabella, indeed, had said to her, on the way home, 'I hope Alex was not too much of a bore when you were left alone with him today. Bushels and crops and hedging and ditching. What can have come over him? Such a man of pleasure as he used to be. No woman was safe from him. Who would have thought that he, of all people, would have become a monk?'

And that, thought Harry, was a strange remark to be made by someone who had been hinting a few nights ago—nay, claiming, that he, Alex, was her lover, and a demanding one at that! Her suspicions that Arabella might have been lying were strengthened by Alex's behaviour as well as Arabella's. He had hardly spoken to her, and, although she had tried to buttonhole him at Allerton, he had held her firmly at arm's length. And now she talked of him as a monk!

Nun'ster she avoided, which did not seem to trouble him. What Harry did not know was that she had yet another protector, and a strange one. The Duke, sighing a little at his seclusion being broken, sent for his heir, Gerald Illingworth, and told him to ask Nun'ster to leave—his presence at Oldheath was offensive.

Gerald tried to argue. The Duke gave him his mild glance, and said in a bored voice, 'Keep him here, by all means, but accept that, if you do, you will inherit my title, but nothing else.'

Stunned, Gerald was compelled to agree. He spoke to Nun'ster, fearful of his reaction, but Nun'ster was amused; his plans were already made—to leave would aid them.

'My dear fellow, think nothing of it,' he said smoothly. 'I hear that he is more capricious than ever these days. Do not put yourself out for me. I need to go to my northern estates.' And he left with great pomp and circumstance.

'Behaving well, for once,' commented Harrendene, who had been informed of the matter by the Duke himself. 'I wonder why?' He said this to the Duke, as well as Gerald Illingworth.

The Duke looked severely at him—at least his mildish glance was severe for the Duke. 'I do not trust him around Cousin Harry, knowing how he behaved to her mother, but I can at least prevent him from troubling her in my own home, if nowhere else. Your wife would do well to look to her own behaviour, Harrendene, my dear old friend. You should remind her of her duties to your name.'

This amused rather than annoyed Dolly. There were times when he wondered where the Duke's information came from, since that gentleman spoke to nobody about anything—rarely even to the Duchess.

Before leaving, Nun'ster gave his orders to Arabella with characteristic arrogance. 'You will do as I bid you,' he said. 'What I ask is little enough. As soon as possible you will ask Mrs Ashburn to ride with you to Ticknor Woods. At the last moment you will cry off. She will be sure to proceed there on her own. Leave the rest to me.'

He did not go far. He put up at an inn some miles away, having sent most of his magnificent train north, and there, as plain Mr Chester, waited for an opportunity to revenge himself on Harry's mother, John Grey and all those who had thwarted him over twenty years ago. He would do it through Henrietta Grey's daughter, and the doing would be the sweeter because the girl was a prize worth any man's winning. And so his men watched the Priory for him, and the comings and goings there.

Harry was happier once Nun'ster had left. She hoped that she had seen the last of him. She missed Alex more than ever. She could hardly wait for him to come to Oldheath, and she knew what her reply would be when he did. No scruples about her own past, or her mother's or her own passionate nature, no fears about Alex and Arabella, or that Alex merely wnted her to regain Racquette, would prevent her from accepting him.

And strangely, once this decision was made, life, as so often, removed her worries over her major fear of her mother's past. She had gone to the library as usual one morning, and the Duke, whom she had not seen for a week, arrived to take morning coffee with her.

He did not speak until Mr Forsythe had served them both, and had withdrawn, then said abruptly, 'I saw that fellow Nun'ster off for you, Cousin Harry. He'll not enter Oldheath again. Illingworth has a poor taste in friends if he needs him.' And then he offered her the book which he was reading—Madame de Maintenon's *Letters*, in a pretty blue and gilt binding—and asked her opinion on a particularly sanctimonious passage to have been written by a lady whose reputation was not actually perfect—or so the Duke said.

Almost as though he had sensed her reservations about herself and her mother's past, he looked hard at her, a strange expression on his face.

'Come, my dear Cousin Harry,' he said, and she followed him through the library to a door in the wall which she had not known existed, it was so cunningly painted.

She found herself in a long corridor, which she guessed led to his own suite of rooms. The corridor was hung with paintings, none of them remarkable, or by great names, but as she passed them she understood that they all related to the Duke's life in some way.

Duchess Emily was there, painted when she was a girl. There was himself, and a recent picture of Gerald. Among them he stopped at a conversation piece, quite small, showing a group of young men carrying fowling-pieces, the Priory's empty window clear in the background.

They were handsome, confident young men, the Duke in the middle of them, and with a shock she recognised Adolphus Harrendene, and Nun'ster, young and personable. On the Duke's left hand side was the man in the miniature which she had found in her mother's possessions. The Duke pointed to him.

'I thought that you should see this,' he told her. 'That is my distant relative, your late father, and this,' he added, indicating another miniature, hanging among a cluster of small portraits of young men and women, 'is your mother.'

Well, there was no doubt of her mother's beauty, and of how little Harry had inherited of it. There was more of her father in her, she thought.

The Duke looked at her severely, as though he had read her mind. 'Your mother was a good woman, which is more important than her beauty. The world does not like to recognise virtue. But it is its own reward.' He sighed, was silent for a few moments, almost as though collecting himself, then said, 'Years ago, in my youth, your father and mother were part of my little circle. We were athletes and scholars then, though I do not seem athletic now. We were all in love with your mother, but she cared only for your father. Nun'ster was the first to offer for her.' He sighed again.

'I suppose that he could not believe that she would refuse him when he had so much more to give her than your father, the poor scholar. He went a little mad when she did. Cursed her and the rest of us, too. When he heard that she had accepted your father he lay in wait for her and carried her off. Dolly Harrendene and your father went after them and rescued her. We arranged between us for your father and mother to be hidden away where he could not find them—successfully, as you know. He was determined to destroy them both. I gave your mother my pearl pendant as a wedding present, and to remind her of the happy days we had all spent together.

'Because he was thwarted, Nun'ster told dreadful lies about us all, destroyed our happy set and your mother's reputation, and embarked on a life of profligacy quite unworthy of his talents. My dear, kind Emily thought that you were troubled in your mind by the echoes of this old scandal, which, she says, still follow you about. You may set your mind at rest, Cousin Harry. I should have given your mother rubies, so great was her virtue, but, I suppose, as the Bible says, a good woman is above rubies.' He fell silent for so long that Harry thought he had finished, until he said, in a melancholy voice, 'Had I not withdrawn from the world, I might have saved you both much unhappiness. Emily tells me that you were left in penury before your marriage. I am greatly to blame.'

'No blame,' insisted Harry. 'We were not rich, but my mother and father were happy, and my mother's second marriage was a contented one.'

He waved a dismissive hand. 'But your condition was hard, and the lies have followed you, and *you* have been lied about too, and I suspect the hand of Nun'ster again. Forget them, I beg of you. Make your decisions in the knowledge that they are false.' He took her hand, and kissed it gently. 'May your life be a happy one, my dear.' And, without another word, he led her back to the door into the library, where she found Mr Forsythe, non-plussed for once, as the Duke had never taken anyone into the corridor before, apart from himself, and the servants who waited on him.

Could the Duke have known of the doubts Nun'ster, Arabella, and Society's gossip had planted in her mind? If so, he had done his best to destroy them. At least that

doubt was removed. What he had said remained with her
for the rest of the day, occupying her mind as she dressed
for her usual afternoon ride with Arabella. They had
planned to go to Ticknor Woods, but, when she found
her way downstairs, Arabella's French maid, a supercili-
ous creature who despised Harry, was waiting for her.
'Milady has a migraine, and does not feel able to ride this
afternoon. She hopes that you will not miss your
exercise.'

Nothing could have pleased Harry more. Riding with
Arabella had been an exercise in politeness, nothing
more. 'Tell your mistress that I hope she will be
recovered soon,' she said briskly, and walked out to
where the two grooms, Knighton and Bagguley, waiting
to escort them, had their horses ready.

Bagguley dismissed, for Arabella had no need of him,
she and Knighton set off together. 'A short ride only
today,' she said, and Knighton, who had received his
orders to guard her carefully, and not to leave her,
nodded companionably. Like most of the servants, he
thought Mrs Ashburn a kind and caring lady. She always
had a pleasant word for him, not like some, and he was
happy to ride with her.

The Duchess watched them go from the window, and
said to Gerald Illingworth, 'I wonder if it is altogether
wise for Harry to go alone, but Knighton is with her,
and he is a good man.'

'Oh, this is not Vauxhall, madam,' Gerald reassured
her. 'Mrs Ashburn should surely be safe enough in the
Nottinghamshire countryside, and they will not go far.'
Arabella, upstairs, also watching Harry ride out, could
have told him differently.

Nun'ster had been waiting patiently in the week since he
had left. Every afternoon, the plain black coach which
he had used at Vauxhall had been driven into a lane on
the woods at the edge of the Duke's estate, and he and

his men had waited for the opportunity to take Harry. He burned for his revenge.

There was the Duke's insult, in turning him out, to pay back now, as well as everything else. He sat in the coach that afternoon, thinking of the past, of Henrietta Manners, of what a glowing beauty she had been, and how he wanted her, and of how they had all thwarted him. Well, Harry would make up for everything. She was, in her way, even more of a prize than her mother. Not beautiful, but something better, and, when he had met her, revenge had seemed sweeter than he had ever thought that it could be. Mistress, or compelled wife, he did not know which prospect was the better. If he ruined her, then she would have to marry him—the prize would be his. He was interrupted suddenly by Blunt, the ugly brute who had led the assault at Vauxhall.

'There's a lady coming from the Priory, and her with only a groom with her, riding towards the woods, my lord.'

'Then be ready for them, man. Chances are that it's the woman we want.' He gave his orders, and his men rode out towards them, nothing lost if it were Caro Illingworth, or Arabella, but, please, let it be her. And as the two riders neared he saw that it was Harry, and that his men would recognise and intercept her as she and the groom turned for home at the boundary fence. He waited in the coach. His men must not, could not fail.

Harry was enjoying her ride. The autumn sun cast the golden light of late afternoon on the Midland hedges, the undulating park, and the stands of trees. She liked most of her fellow guests, but it was pleasant to be away from them for a little. Knighton rode up beside her, and proposed that they return. 'I have my orders, madam. The Duchess does not wish you to go too far.'

Harry did not argue with him. He had his duty, as she had hers, not to be foolish, or to put herself into danger.

She could not think that danger lurked here in this smiling countryside, and, as she thought this, danger struck.

Three horsemen emerged from the trees, and rode at them. The leader reached for Harry, plucked her from the saddle, and threw her across his. Knighton they struck down before he could defend himself, or escape. He lay on the ground, groaning, as his horse bolted after Harry's, and one of the ruffians dismounted and struck him, as he lay helpless, with the bludgeon he had used for the first blow.

Harry's captors made for the lane which ran through Ticknor Woods.

CHAPTER TWENTY-ONE

IN THE placid, orderly life of Oldheath, no one at first noticed that Knighton and Harry were long in returning.

The Duchess was busy with Stephens, the agent, and then retired to her room to rest a little before the evening. She had letters to write, not official ones, and when that task was done she walked in her garden, admiring the late show of flowers.

Harry was not absent from her thoughts. Indeed, she was thinking with pleasure that on the visit to Allerton both Harry and Alex had found enjoyment in one another's company again. Harry had told her that Alex was coming over to Oldheath before she left for Racquette, and the Duchess hoped that the visit meant what she thought it did. Alex deserved a good and loving wife, not a predatory creature like Arabella.

The Duchess contemplated with some relief the news that Adolphus Harrendene had given her that morning. He intended to leave for Matcham before the week was out. He had seen and spoken to the Duke more than once, a thing remarkable in itself, and felt that he had done his duty to his old friend. Emily thought that she could hardly say that she was sorry to see Arabella go, but murmured some polite nothings, which she felt were hardly sufficient to deceive poor Dolly as to her true feelings.

So, all in all, things were going well. The harvest was in, and, although the villagers were surly, Stephens seemed to think that matters were settling down, which was a relief. Only Hannah Pye began to worry as time went by and Miss Harry did not return.

Afterwards Harry was to remember that her first reaction had been one of an overwhelming fear, as she was thrown like a bundle across the saddle of the leading ruffian, and was galloped away, leaving poor Knighton sprawled on the ground. Mingled with her fear for herself was her fear for him.

She had at first thought her attackers to be Luddites, who had been reported to be on the prowl, but, as they made for the road to the north, which ran along the far boundary of the Duke's estate, she saw that waiting there for them was a plain black coach. Even in her pain and fright it was plain to her that Luddite peasants would not own a coach and four splendid horses.

Without ceremony she was bundled from the horse's back, the coach door was opened, and she was pitched into it, head first.

'Well, well,' drawled a hated voice. 'What have we here? The lady herself. Welcome, dear Cousin Harry.'

Nun'ster, it was Nun'ster! She sat up on the floor, and glared at him. 'Release me at once,' she said, rage almost replacing fright. 'I have no wish to be with you. You dishonour yourself as well as me by such conduct.'

He clapped his hands together as though he were at a play. 'Bravo, my dear,' he sneered, 'I always knew that you had spirit. Our final encounter will be all the sweeter for it. Allow me to assist you to your seat.'

'Certainly not,' said Harry, scrambling somehow on to the cushions opposite to him, 'I have no wish to touch you. I advise you to let me go. No good can come of such conduct.'

They were already jolting along the rough road, away from the Priory, and his amusement was plain as the late afternoon sun entered the coach. 'It is my wishes, not yours, which obtain here. I think that you will change your tune when we reach our tête-à-tête. I know how to pleasure pretty ladies, and, mark me, opposition is a sauce to any feast. I intend to enjoy you, Cousin Harry, and take my time about it, too. I would advise you to do the same. But, no, continue to oppose me, and complete my pleasure. If you do not care for me I give you leave to think of Alex Templestowe as we grapple.'

Harry wanted to shriek, to scream, and, as they fled through a small village, contemplated putting her head out of the window and calling for help. He seemed to know what she was at, and smiled lazily. 'Do not you think of escape. There is no way out, I assure you. You are my naughty daughter being taken home after erring behaviour, and so I shall tell any servant at the inn whom you might hope to suborn. No, accept your fate, my dear. Enjoy yourself and please me. Accept further, that, after I am done with you, no one but myself will want you. Really please me, and I might even think of marriage. I need an heir, if only to spite my present one. Yes, you would make a good mother, after suitable taming, that is. You are inclined to speak your mind too much at present. But I can soon undertake to cure you of that. A little spirit is a good thing. Too much could be a bore.'

Such coldly smiling malevolence chilled Harry. She tried to calm herself, to sit opposite to him without giving him any indication of her fear and fright. She would not speak; to do so might provoke him into further insult.

'Come,' he said, 'that's better. You learn quickly, I see. Not like your mother.'

Her head lifted. 'Do not speak of her. I believe you to lie about her. Let it be enough that you have me.' And her mind was like a squirrel running round a cage as she thought of ways and means of escape. He had spoken of an inn. There might be opportunity there.

Again, it was as though he sensed her thoughts. He was lying back against the cushions, and savouring her. 'Yes, we are making for an inn. We head for Doncaster, but that will be tomorrow, after we have enjoyed tonight.'

'Are you not afraid of chase?' she asked, as cold as he.

'No, indeed. Who is there to know that it is I who

have taken you? Ten to one your would-be rescuers will
fly in the wrong direction. No, I think we can safely say
that you are at *point non plus* with me.'

Harry closed her eyes and lay back. She must rest. She
was already bruised and tired, and must recover. For
some reason she could not understand she kept having a
vision of Gilly. He was lying back against his pillow, face
haggard, laughing, and saying something to her. What
could it be? What forgotten memory teased her? She
would have thought that Alex would have occupied her
mind, but all she could think of was the most bitter
regret that Nun'ster was about to destroy all her hopes
for a future with him.

Courage, she could hear Gilly saying. Courage, but
why? It was true that courage was what she needed. The
vision of him wavered and faded. Nun'ster was leaning
forward. He had poured brandy from a silver flask into a
small cup, and was holding it out to her. 'Come. You
look weary. This will help you.'

Harry took the cup, held it a minute, and then tossed
the brandy in his face. 'No poisoned cup for me,' she
asserted, which might be Drury Lane heroics, but
expressed her feelings. She had no wish to be fuddled—
and an easy prey.

His smile never wavered as he wiped his face. 'You
shall pay for that useless gesture, and later drink as much
as will please me, not you. Later,' he repeated.

After that he ceased to trouble her, closing his eyes,
and lying back, and, as she moved towards the door-
handle, murmured, 'But don't try to throw yourself out.
I do not want the trouble of transporting a dead female
across country, or of leaving you to expire in a ditch,
either.'

Delaying tactics are best, she could almost hear Gilly
saying. Don't fight him. Go along with him, and look for
an opportunity. He is right. Don't risk your neck. Death
before dishonour is clever on the stage or in a novel, not
nearly so sensible in real life. Rest.

Which she did, and, despite the fear which made her feel so sick that vomiting seemed possible, she actually dozed. So that, opening his eyes, he looked at her, and admired her gallant spirit, and thought of the pleasure to come in breaking it.

Alex Templestowe rode over to Oldheath in the late afternoon. He was wearing his working clothes, and looked like a gamekeeper, but Evans accompanied him, and his fashionable toilet was in his saddle-bags. He only intended to stay overnight, make his offer, which he was now sure would be accepted, and return to Allerton ready to begin preparations for the wedding for which his kind aunt had waited for so long. He had seldom felt so happy. In his head was a picture of Harry, standing at the farm gate, the straw he had given her in her mouth, laughing up at him.

The Duchess and Hannah heard the echoing hoofbeats of a pair of riders, and both exclaimed, 'At last!' thinking that it was Harry and Knighton, whose return had long been expected. The Duchess met Alex as he dismounted outside the main doorway and said, 'Oh, Alex. I am sorry to sound unwelcoming, but I so hoped that you were Harry and Knighton. They rode out earlier this afternoon, and have not yet returned. Stephens has sent Bagguley and some of the stable lads to look for them. We are beginning to fear an accident.'

This was a stunning blow. All Alex's imaginings had included a vision of a Harry running to meet him, either in the hall, or down the stairs, or, perhaps, standing in the door of the drawing-room, a welcome on her face.

'Not returned?' he said, and prepared to remount.

The Duchess put her hand on his arm. 'No,' she said. 'That would be needless. There are two parties looking for them. Best to wait.'

Adolphus Harrendene and Arabella were in the Duchess's little sitting-room, Arabella saying, 'I am sure

that there is no need to worry——' before her husband
cut in coldly,

'Pray do not be ridiculous, madam. I do not understand why you did not accompany her as was arranged
this morning.'

Arabella gave him her shoulder. 'You know that I had
a headache. . .'

'I know that you said that you had one,' was his stern
reply. He looked at Alex. 'I do not like to think of them
out in this weather.' For it had begun to rain again, and,
early though it was, was growing dark.

They were arriving at an inn, and the cessation of the
coach's jolting woke Harry from her half-sleep. For a
moment she contemplated refusing to leave the coach,
and then thought that this might lead to more draining
of strength. She meant to avoid having to take Nun'ster's
arm, but he gave her no chance to escape contact with
him, for on leaving the coach he took her firmly by the
wrist to lead her through the inn yard, and into the inn
parlour which opened off a room where rustics were
already drinking.

The eyes on them were incurious. Great ones came
and went. The innkeeper bowed and scraped before
Nun'ster, said that his rooms were ready as his man had
earlier ordered, that food would be sent up, and—— But
before he could say more Nun'ster was by him, and
mounting the stairs, drawling, 'I leave all that to under-
lings; deal with my man, if you would.'

Harry was dragged along behind him. Mutinously, she
made herself as dead a weight as possible, but the
strength which he displayed made her dismally aware of
the great physical difference betweeen a big man and a
woman who was not of the largest.

At any other time she would have found the rooms
pleasant. They were cleaner than most, and tastefully
furnished. The bedroom opened off a small sitting-room,
where a table was already set for a meal. There were

bottles of wine on a small sideboard, and pictures on the walls—Morland prints in pretty gilt frames. The room's charm mocked her situation and her fears. I am General Fabius, she reminded herself, my motto is patience, and lead the enemy on, although how she could defeat Nun'ster she could not think.

He was loosening his cravat, and then offered to remove her short riding-coat. Again she contemplated refusal, but rejected it, allowing him to take it from her, stroking her neck as he did so, the touch making her cringe, and then accepting the chair he pulled up.

There was a crackling fire in the grate, and he placed one booted foot on the fender. He was plainly at ease, and his eyes raked her. 'Allow me to remove your boots, my dear.'

'No.' She retreated from him, tucking her feet beneath her chair.

'Oh, rest easy, my dear. I have no intention of touching you yet. We shall eat and drink, or rather you will drink, and then, why, only then, shall we enjoy ourselves. We have the night before us.' He constituted himself her boot-boy, smiling up at her, and caressing her ankles with his hands, before standing her footwear in the corner. He pulled the bell, and his man Grimes appeared, insolent eyes sliding over Harry, and she wondered drearily how many times he had assisted in such sordid adventures.

'Tell that gross fool downstairs that we shall be ready to eat——' and he pulled out his watch '—in about a half-hour. Before you go you will pour some wine for us both. A small glass for myself, but you will favour Mrs Ashburn with a large one.'

Grimes's eyes as he carried Nun'ster's orders out were as lascivious as his master's. He caught Harry's breast with his hand, as he placed the glass before her, and Nun'ster smiled at it.

'My servant favours you, I think,' he remarked, raising his glass in a mock toast.

It was not the landlord, but Grimes who brought their food up, slowly, over the next hour. It was good country fare, and excellent. A great tureen of vegetable soup, a game pie, steam rising from the hole in its golden crust, and potatoes, baked in the inn's oven, oozing butter. Afterwards there was a syllabub, in a crystal dish. Nun'ster ate slowly, with great enjoyment, commending the food to her as he did so.

Indeed, in better circumstances Harry would have enjoyed it, and the large loaf of bread, farm butter, and Stilton cheese which came at the end. But she had no appetite at all, and, despite Nun'ster's frequent exclamations as to the excellence of the meal, ate hardly anything, and it might as well have been straw for all the good she gained from it.

Mixed with the sickening terror which grew in her every minute were her memories of the starving children in the villages they had left behind. Such plentitude seemed indecent, in the face of their suffering and her own plight. She contented herself with looking around the room, and wondering what she might use as a weapon against him. There was little enough to hand. And time seemed alternately to shorten and to lengthen. Even after the meal was done, he showed no eagerness to proceed further. Sprawled in his chair, one leg across the seat of another, his glass in his hand, cravat gone, shirt unbuttoned, he persisted in behaving almost as though they were an old married couple. She had no doubt that he was deliberately prolonging her agony, and she was determined to show no breach in her courage. Her one hope was that they would have missed her at the Priory, that Knighton might be found, that they would be looking for her. . . She echoed her tormentor's small talk, and smiled with stiff lips, refusing further wine from her captor. Nun'ster was a particularly large cat toying with a very small mouse which occasionally squeaked defiance at him.

'Expectation is all,' he announced. 'Possession, now,

while one's end, can be over too soon,' and Harry's stretched nerves were vibrating as he spoke. She replied mechanically to him, her mind ceaselessly revolving every possibility of escape. She had rejected table-knives as weapons—too small—and an attempt to attack him while Grimes hovered outside would merely serve to exchange one tormentor for another, probably worse. Surely he would soon dismiss him for the night, and then she would only have Nun'ster to deal with?

He was busy attacking her mother's reputation, but this was a useless tactic. He could not disturb her with that, not since the Duke had told her what she knew to be the truth.

'You defile her memory,' she flashed at him. 'You judge others by your own black heart. Remember that you were young once. Think of all that you threw away.'

'Oh, indeed, a pretty advocate you make. What a pity that women are not allowed to stand at the bar. You would be a very Portia. Plead on, my dear. The entertainment you provide is better than I thought. I see that you please me more than your mother. Her understanding was not inferior, but could not hold a candle to yours. You will make a splendid mother for my sons. I suppose that it was that poor boy you married, Gilbert Ashburn, who trained you. I heard that his intellect was beyond reproach.'

Harry stared at him. By naming Gilly he had unwittingly unlocked a memory for her which she could use against him. She'd known that Gilly had something to tell her which would help her, but she had not been able to think what. Nun'ster, by mentioning him so unexpectedly, had broken through her mental fog, and she saw Gilly plain before her, lying in the sunlight in his bedroom, and she was speaking to him.

Nun'ster and the room about her faded, his voice came from a great distance. They had been talking, she and Gilly, of a poor woman raped and half killed in a neighbouring village, and Gilly had said to her, 'I should not like to think of that happening to you.'

'But how should I prevent it? A woman must always be at a disadvantage in such a case.'

'That is not always true,' he had told her gravely. 'There is one way by which you might defend yourself. But you would need to have great resolution and strength of mind—and luck. I believe that you possess the first two, and these might provide you with the third. . .' He paused, and said, 'I must not distress you but, however weak and ill I may be, I am still a man, and I must speak plainly. A man is most vulnerable, Harry, where he gains his greatest pleasure. You understand me? Remember Peel?'

She nodded. Yes, she remembered Peel. Remembered how he had screamed when the bull had butted him—there. Remembered how he had fallen in the field, and the village children had laughed, and Gilly had said, 'Come away. The poor brute is badly damaged.' It was when they were little, and he had explained to her why Peel was to be pitied.

'So, if you are attacked you must try to injure him by striking him hard. . .in his vulnerables. . .' at this they had both laughed nervously '. . .with your knee, or some object to hand, and then, when he is lost in pain—it may not be long—you must strike him again, over the head preferably, with whatever you can find. And both times you must have no pity. Strike to kill—you will not—but you will do him such a hurt that you may escape before he recovers. A poker, a vase, a jug, an ornament, anything which does him an injury. You understand?'

She had shivered, and nodded obediently. 'But I shall never need to know this,' she had objected.

He had taken her hand and looked hard at her. 'Harry, in this life we never know what we may need. When we were young I never thought to be the helpless invalid I am. Even five years ago I thought that one day you might truly be my wife, and now I am dying and you are still my sister. Remember what I have told you.'

Well, she had pushed it away. She did not want to know of such things. But she needed to know now. And she thanked Nun'ster for provoking the memory. And, as she thought this, Gilly faded, and it was Alex she saw, as he had stood at the farm gate, laughing at her and putting the straw in his mouth. Oh, she must somehow thwart Nun'ster; she must. For her future lay with Alex, and following Gilly's advice might secure that future for her. She must hope, for without hope she was lost—she was truly the mouse which the cat toyed with. Surely an opportunity would come, and she thought of Alex and wondered what he was doing.

Alex could not rest. He paced the small room, waiting desperately for news of Harry and her groom. They had now been missing for so long that no one could delude themselves. Some mischance, some accident had come to them. There was an urgent knocking on the door, and both Adolphus and Alex started up, but the person who entered bore no news of Harry—in fact, brought news that was to dismay them all. It was Hannah Pye, Harry's old maid from Netherdene.

'Madam,' she said to the Duchess, and her curtsy was hardly polite. 'I am afeared that someone has done Miss Harry a harm.'

'No, Hannah,' replied the Duchess firmly. 'You are right to worry over your mistress, but an accident, surely.'

'No,' insisted Hannah baldly, breaching all laws of servantly etiquette. 'Not an accident, but something like Vauxhall. I am afeared that Lord Nun'ster has taken her.'

By now all the Duchess's guests had assembled, and they all stared at her.

'Nun'ster?' repeated the Duchess faintly. 'Now why

in the world should you think him responsible for Vauxhall? And he left here days ago.'

Before Hannah could reply, there was the sound of horses' hoofs, running feet, and shouting outside, and Stephens burst into the room without ceremony.

'Forgive me, Your Grace, but the matter is urgent. We have found Knighton near Ticknor Woods. He is badly hurt, but was conscious enough to tell us that men made away with Mrs Ashburn, after attacking him, and carried her off to a waiting coach which then drove off north.'

Uproar reigned. Hannah said loudly, 'It is as I said. It is Lord Nun'ster. He threatened Miss Harry when she refused him, but she would not take him seriously.'

'Refused him?' cried a dozen voices at once. 'He proposed!' said the Duchess and Alex together. 'But she never——'

'Told you,' finished Hannah angrily. 'Of course not, bearing in mind how you all treated her. But he did. And what's more, it's my belief that madam there——' and she swung round and pointed at Arabella '—helped him to make away with her, both at Vauxhall and here. Oh, I've heard that French maid of hers, and his man Grimes, laughing together back in London,' she finished sturdily. 'Thought she'd get *him* back——' pointing to Alex '—if she helped that man run off with Miss Harry. Oh, I blame myself; I should have put two and two together before.' And she started to cry, throwing her apron over her head.

The night's wonders were not yet over. As Hannah had finished speaking the door opened, and the Duke stood there. He had been told that Mrs Ashburn was missing, and had broken the seclusion of many years to come to find out what was being done to find her.

'What nonsense,' began Arabella, face white, only to have her husband, his own face suddenly unrecognisable, grasp her by the wrist, saying,

'But it is true, is it not, Arabella? Answer me.'

Arabella replied desperately, addressing both the Duke, whose mild gaze was on her, as well as her husband, 'Why attack me? Why suppose Mrs Ashburn totally innocent in this matter? For all we know she might have gone with Nun'ster willingly.'

The stares were turned on Arabella. The Duchess said, 'No, I will not believe that,' and the Duke lifted his head, and spoke with his usual lack of interest in what he was saying.

'Harrendene, my old friend, you should put a bridle on your wife's tongue. She is careless in what she says.'

Harrendene's response was to take his wife by the arm as, colour high, she began to answer the Duke. 'Be quiet——' he ordered, but he in his turn was interrupted by Hannah, who was appalled at what Arabella had said.

'Ask her. She knows. If not, send for her maid. She knows the truth. She was laughing just now about your pretended headache, leaving Miss Harry to go out alone. Yes, my fine madam, it is you who have helped to ruin Miss Harry.'

The Duchess said, her face ashen, 'I know she does not like Harry, but why. . .?' And then she looked at Alex, who stood, grey-faced, his eyes on Arabella. 'Of course,' she said, 'of course.'

'She knows that I am telling the truth,' repeated Hannah defiantly.

Harrendene turned to Arabella. His face was white. 'Answer me, Arabella; is she telling the truth?'

'What a question!' she began hardly. 'Who can believe a word a stupid servant says. . .?'

'Oh, but I do,' said the Duke gently, and for the first time there was authority in his voice. 'Tell me, why should she lie? I know only too well what Nun'ster is capable of, and the servants always know more than we do.'

'Yes,' agreed Harrendene grimly. 'You have the right of it.' He turned to Alex. 'If it is Nun'ster, and everything points that way, he will take the road due north, towards his home, and you and I must follow him up it, if we are to find her before it is too late.'

He swung round to confront his wife, who stood there, her world in ruins. Whatever else, now that what she had done was known, she had lost Alex, and forever. And she had lost Harrendene, too, and the world of fashion which she had dominated for so long. She would never be received again.

For Harrendene said, his face hard as she had never seen it, 'Arabella, you will go to my room, not yours, and you will await me there, and you will go at once, without delay; I will deal with you when I return.'

Every eye was on her, and every eye was accusing. She flung her head back and stared defiantly at him.

'No,' she flashed at him. 'I will not.'

'Oh, but you will, or I shall turn you out of doors, now, instantly, into the rain; I would not hesitate to treat you as you have treated poor Harry,' he said. 'I warned you and warned you, and you would not listen. Do not detain me; I must try to undo what you have done,' he told her, as she grasped at his arm, her face an anguish of pain, but it was Alex she was looking towards, not her husband.

Alex had turned away from her; he could not bear to look at her again. She was odious to him.

The Duke ordered, in his mild voice, 'You must go after Cousin Harry at once. I cannot bear that this should have happened to her on my land. If he has made away with her successfully, I shall pursue him through every court in the land.'

They were the last words Alex heard as he and Harrendene ran from the room. 'We must plan what we are about to do,' said Alex. 'Campaigning taught me that preparation is everything. We must go on horseback to make as fast a time as possible, and Evans and your man must follow in a chaise. If Knighton was right, and Hannah is to be believed, and it is Nun'ster, he will be heading north for his place near Ripon. The first posthouse on the road will tell us whether he has gone through, and after that. . .'

'We stop at every inn we reach, and look for his carriage in the yard. He will not be expecting us, and on horseback we can hope to overtake him,' continued Harrendene. 'Alex, I am so sorry that it is my wife who——'

'Don't apologise for Arabella,' said Alex. 'She is beyond your or any man's control. I can only thank God that she refused me when I was in Spain. To do this to Harry, who has never harmed a soul!'

'My responsibility, though,' returned Harrendene.

Then they spoke only of their journey, Alex saying, 'We will go as hard and fast as we can, only God grant that we shall be going in the right direction. To think of her with him. . .'

'He failed with the mother, and now means to succeed with the daughter,' said Harrendene, as they mounted fresh horses, and finally rode down the long drive and through the Priory gates, Alex facing a hard night, after a hard and difficult day.

CHAPTER TWENTY-TWO

I CANNOT expect anyone to come to save me, thought Harry, unaware that Alex and Harrendene were already well on their way towards the inn, and therefore I must remember what Gilly said, and try to save myself.

Nun'ster had begun to yawn and stretch in a most unmannerly way, hinting at a desire to retire. He had his eye on her, and presently put his head out of the door, and she heard him dismiss Grimes with, 'You may entertain yourself, now, Grimes. Mind, I wish to leave early tomorrow, so do not loiter about. Hot shaving-water by six, and your sharpest razor. Mrs Ashburn will desire chocolate, too, first thing, I have no doubt. It's a good restorative for tired bodies,' and he turned to grin at her as he finished.

He put out a hand, after he had shut the door.

'Come, let's abed. I wish to reach home tomorrow, and I have had enough of teasing you. Your appetite should be sufficiently whetted by now.'

Harry hung back, so he gripped her by the wrist and pulled her through the door and into the bedroom. His strength shocked her, and she knew that only guile could save her.

He clutched her to him and tried to kiss her lips; she turned her face aside at the last minute, so he caught her neck instead. His lightest touch was hateful to her. If she had feared that she was a wanton who burned with passion at any man's touch, she now knew that fear was needless. It was Alex to whom she responded, and no one else. Nun'ster took her roughly by the chin, and said again, 'Come, do not make me use force. You will not like it. Resign yourself, my dear. Why fight what you cannot prevent? Besides, I mean to marry you, when I have taken my pleasure. Think of it—a Marchioness's coronet for one night's work—which could be pleasure if you used your splendid understanding properly.' And he kissed her roughly on the lips before pushing her on to the bed.

Guile, she must use guile. She leaned back against the pillows. On the wall opposite, above the mantelpiece, was a sampler embroidered with the words 'God bless our home'. What a singularly inapposite message, she thought irrelevantly. There was a small wash-stand by the bed, with a bowl and a large jug of water on it. Then inspiration struck.

'You are right,' she said, licking her bruised lips and smiling up at him. 'Why fight the inevitable? A moment, and I shall be ready for you.' And she began to unfasten the top buttons of her riding habit.

His whole demeanour changed, and became easier. 'I said that you had great understanding. I believe we shall deal well together.' Watching him, she saw the wariness with which he had treated her ooze out of him.

'I was a fool,' she said, 'to resist you.' And now she was halfway down the buttons, and she stopped, giving him a smile borrowed from Arabella's repertoire—lasciv-ious and inviting.

'Do not you think I deserve a better kiss than the last you offered me?' And she leaned forward, her face soft, and eyes half closed, appalled at her own ability to seduce, and half understanding why Arabella found such power pleasant, for his face had softened too, and he leaned forward to give her the kiss she demanded, quite unwary, so that, as, instead of the kiss, she fastened her teeth hard in his top lip, he was unready for her attack.

Blood streaming from his mouth, shocked more than pained, he reared back, his hands flying up, and as he did so Harry, fighting down revulsion, brought up her knee, as Gilly had told her, with all her strength into his unprotected body.

He fell forward against the bed, crying out with pain,

fortunately missing her, so that she sprang up, and,
seizing the heavy water-jug from the wash-stand, brought
it down with all her strength on his unprotected head as
he turned to face her.

The jug shattered, water and blood ran down his grey,
shocked face, and he slipped from the bed to the floor,
where he lay unmoving. Her first thought was, Gilly was
wrong; I have killed him. And I do not care. Neverthe-
less she knelt by him, to find the pulse still fluttering in
his wrist, although he was quite unconscious, his lips
livid.

What to do? She was in her stockinged feet. She could
not simply run from the inn into the September night;
that would be to invite further trouble. Nor could she
leave him to die. She was too inexperienced to know
whether or not she had really dealt him a mortal blow.

She rose, rebuttoning her habit. It would not do to
appear a slut. She must intimidate the landlord, try to
obtain a surgeon, and the means of returning to Oldheath
before her reputation was quite gone. She had no notion
of what he and Grimes might have said of her to the
landlord, but guile had laid Nun'ster low, and further
guile might bring her through this.

Her late assailant still lay unconscious under the ironic
sampler. She walked to the door, and ran lightly downstairs. Now to confront mine host.

Alex and Harrendene had learned at the first posthouse
of a coach with an older man and a young woman in it
changing horses some time earlier in the evening. By the
description it was Nun'ster and Harry. 'So Hannah was
telling the truth,' said Alex.

'Did you doubt it?' asked Harrendene, before they
rode on. 'It is as the Duke said. The servants always
know more than we do.' Alex looked across at him. His
usually pleasant face was stern, and he wondered what
fate awaited Arabella when they returned to the Priory.
Like the Duchess, he knew why Arabella had done what

she did, and was shocked by it. But Harry in Nun'ster's power was all that concerned him. Arabella had forfeited his consideration long ago.

The next inn they came to was not open, and when they knocked the landlord came out and swore at them. There was death in the house, he said, and, no, he had no horses—they'd best travel on. The White Horse was not far, and, 'No, I've not observed a coach going through, damn you; leave me alone.'

So they pressed on, and the White Horse was further than he had said. They had paused for a moment, and Alex had pulled out his watch. There was a moon peering through low cloud, and it was barely nine of the clock, which shocked him. So much had happened in so short a time.

But the White Horse finally came in view, at the bottom of slight hill, and as they rode towards it Alex prayed that this might be the one; and, yes, there was a coach in the yard, and a man by it in a doorway, a girl in his arms, and as Alex made for him he saw that it was Nun'ster's man Grimes.

He recognised Alex and, abandoning the girl, let out a yell, but Alex had him by the neckcloth, and hissed into his face, 'Your master is here, and Mrs Ashburn?'

'Since you know so much, the answer is yes,' choked Grimes. 'But I doubt whether you're in time to save your precious piece, my lord.'

Alex knocked him flying, and then, Harrendene following, entered the inn through the door from the yard. They were in a small passage, giving way to the kitchen on one side, and the public rooms on the other. They pushed through the door to the bar, and they could hear Harry's voice, raised and peremptory.

'But I must have a doctor, or a surgeon, at once. At once, I say. You fool; what do you think the Duke will have to say to you when he hears of your misconduct?'

Alex burst through the last door to find himself in the inn parlour, the landlord standing in front of the fire, and Harry confronting him, in her stockinged feet, but otherwise fully clad, thank God, her face scarlet with anger, and the landlord laughing at her.

Alex caught her in his arms. 'A doctor, my darling, and a surgeon, you shall have twenty of them. What has that swine done to you? And you,' he added, turning to the landlord, who was staring at him, mouth open, 'why are you not doing as she asks?'

'And who the devil may you be?' said the landlord, having recovered himself a little, staring at Alex in his rough working clothes. 'And why should I trouble with a gentleman's doxy——?'

He got no further. Harrendene, who had followed Alex in, took him by the throat, a most unHarrendenelike act, and said softly, 'I am Lord Harrendene, this is the Earl of Templestowe, and the lady to whom you referred so unpleasantly is his lord-ship's cousin. Unless you send for a doctor for her immediately, I shall thrash you senseless. Now, summon your barman, and send for assistance.'

Harry, delighted to find herself so tenderly embraced by Alex, said earnestly, as he murmured brokenly over her, while Harrendene demanded to know where that cur was, so that he might thrash him, too, 'Oh, but you mistake; it is not I who need a doctor, you know. It is Nun'ster. I fear I might have killed him. I am not hurt at all. He had scarcely touched me before I knocked him unconscious.'

Both men stared at her, and Alex held her away from him, relieved to find her unharmed, but barely giving credibility to her story. 'My darling, you knocked him unconscious? Are you sure that you are not delirious?'

'No, indeed. I think you had both better go upstairs and see after him. I would not like to think myself a murderess, even to save my honour.'

Harrendene began to laugh, his first pleasant moment in the whole sorry evening. 'So we shall, my dear. Poor Alex; he has been riding through the night to save you, and he finds that you have saved yourself. Come, let us go and find what the enterprising Mrs Ashburn has done to her abductor.'

They mounted the stairs, and entered the bedroom to discover Nun'ster stirring. He lifted his head as they came in, and Harrendene dropped on his knees beside him. 'Well, well,' he drawled, 'what have we here?' His glance took in the shattered water-jug, the blood on Nun'ster's face and lip, and his greyish-yellow countenance. 'Never tell me the great seducer was overthrown by a kitten?' His amusement was so patent that the man on the floor writhed beneath it.

Harry, hovering behind them, observed fervently, 'He is not dead, then. I am so relieved. I had not quite meant to kill him.'

'Take her away, Alex,' said Harrendene. 'I shall guard this ruined clown until the surgeon comes to mend his head for him.'

Alex's look for Harry as he led her into the inn parlour was almost one of awe. 'How came you to make such a mess of him?'

Harry hung her head and coloured a little. 'Do not ask me. It was not very ladylike. It was something Gilly told me to do if ever I were attacked. It worked very well, except I did not know that I should hurt him as badly as I did. I thought that I had killed him, when I only meant to stun him.'

Alex began to laugh helplessly. 'Gilly told you. . .my cousin told you. . .? Oh, yes, by the look of him I can guess what you did to him. God bless Cousin Gilbert. You brick, you absolute brick. He did not know what he was at when he made away with you. Oh, my courageous darling.' And before he could stop himself he put his arms around her, and began to kiss her vigorously. Her response was equally rapid and passionate, and what would have happened had the landlord and the surgeon not arrived, Harry thought afterwards, did not bear thinking of—or perhaps it did.

'What am I doing?' he exclaimed. 'Here has Nun'ster been assaulting you, and the moment I arrive I am as bad as he.'

'Oh, no,' replied Harry, 'not at all. It is not at all the same. I could not bear him to touch me. Now you, on the other hand. . .' She fell silent, blushing at what she had almost said. How strange it was, that what filled her with the utmost revulsion when it was Nun'ster should be so utterly different when it was Alex who had his arms around her, and was murmuring endearments into her ear.

'No,' said Alex slowly. 'I am being unfair. We shall get that fat barrel to bring us something to eat and drink, and then when Evans, and Harrendene's man, arrive, we shall drive back to Oldheath. And in the morning, I shall——' And he stopped, amusement playing on his face.

'Yes?' prompted Harry. 'In the morning. . .?'

'In the morning I shall ask Mrs Gilbert Ashburn a question, and I think I know what the answer will be.'

'Well, I shall not break a water-jug over your head, that is certain,' replied Harry, as Harrendene came in, and said,

'The surgeon is looking after Nun'ster. I propose that we have something to eat, and then return home.' He looked at Harry. 'You are a remarkable young lady, Mrs Ashburn, and have planted such a facer on Nun'ster as almost makes me sorry for him. He is quite ruined, and likely marked for life. When this unlikely downfall is bruited abroad he will not be taken seriously again. Society will not know him, and women will laugh at him.'

The landlord, now servile in his manner, brought them food, and they ate and drank as they waited for the carriage to arrive, Alex smiling at Harry across the table, and each of them thinking only of the other and the future.

* * *

Later, lying in the crook of Alex's arm in the chaise, Evans driving them, Adolphus Harrendene having hired a carriage to take him to Oldheath, saying that they did not want or need his company, Harry wondered sleepily whether this was a dream from which she might presently wake.

She had been amused at Evans's expression of surly indifference as he had helped her into the carriage. He had lost his master to the women at last, but, if the Colonel must marry, then better he settled himself with someone who had paid Nun'ster out for all the poor servant girls he had exploited over the years, rather than with some stiff, fine lady who would have had hysterics at the thought. The sight of the ruined would-be seducer quite made up for having a Lady Templestowe to bear with.

Harry, after some small protest— 'I really am in splendid fettle'—allowed Alex to cosset her. Feeling the strong beat of his heart against her cheek, his lips against her hair, she thought how strange it was that, after all the passion which had passed between them, they were content to sit quietly together, simply to hold one another being quite enough.

Once she stirred and said, sleepily, 'How did you find out that Nun'ster had kidnapped me? You know that he proposed to me and I refused him?'

'Yes,' replied Alex, 'Hannah told us.' And briefly he informed her of all that had passed at Oldheath, once it was known that she had been kidnapped.

He thought she slept after that, but she suddenly stirred, and said, her voice low, 'Poor Arabella.'

'Poor Arabella? You can say that?'

'Oh, she made a wrong choice when she thought that she could have Lord Harrendene and marriage and you as well, outside it. She never knew you, did she?'

No, he thought, as Harry fell silent, her hand in the hand of the man she loved, if Arabella never understood me, then I never understood myself, either. Simple passion is not enough, and what an empty life I should have had if she had accepted me after all. I have been spared that, thank God.

He tightened his hold on Harry a little, and kissed her again. In this moment out of time, neither felt passion—that would come later—only a kind of fulfilment beyond the body's needs.

He had intended to propose to her in the morning, but suddenly he felt that he wished to avoid anything which might remind either of them of his previous failed offer. What better time than now, when each had accepted the other, when all doubts about their feelings had disappeared, when they were alone together, the rest of the world forgotten? Neither his wrong suspicions of her nature and character, nor Harry's doubts about her own and her mother's reputations, or Arabella's hints, mattered any more, or could matter, as he felt her warm and contented beside him, as though they were already an old married couple, secure in one another.

'My darling,' he said, wondering whether she already slept.

'Alex?' And her voice was warm and loving.

'My darling, I meant to come to you tomorrow, dressed in my glory, and you in yours, on my knees in the garden-room, and ask you to marry me; but what better time than now? Now we are ourselves, not our valet's nor our lady's maid's possessions, but two poor human beings who have at last found one another. Harry, my dear, I don't really need to ask you, but I will. You will be my wife, will you not? I saw your answer in your face at Allerton. I promise you that you will never regret it.'

He turned her face towards him to kiss it, and she thought for a moment of the past before she accepted the present. Life with Gilly would have been a canter through a pleasant parkland, and what awaited her with Alex was a steeplechase over difficult country with a proud and passionate man who would love her, and torment her a little, and she would need all her character and strength to match him. But what she had felt for Gilly was a sisterly love—for Alex it was different again. Her passion matched his, and burned with an equal fire. It was as though Gilly had saluted her and at last ridden out of her life, but not her memories.

Alex was murmuring into her hair. 'Oh, Harry, my love, my love. I promise you, you'll have no regrets. I know I'm not an easy man, but, oh, Harry, I want you for my wife, to be my companion as well as my love. You must know how much I love you.'

'As I love you,' she said, and, held against his heart, Cousin Harry came at last into her true inheritance.

The other exciting

MASQUERADE
Historical

available this month is:

THE MANSINI SECRET
Louisa Gray

Stranded in Italy by her father's death, Lady Cecilia
Sherringham was witness to a murder, which
brought her to the notice of Federigo, Prince
d'Aquilano. He was loth to let her leave his city, for
few people stood up to him as Cecilia did, and real
friends were even rarer in his turbulent world.

But lurking danger threatened their lives, and it
seemed the desperation to keep the Mansini
secret from public gaze might yet keep them
apart . . .

TWO
HISTORICAL ROMANCES

&
TWO
FREE GIFTS!